Lilies on Her Grave

L. N. Costley

Preface

Content warning:

This book is intended for mature audiences, and contains scenes of:

Abuse
    Drug use
    Profanity
    Sexual assault
    Sexual situations
    Violence

To my wife
For supporting this crazy dream.

Chapter 1

Awakenings

Lilly Barnes was dead, she just didn't know it. A tight pressure coiled itself around her neck, like a boa constrictor squeezing the life from its prey. Clutching at her throat, she desperately tried to clear her airway as her breathing grew more labored with each fading heartbeat.

She struggled to open her eyes just a fraction of an inch, the accomplishment costing her. The blurred image of a dark figure loomed in front of her, their shadowy features distorted and lost within the ever-closing darkness, though it was so close she felt its rancid breath upon her face. Her eyes yearned to close again. She fought with all her might, but it was no use.

Lilly's world became as dark as the void.

A slight breath of fresh air caressed the soft skin of her face, carrying with it the scent of earth and pine. Was she outside? She had been. She was almost certain of it, but a thick fog blanketed her mind, and she couldn't recall where she had been just moments before.

Tree limbs softly creaked above her, their leaves rustling back and forth gently. She was definitely outside. Tilting her head, her ears strained against the darkness, but no other sounds called out to her. Then, another sense came to life as a strange scent tickled her nose. The aroma seemed vaguely familiar. Something from her past? A cologne? Or maybe after-shave? The harder she pondered the scent, the more memories of her grandfather swam to the surface of her mind. Yes, that was it. The same scent always greeted her whenever she hugged him. It was his aftershave, Old Spice. The smell and the thought of her grandfather left her as quickly as they had come.

Lilly's world was as dark as the void.

She stood there listening to the eerie stillness for what felt like an eternity before a loud, exhaling breath pierced through the darkness.

"Hello?" she called out. "Is someone there?"

The sound of something metallic being raked across, or maybe pushed *into* dirt, rang out through the void, followed by a shallow thud.

Pressure pushed down upon Lilly's chest as she labored for breath. Dreaded panic took form in the pit of her stomach. One that radiated outward, causing her heart to race wildly out of control, and for the first time, she sensed something was terribly wrong.

Ear-piercing static exploded into existence, as if someone had flipped on a switch. The volume intensified, drowning out everything else. A scream ripped from her throat, but the static overwhelmed her voice, swallowing it within the chaotic whirl-wind raging inside her skull.

The tormenting squelch climaxed in an unexpected erup-tion of color, and Lilly found herself standing in a small clearing somewhere deep in a dense forest. Above her, dark, luminous clouds raced across the heavens upon an unfelt wind.

The world around her looked odd. It reminded her of the first time she had experienced a solar eclipse. When the moon had blocked out the light of the sun, casting the entire world in an eerie shadow.

The metallic sound from earlier reached her ears again.

Turning around, she found a man standing behind her. His back was to her, but she could still make out a few of his features. He stood at least six feet tall, almost a half-foot taller than her, and his body was thick. Not with the defined muscles of a bodybuilder, but more like a big construction worker. Someone naturally strong.

A black baseball hat covered his neatly cropped brown hair. An ordinary brown jacket, blue jeans, and a pair of heavily worn work boots rounded out his wardrobe while his black-leather-gloved hands wrapped tightly around the long wooden shaft of a shovel.

The man pushed the shovel into a pile of dirt near his feet, then gracefully swung it around and tossed a scoop full of fresh earth into a hole in the ground. The hole measured two feet in width and almost four feet in length. From her vantage point, Lilly had no idea of its depth or what lay within.

"What are you doing?" she asked, her tone a tad interrogative.

The man ignored her and tossed another scoop full of dirt into the hole before thrusting the shovel deep into the pile of dirt. Wiping a generous amount of sweat from his brow, he blew out an exhaustive breath.

"I said, 'what are you doing?'" Lilly asked again, this time a little louder. She reached out to touch the man on the shoulder and was taken aback when her fingers passed through him as though he wasn't even there. "What the...?" The moisture in her mouth evaporated, leaving in its wake a vast desert as a heavy weight fell into the pit of her stomach.

Lifting his head, the man's eyes scanned the area around them, and in doing so, looked right *through* Lilly, giving her the first glimpse of his face. The lines etched into his white skin said he was somewhere in his mid-fifties, and his upper lip was adorned with a thick brown mustache, while the remnants of a small cut graced his lower lip. A pair of thick, black-framed glasses with even thicker lens rested on the bridge of his wide nose. A hint of familiarity hung about him, but that dense blanket of fog covering her consciousness had yet to burn away.

Turning his attention back to the hole, the man removed a pocketknife from his front pants pocket. It had a black handle made of bone, with two blades, one on each side. The knife seemed small in the man's large hand. Extending one of the blades, he jumped into the hole, its lip reaching the top of his knees. Bending low, he used the knife to cut something, but again, from her vantage point, Lilly had no idea what.

When the man straightened, Lilly saw a strand of long blonde hair grasped in his left hand. Long blonde hair identical to hers. Raising the lock of hair to his nose, he inhaled deeply, holding the breath and savoring the scent. A slight quiver of ecstasy pulsed through his lips. Taking a small plastic bag from his back pocket, he placed the lock of hair safely inside before gently replacing the bag into his pocket. Climbing out of the hole, the man grabbed the shovel and recommenced with his laborious task.

A nagging feeling rose in the back of Lilly's mind, telling her not to step any closer to the hole. The hole she knew she had to look into. She didn't want to. What she wanted to do was to turn around and run as far away from this all-too-creepy scene as fast as her legs would carry her, but she felt herself being drawn forward.

Closing her eyes, she took a deep breath to calm her nerves before taking several long strides forward, bringing her to the very edge of the hole. She needed to do this, she told herself, as the sound of the shovel being pushed into the dirt again made her wince. Forcing her eyes open, she peered into the hole. A slight gasp escaped her lips when she found her own face staring up at her from the depths of the hole.

The feeling of being punched in the stomach caused her to double over and purge the air from her lungs.

Her blue eyes were open and soulless. A white film had formed over her pupils, giving them a hazy appearance as they stared off into nothingness. Her once-red lips were now a blackish purple, while her skin had a waxy sheen to it. Her blonde hair had lost its once-golden luster as a large matted tangle of blood and hair stubbornly protruded from the left side of her head. Dirt covered most of her body now, except for her bare left arm, which seemed odd to her, of all things, because she had on a pink long-sleeved running shirt.

With a slight trembling in her lips, she fell to her knees, tears cascading down her cheeks. A shovel full of dirt landed on her face. "No, no, no!" she whimpered, trying to brush the dirt away. Sheer terror filled her heart when her fingers passed awkwardly through the dirt and her face.

Fear turned into a blinding rage. Springing to her feet, she charged the man, who was nearly finished with his task. The task of burying her in a shallow grave. Her father had made sure she could take care of herself. Enrolling her in a self-defense class when she turned sixteen. It was there she had learned to fight, so that's what she did.

"You bastard!" she yelled, cocking her right arm back and balling her hand into a fist. She swung at the man's face with all of the strength her anger could muster, but like the dirt, her fist passed right through him. She screamed louder. Harder. Spittle spewed from her mouth, covering her lips.

The rage continued to pour from her body. She threw punch after punch until what strength she had left evaporated, causing her to collapse once again to the hard earth. The man spread out the remaining dirt before picking up a small push broom from the edge of the clearing. After the dirt around her grave had been swept clean, erasing all signs of anyone ever having been there, the man covered the area with leaves, trying his best to make the area appear undisturbed. Hoisting the shovel onto his shoulder, he used the broom to sweep away his footprints as he made his way to the edge of the clearing.

"I won't let you get away with this, you mother fucker," Lilly screamed, forcing herself to her feet.

She made it about ten feet past her grave when an overwhelming sense of foreboding washed over her, causing her to stop the pursuit of her killer. Why was she stopping? The man who had murdered her was slipping away, and that was something she could not allow. Something she *would not* allow. She pushed forward, but the sense of dread increased tenfold with each step. A thousand tiny needles, each one hotter than the sun itself, prickled her all over her entire body. Overwhelmed, her body crumpled to the ground in defeat. Taking what little anger she had left, she let out an ear-shattering scream.

The man stopped dead in his tracks and glanced back over his shoulder in the direction of Lilly and her grave. Squinting, he stared hard through the thick lens of his glasses for several long seconds before moving on and disappearing among the trees.

"I don't understand," Lilly said, her voice quivering faintly. Wiping away the tears from her face, she lifted her head skyward, as if expecting some heavenly answer to be cast down upon her, but the ever-racing dark clouds were all that she saw.

Music blared through her ear buds as she glanced down at her GPS running watch. Two and a half miles at a nine-minute mile pace. Her breathing felt strong and under control. College midterms were a few days away, and after studying for the past week and a half, her mind needed a break. Something brushed against her leg, causing her to lose focus. Glancing down, she was surprised to find a yellow puppy with long floppy ears running next to her.

"Hi there, cutie." She stopped to pet the puppy, who eagerly jumped up and licked her face. She laughed as the puppy wagged its tail so hard that it was practically falling over. "What are you doing out here by yourself?"

"Gunner!"

Lilly looked up and saw a man walking toward her, carrying a dog leash in one hand. He wore thick, black-framed glasses and a black baseball hat. His brown mustache-framed lips smiled upon seeing her.

"Is this your dog?" she asked between laughs, pushing the puppy back a bit as it tried to lick her face clean.

"Thank you so much," the man said. "He got off his leash and ran off. I'm not as fast as I used to be." He kneeled and grabbed the puppy by his collar. "I was beginning to worry."

"Glad to help." Lilly gave the puppy one last pet. "What kind of dog is he?"

"He's a yellow lab."

The puppy began to twist and turn, trying to break free of his owner's grasp.

"Gunner, calm down," the man said, tightening his grip and causing the puppy to cry out.

"Hey!" Lilly said.

The man let go of the puppy's collar at the sound of Lilly's voice and watched as the dog ran off down a small foot-worn path leading into the woods. "Sorry, I wasn't trying to hurt him," he explained, slowly getting to his feet.

"I'll get him." Lilly sighed, feeling a bit responsible. She took off after the puppy and found him lying down not far from the road. "There you are," she said as the puppy ran to her. "Let's get you back to your owner." She scooped the puppy up in her arms

before he could run off again. A powerful arm wrapped itself around her neck and pulled her tight into the man's body.

Lilly tried to scream but couldn't find her voice as it became a battle to breathe. She felt a slight twinge of pain in the right side of her neck. She knew what was happening and knew from her self-defense classes that the most important thing was for her to try to remain calm. If she let her fear overwhelm her, he would win. Dropping the puppy, she grabbed the burly arm around her neck and pulled it downward, allowing a small amount of air to reach her starving lungs. Lowering her center of gravity and lifting her right leg, she slammed her heel down with all the force she could find. The man let out a grunt as Lilly felt his grip on her loosen just enough. She raised her right arm and slammed it backward, elbow first, into the man's ribs.

That did it, she thought, spinning free from her attacker's grip. She had to get back to the road. Back to where there might be someone, anyone, who could help her, but she found the man towering in front of her, blocking her path of escape. Lilly's head became fuzzy, and her vision blurred. Cocking her fist back, she punched the man square in the face. His head snapped back, giving her the distraction she desperately needed. She side-stepped her attacker and moved to rush past him, only to find a powerful hand grabbing her left arm and dragging her backward. Lilly tried to scream. Tried to fight. There was a flash of green light, and searing pain exploded from within the left side of her head.

Lilly Barnes was nineteen when she was murdered and buried in the woods where no one would ever find her.

Chapter 2

Giving the Dog a Bone

Lilly had no idea how long she had been sitting in the forest. Her tears had dried up some time ago, but the anger toward the man who had buried her still simmered deep within her. The strange solar shadow and the dark racing clouds remained unchanged.

She paced out the distance from her grave to the invisible wall of overwhelming dread keeping her from leaving the scene of the crime. It measured roughly twenty feet in diameter and encompassed the entire burial site. No matter how hard she tried to get past that distance, she found it impossible to do, giving her the distinct impression something horrible would befall her if she left. The idea that she was even thinking about her *gravesite* sent a surreal shiver cascading down her spine. She kept waiting for this hellish nightmare to end, but the alarm clock never went off.

It did not take long for her to grow bored of sitting around. She needed to do something to keep from going insane. She tried to dig her body out again, but as before, her fingers passed through the dirt. In the end, not a single twig or fallen leaf had been disturbed.

Her thoughts drifted to her parents. Did they even know she was missing? Did anyone except for the man who had killed her? They had to have known by now, she thought, glancing up at the darkened sky. *How long have I been here?* It felt as if days had passed, but with no sun or moon to judge the passing of time, she had no way to tell.

Even if her parents were looking for her, they would never find her out here in the woods. They knew she would have been running at the park in her hometown of Olivet, Michigan, but the park was over five hundred and sixty acres of heavy woods with numerous nature trails. *If* she was even still in the park.

Slamming her fist down on the ground, she sprang to her feet and let out a frustrated scream. She knew no one would hear her, but the act gave her a small sense of reprieve. Why was she even still here? She hadn't been a bad person in life, so surely her soul should be going to heaven, but why hadn't it? What if there wasn't a heaven or a hell? What if this was it?

Rustling leaves pierced the eerie stillness like a lighthouse in the fog. Lilly stood and looked through the trees for the source of the sound, and after a few minutes, a medium black-and-white dog came trotting into view. Her first thought was the man had returned and brought his puppy with him, filling her heart with fear. But Gunner had been yellow, not black-and-white. Lilly sighed a breath of relief.

The dog moved closer to where she stood. Close enough for Lilly to see it was wearing a collar. Maybe its owner was out here too. But would its owner be able to see her? she wondered, remembering how her killer had looked right through her.

The dog stopped at the edge of the clearing, the hackles on

its back raising. Sniffing the air, a low growl rumbled from its throat.

"Right back at ya," Lilly huffed.

The dog's ears perked up at the sound of Lilly's voice, its head tilting slightly in confusion.

Her eyes widened as a shimmer of hope fluttered in her unbeating heart. "You can see me, can't you?"

The dog shifted its head to the other side and let out a slight whimpering sound, its tail slowly wagging back and forth a couple of times.

"You can!" Lilly cried out, the unexpected change in the volume of her voice causing the dog to take a few cautious steps away from her. "Hey, it's ok. It's ok," she reassured in a calming voice. "Come here," she said, bending her knees and clapping her hands.

The dog took a wary step forward, sniffing the air again while keeping its hackles raised as a warning.

"That's it. I won't hurt you," she promised, holding out her hand. The dog inched closer and sniffed the dead girl's hand for several seconds before sniffing vigorously at the ground.

"Can you smell me?"

The rate of sniffing increased as the dog circled the area above Lilly's body.

"That's it, that's it," she said, reaching down and patting the ground.

The dog pawed at the earth.

"Wrigley!" came a man's voice.

Lilly's heart skipped a beat when she saw the man enter the clearing, heightening her anxiety, but a sense of relief washed over her upon seeing his face. This man had a full brown beard, and his body type was nowhere near the same as her killer's.

The dog saw its master and lowered its head submissively

before slowly walking back to its owner with its tail between its legs.

Lilly's one chance at being found was slipping away. She needed to do something and fast, but what? "Wrigley!" she called out.

The dog came to a skidding halt upon hearing its name.

"Come here," she said, throwing in a little whistle for good measure.

Wrigley ran back to the hole and continued to dig at the earth.

"Come on, you're getting all dirty," the dog's owner said, but the dog wasn't listening. The man walked over and grabbed the dog's collar, pulling it away from the hole.

"Come on, Wrigley," Lilly called out again. "Keep digging."

The dog twisted about, trying to break free of its owner's grip. "What are you doing?" he asked. Wrigley managed to slip out of his collar and immediately ran back to the hole, digging at the dirt at a feverish pace.

"Wrigley!" the owner scolded. Grabbing the dog by the scruff of its neck, he tried to pull the animal away again, but the dog resisted the effort and kept digging.

"That's it, you're almost there," Lilly cheered the dog on. "Find me, find me."

"Wrigley, I said enough," the man commanded, taking a firm stance and pulling the dog away from the hole. The dog turned and nipped at his owner's hand. Not hard enough to break the skin, but hard enough to say, "Let me go," causing the man to take a step back, allowing the dog to stick its head back into the hole.

"What's gotten into you?" the man asked, rubbing his hand. The dog answered by pulling something free from the hole and dropping it at his owner's feet. The man's eyes drifted to the prize his dog had worked so diligently to procure from the ground and gasped at the sight of a skeletal foot.

"Good boy, Wrigley!" Lilly cheered.

~

BEFORE LONG, Lilly's once-empty clearing became overcrowded with people. A police officer cordoned off the area with yellow caution tape. Others took pictures, while others still had slowly and methodically removed all of the leaves covering her grave. Investigators in white decontamination suits sifted through the dirt as Lilly's body, piece by piece, was slowly unearthed.

The pungent smell of decaying flesh reached her nose and made her gag. She felt so morbid watching them dig up *her* body. Large lights were set up around the clearing, telling her that nightfall must have come, although the sky above her never changed. Wanting a change of scenery, she made her way over to the edge of the clearing where Wrigley's owner was talking to a man dressed in a gray suit.

"Mr. Haas, I'm Detective Brandt," the man in the suit said as Lilly approached them. "Can you tell me what happened?"

"I was out walking the trails with my dog when he took off into the woods. I ran after him and found him here digging in the ground. Then he pulled out that foot. Was that thing...real?"

"I'm afraid so," answered Detective Brandt, handing the man a business card. "If you remember anything else, please don't hesitate to call. An officer will walk you back to the head of the trail." Mike Brandt placed his hands deep into his pants pockets and watched as the evidence technicians took the last of the body, a grizzly-looking skull with strands of long blonde hair, out of the hole and placed it in a black body bag with the rest of the remains.

MIKE RAN a hand over his bald head and gave it a hard rub. Twenty years with the Auglaize County Sheriff's Department, and he had never investigated anything like this before. Things like this weren't unheard of in rural Ohio, but they were rare, and while he had investigated a fair number of homicides in his career, they were nothing like this. This was not a spur-of-the-moment killing, where the ones responsible fled the scene as soon as the bullet casings hit the floor. This killer had taken their time to dispose of the body, which meant the killer had a plan, and judging by the condition of the remains, that plan had taken place some time ago. If not for the dog, how long would this body have gone undisturbed?

A man in a white suit approached Mike and took off his mask. "We're wrapping things up here, Detective."

"Find anything useful?"

"A partial footprint on the far side of the grave. Probably made by some kind of work boot, but I don't think there's enough to be of any use."

"What about the body?"

"Female, judging by the hair. Mostly skeletal. We didn't find any clothing or jewelry either. Won't know much more until the autopsy is done."

Mike blew out a frustrated breath. "All right, get her to the morgue. Tell the doc I'll be there when I can."

The man nodded and walked over to an ambulance stretcher, where another tech was securing the body bag to the stretcher.

Detective Brandt took a hard look at the crime scene. They

were deep in the woods. At least a mile from the dirt road serving as the nearest thoroughfare. Nothing out here but deer and mosquitos. The killer would have had all the privacy they needed and all the time in the world to bury the body the right way. The clearing didn't have any useful footprints, and the grave had been camouflaged with leaves to make it blend in with the surrounding area. How familiar was the killer with this area? Mike mentally thumbed through a long list of recent cases but didn't recall any fresh missing person's files. A frightening idea made its way into his head, causing him to take out his cell phone. "We're going to need some cadaver dogs out here."

WHAT'S A CADAVER DOG? Lilly thought, still eavesdropping on Detective Brandt's conversation. The two evidence techs wheeled the stretcher holding Lilly's remains past her, each trying their best to navigate the rough terrain of the forest floor. What was she supposed to do now? Should she follow her body or stay with the detective? On the one hand, she wanted to stay with the detective in case he discovered anything else, but she quickly became overwhelmed by that feeling of dread the farther the stretcher moved away from her.

"Twenty feet," she said, realizing the wall hadn't been put there to keep her trapped in the forest but to keep her spirit attached to her body. But for how long?

The two evidence techs finally reached the road, where they found a van from the coroner's office waiting for them. Lilly had to move fast to slip past the two techs as they loaded her body into the back of the van.

"She's all yours," said one of the techs, slapping the back of the van with his hand. "Detective Brandt'll meet you guys down there." The van lurched forward, causing Lilly to stumble around the back of the van and nearly fall over. She cautiously lowered herself to the cold metal floor, questioning how a ghost could lose her balance, while the van proceeded to hit every hole in the road.

Eventually, the van slowed and came to a stop. Its backup alarm engaged as the van slowly reversed for a few seconds before coming to a stop again. The back doors swung open, revealing a scrawny guy somewhere in his twenties. He had short red hair, a face full of zits, and wore a long white lab coat with a name tag that read Brad.

"Final stop, the morgue," he said in a sarcastic tone, pulling the stretcher from the back of the van.

Lilly climbed out of the van and saw they were in the loading dock of an old brick hospital. She stood there for a few seconds, trying to take in her new surroundings, before rushing after Brad, who wheeled the stretcher into the building.

Lilly followed a few steps behind, making sure to stay within the twenty-foot range of her body. She could smell Brad's body odor, his zit medication, and the bouquet of sterilization and death that permeated from the walls of the old building.

Brad maneuvered the stretcher down several long, darkened hallways, his footsteps echoing ominously off the walls, until he came to the door that read Exam Room One in white lettering. Pushing a large button on the wall, the heavy door swung open as the room's lights flickered on automatically.

In the center of the room sat a large stainless steel table. The outer edge of the table resembled a picture frame. The inside of the table was recessed a few inches and had small holes cut throughout its surface. A large light hung from the ceiling, directly above the table, and at its foot rested a metal sink with an attached spray nozzle.

Brad swung the stretcher around and pushed it over to the wall on the left side of the room. The wall held six metal doors, stacked two high and three long. Having watched a number of crime dramas on television, all of which had at least one episode involving a medical examiner, Lilly knew the metal doors were part of a large refrigeration system used to keep dead bodies, like hers, cold to prevent further decomposition. Brad opened door number three and pulled out a long metal shelf. After sliding the body bag on the metal shelf, he pushed it back into the cooler and closed the door before wheeling the stretcher out of the room and vanishing from sight.

Lilly stood in the farthest corner of the room, wanting to be as far away from the exam table as she possibly could. She stood there solemnly for several minutes until the lights automatically shut off, leaving her all alone in the dark morgue.

Chapter 3

New Friends

The lights in Exam Room One came to life when Brad strode casually into the room. He whistled along to the music blaring from the headphones in his ears, oblivious to the world. Lilly, who sat in the far corner of the room with her knees tucked up to her chest and her crossed arms resting on top of them, slowly lifted her head. The big round clock on the wall read nine o'clock. It had ticked relentlessly through the night, with the old brick walls of the exam room twisting the sound into a creepy, echoing noise that had come close to driving her mad.

Brad opened the cooler containing Lilly's body. After slipping on a pair of latex gloves and a face mask, he pulled out the long metal shelf and unzipped the bag. Slowly and meticulously, he removed her remains and gently placed them on the metal table. The door to the exam room opened again. This time, a short, round Hispanic man wearing blue scrubs walked into the room.

"Morning, Dr. Ortiz," Brad called out.

"Good morning, Brad," the doctor replied. "This is our Jane Doe, I take it?"

"Yes, sir." Brad checked the body bag one last time before folding it up and placing it off to the side.

"And Detective Brandt?" Dr. Ortiz walked over to get a better view of Lilly's remains.

"No idea," Brad responded, turning on the big bright light above the table.

"Well, I'm not going to wait around all day. Let's get started."

Lilly had no intention of watching what was going to happen next, so she lowered her head back onto her arms and closed her eyes. She heard an array of sounds come to life. Metal hitting metal. A saw. Running water from the sink. She had no idea how long this went on, but it felt like it was never going to end.

The exam room door opened again.

Tilting her head ever so slightly to the side, Lilly caught a glimpse of Detective Brandt entering the room.

"Sorry I'm late," he said, slipping on a face mask and a pair of latex gloves. "What'd I miss?"

"Everything, I'm afraid," the doctor said. "Just finishing up."

"Yeah, sorry about that. Had to make sure no one else was out there."

Lilly lifted her head. Detective Brandt's statement caught her off guard. The idea of there being other bodies in the woods aside from her own had not even crossed her mind, and if there were others out there, were they like her? She didn't recall seeing anyone else in the woods, but she had been confined to the small clearing, and the forest was a big place.

"Was there?" Dr. Ortiz asked, taking off his mask and gloves.

"Thankfully, no," Brandt answered. "We had cadaver dogs check several square miles around the area where she was discovered."

"That's a relief," the doctor said, picking up a clipboard and scribbling something on it.

"So, what did you find out?"

"You might want to get up and stand a little bit closer, so you can hear what they're saying," came a voice Lilly hadn't heard before.

Turning her head, she found the most peculiar man standing next to her. He had on an old, tattered brown jacket, a gray hooded sweatshirt underneath it, and a pair of dark green corduroy pants with a large hole over the right knee. A bright yellow backpack rested on his back. His skin had the same hue as freshly fallen snow, and his head was as bald as a baby's ass.

"Here, let me help you up." The man offered her a hand. Lilly noted a black metal ring with a large blood-red ruby in the center on the ring finger of his right hand. It reminded her of her class ring from high school, but the sides of his ring were void of any writing or symbols.

"Who the hell are you?" she asked. "And how can you see me?"

The man stood there gawking at Lilly, growing more impatient with each passing second as he continued to hold his hand out to her. With an annoyed sigh, she reached out, and to her surprise, she discovered she could grab the hand presented to her. The man pulled her to her feet and pushed her toward the exam room table.

"The victim is female, between fifteen and twenty years old. Caucasian, and given the lack of flesh, I am confident she has been buried for at least six months. Now for the interesting part. Do you see this spot right here?" Dr. Ortiz pointed to a spot on the left side of Lilly's skull, near her temple.

The odd man pushed Lilly right up behind the detective, so she could get a good look at the small half-orb-shaped indent in the bone, along with several spider-webbing cracks radiating out from the center of the indent.

"And if you look right here," the doctor said, moving to the top of Lilly's body.

Lilly followed the doctor's movement and found the top portion of her skull had been removed, which the mere sight of caused her involuntary gag reflex to kick in. "Wait, did he say six months?"

"Shhh," the odd man scolded, pointing back to the inside of Lilly's skull, where she found a dark red stain upon the white bone on the other side of the orb-shaped indent.

"Is that the cause of death?" Detective Brandt asked.

"It's hard to say," the doctor said. "It's definitely a point of blunt force trauma. The impact was hard enough to fracture the skull and cause a significant brain hemorrhage. The blow would have certainly caused loss of consciousness, a concussion, and most assuredly, given the size of the hemorrhage, put her in a coma.

"Given the state of the body, though, I am not able to give you anything more definite. The hyoid bone is intact, but that doesn't mean she wasn't strangled, and I did not find any tool or weapon marks on any of her bones, but it does appear some of her hair was removed. Right here." The doctor pointed to a portion of Lilly's hair on the right side of her head. "And the body was also free of any foreign DNA. With all that being said, I would say the point of blunt force trauma certainly assisted in her death, so I'm ruling this a homicide."

"So, you've got nothing other than a small dent in her skull and some missing hair?"

"Being in the ground, unprotected for six months, will

destroy all traces of forensics," Dr. Ortiz reminded Brandt. "Any idea who she is?"

"None," Brandt answered. "We don't have any open missing person cases, and the surrounding counties aren't missing any young white females. I'll put what I've got into the national database and hope we get a hit. It's been a pleasure," he added, walking out of the exam room.

Lilly stood there staring at her decomposed body. Brad finished a few things with her body before placing it back in the cooler while Dr. Ortiz washed up. Before she knew it, both men had walked out of the room, leaving her alone with the odd-looking man, who had not left her side.

"Tough break," he said. "A lot to absorb, huh?"

Lilly turned her head and gave the man a frustrated scowl. "Who are you again? And what are you doing here? No... Let me rephrase that... What am *I* doing here?"

"The name's Fred," the man said, extending his hand again.

This time, Lilly did not accept the invitation.

"Ouch. No need to get your panties in a bunch."

"My what?" Lilly said, raising her voice.

"Fine," Fred said. "I was just trying to give you a few moments to absorb what has happened to you, and..."

"Time to absorb?" Lilly's voice filled with anger. "According to the doctor, I've been buried in the ground for six months, all of which *I* was stuck sitting next to *my* dead body, so forgive me for saying this, but I've had plenty of time to *absorb*."

Fred stared at her for a moment before taking out an old pocket watch and checking the time. "I don't have time for this shit," he said, placing the watch back into his pocket.

"I'm sorry," Lilly stated sarcastically. "Are you late for something?"

"Yes, as a matter of fact, I am," Fred retorted bluntly. "So, if you want the guided tour, you'd better keep up," he added, walking out of the exam room.

Lilly stared in disbelief but shook it off when Fred told her to get moving. She quickly approached the door but stopped and hesitantly reached out a hand. She watched as it passed right through the exam room door. Taking a deep breath, she stepped *through* the door and out into the hall, where she found Fred waiting for her.

"Ok, newbie, listen up because I don't like repeating myself. You're dead," he began, moving down the deserted hall.

"Duh. Six months, remember?" Her voice was full of sarcasm.

Fred whirled around, the top of his pale bald head flushing red. "Unfortunately, our system isn't always perfect. Sometimes spirits get overlooked, and things like this happen. We have been under our minimum staffing requirements for the past two centuries. In an ideal world, someone should have greeted you at your TOD and explained the rules to you."

"TOD?" Lilly asked.

"Time of death," Fred said. "You should never have been left out there for that long on your own, so for that, I do apologize. I'm not even the one who's supposed to be doing this. I'm strictly an East Coast reaper, but I'm doing someone a favor, so drop the attitude, and I'll do my best to get you on your way." He resumed his trek.

"You're a reaper?" Lilly did her best to keep up. "Like the grim reaper?"

"I'm just one of many, sweetheart." Fred came to a stop in front of a row of elevator doors. He swung his backpack off his shoulders and retrieved a purple spiral notebook. He flipped through the pages until he found the one he wanted and ran a finger down its surface, stopping about halfway down. "Sixth floor," he said before stuffing the notebook back into his backpack. "You're what we in the business call a purg."

"A what?"

"A purg. Because you're technically in purgatory. You have some unfinished business keeping you grounded," Fred told her as an elevator door opened. Fred hastily stepped in, followed by Lilly.

"Why are we taking the elevator?"

"Because I don't like taking the stairs." Fred stood there with an impatient expression etched upon his face.

"Well, aren't you going to push the button?" Lilly asked, watching the elevator doors close.

"Oh, right," Fred remarked. "Can you do it for me? We need to go to the first floor first and cut through the ER, so we can take a different elevator to the critical care unit."

Lilly went to push the button for the first floor. Her face flushed with irritation when her finger passed through it. Fred burst out in a fit of laughter. "Oh man, that never gets old," he said, pushing the button for the first floor.

"How come you can push it and I can't?"

"Because I'm not a ghost," Fred replied. "It's like this, Purg. The laws of physics still apply to you, but only about 25 percent of the time. You can't float around like you see ghosts do on TV. You're stuck on the ground. You can't interact with anything, which means you can walk through walls and shit, but only because you can't turn a doorknob. Oh, and nobody can see or hear you, if you hadn't already figured that out. Understand?"

"I guess," Lilly answered skeptically.

"Ok, try this one," Fred tried to explain. "If you would have walked through the elevator doors, without them being open, and the elevator car wasn't here waiting, you would have fallen into the bottom of the shaft, where you'd be stuck, because even though you could walk through the walls, there's no real exit down there, and you can't walk *through* the ground."

The elevator doors opened, and Fred took off like a shot, not waiting to see if Lilly followed. The doors started to close, and Lilly barely made it off the elevator in time. She spotted Fred's bright yellow backpack halfway down the hall and took off after him but found her path obstructed by hospital staff going about their daily routines. She dodged and sidestepped her way through the hall until a high-pitched tone coming from one of the ER rooms caught her attention.

Lilly barely had time to move out of the way as an army of nurses rushed into the room. Peeking inside to see what all the commotion was about, she saw a young man on a hospital bed. He was in his mid-twenties and had jet-black hair, while his white skin held several tattoos on both of his arms. One of the nurses started to perform CPR while the man's spirit materialized at the foot of the bed, where he watched in bewilderment as the nursing staff desperately tried to save his life.

His confused brown eyes met Lilly's as the two stared at each other. He was taller than her by at least half a foot. His body looked a little scrawny, but not starving scrawny. Maybe scrawny wasn't the right word she was looking for. Wiry seemed more appropriate. She felt someone grab her arm and turned to find Fred giving her an annoyed stare. "Are you here for him?" she asked.

Fred peered into the room, and the man's expression turned sour upon seeing Death. "No," the reaper replied.

A nurse yelled, "Clear!" before giving the man's heart a shock from a defibrillator. The man's spirit faded from sight as the heart rate monitor beeped with life.

"We're going to the sixth floor, remember?"

Lilly followed Fred as they made their way through the hospital. She noticed that even though the hallways were bustling with people, everyone moved out of the reaper's way. She also noted not one of them ever made eye contact with him.

"Here we are," Fred said, strolling into room six twenty-four.

On the bed lay an older man with mostly gray hair. His white skin was littered with brown spots. An oxygen hose lay under his nose while an array of other tubes and wires protruded from his body.

"Lilly, meet Chuck Jennings," Fred said, slipping off his backpack and retrieving his purple notebook. "Jennings... Jennings..." he mumbled, flipping through the pages. "Jennings. TOD is at 3:09 a.m." He reached into his pocket and pulled out his pocket watch. "Two minutes to spare," he said, replacing the watch from where he had retrieved it. "You might want to stand over here," the reaper instructed, moving off to a far corner of the room.

"Why?"

"Because in two minutes, a butt-load of people are gonna come rushing in here."

"You said they couldn't see me."

"They can't," Fred answered. "But do you really want a bunch of strangers walking *through* you? Besides, I need the room to work." He reached once more into his backpack and pulled out a bathroom scale, which he placed on the floor in front of him.

"What's that for?"

"Gotta weigh the man's soul now, don't I?"

Lilly gazed at the reaper with a dumbfounded expression. She started to say something she knew Fred would find annoying but closed her mouth when Chuck Jennings flat-lined. A handful of nurses rushed in and began CPR. Just like in the ER room, the man's spirit appeared at the foot of his bed.

"Is that me?" Chuck asked. "What's going on?"

"Sir?" Fred called out.

Chuck turned and locked eyes with the reaper. "I knew this day would come," he said, shaking his head solemnly.

"If you would be so kind," Fred said, motioning to his scale. "Your soul has to be weighed before judgment can be passed."

"What...happens after that?" Chuck asked hesitantly.

"Once the scale has rendered a verdict, I will assist you in reaching your final destination."

"Which is where, exactly?"

"There are only two options," Fred answered, motioning toward the scale.

The man stepped forward and began to place one foot upon the scale but stopped shy of its surface. He held his foot there for several long seconds before placing it back down on the ground. "I can't do this."

"You don't have a choice." Fred motioned to the scale once again.

"There must be some kind of mistake," Chuck argued. "I've led a very giving life. To my church. To my family. To my community. There should be no judgment! I demand to speak with your supervisor!"

"Yes, you did do all of those things you mentioned, but how did you serve Max Evans?"

"Who?"

"Cut the shit, Mr. Jennings. You *know* who you're talking to. You hit that little boy with your car, killing him, and just drove off. Didn't even stop."

"But I was drunk," Chuck pleaded. "I didn't even know I hit something. I mean... I saw the dent in my car the next morning, but...."

"You didn't hit something. You hit some*one*," Fred corrected as he began to lose his patience. "If it were up to me, I would bypass the scale altogether and send you straight to hell, but management says we have to follow protocol. Now get on the scale. I'm not going to ask you again."

"How do I know those things are even accurate?" Chuck asked, trying his best to stall.

"I can assure you they are routinely calibrated by an independent third party," Fred motioned to the scale again, the top of his bald head growing a bright shade of red.

Chuck shook his head again. "Nope, not gonna happen. I demand to speak to your supervisor."

Fred's hand became a blur of movement as he reached out lightning-fast. Lilly watched in amazement as Fred's hand passed right through Chuck Jennings's chest. Chuck cried out in surprise as the reaper's hand closed around his spinal cord.

"You can't do this," Chuck protested as Fred easily hoisted the man into the air before setting him down on the scale. The dial, which was half white and half red, began to spin. It did not take long before it stopped, red filling the entire display window.

"Fuck," the man whispered.

Reality came to a screeching stop. Everyone and everything ceased to exist within the stream of time. A sinister laugh echoed throughout the room. Every inky shadow cast by the living slithered to one corner of the room, making it as black as the void itself. Two glowing red eyes took form within the darkness. A loud gulp managed to escape Chuck's throat as a figure emerged from the shadows. It was a demon from the very bowels of hell, standing seven feet tall with blackened and blistered skin. Its once-red, glowing eyes were now yellow and staring intensely at Chuck. A pair of pants made from human flesh covered its lower half, while a shirt of rusty chain mail protected its muscular torso. The demon let out a thunderous roar as it extended its leathery wings and gave them a mighty flap.

"Fuck me," Chuck whispered again.

The demon moved with supernatural speed and came to stand dangerously close to Chuck. "Oh, there'll be plenty of time for that," the demon hissed. If Chuck had been alive, he would have surely shat himself, but since he was dead, he did not have that luxury. The demon looked directly at Lilly, who also let out a gulp, while it sniffed the air around her. It flashed her an evil grin before turning its attention to the reaper. "Fred! How the hell are you, brother?"

"You know, overworked and underpaid."

"Looks like they're working you to death." The demon let out a hearty laugh. "They got you greeting purgs now?" He nodded in Lilly's direction.

"Doin' a favor for someone," Fred replied.

"I heard it had to do with that incident in the East River."

"Who told you that?"

"I have my sources," the demon said.

"It was Gladus, wasn't it? Fucking Gladus."

The demon shrugged.

"This one believes there's been some kind of mistake," Fred said, purposely changing the subject.

"They always do," the demon said. "Let me guess, you want to speak to a supervisor?"

Chuck slowly nodded.

"I can arrange that," said the demon, bringing a nervous smile to Chuck's lips. The demon punched his fist through poor Chuck's chest and grabbed his spinal cord, much like Fred had, but this time the hand didn't simply pass through the dead man's skin; it was thrust through. Blood sprayed everywhere as Chuck screamed in horror and pain. The demon lifted Chuck into the air and began to walk back to the shadow-saturated corner. "Catch ya later, Fred," the demon called out over Chuck's screams. "Good luck, Purg," he added before the two of them disappeared within the blackness, causing the doorway to hell to fade from existence.

The river of time flowed forward once again as if nothing had happened.

Lilly was at a loss for words. Being a ghost and learning that she had to complete her unfinished business before she could cross over cemented the fact that there was indeed an afterlife, but up until this very moment, she had never thought about what that had actually meant. If something like a demon was real, then that meant God was also very real, and while she had attended church with her parents all her life, she had never really given much thought to her own belief in the Almighty. Until now. She suddenly felt sorry for Chuck Jennings, knowing what his fate would be, but deep down, Lilly found herself wanting to be there when her killer's time came. Did that make her evil or just human?

Chapter 4

Follow the Light

"What just happened?" Lilly asked once everything had returned to normal.

When she didn't get an answer, she turned in time to catch the reaper hastily leaving the room. When she finally caught up with him, Fred stood in front of the elevators again.

"What was that back there?" she asked again as the elevator doors opened.

"What?" Fred stepped in and waited for Lilly to do the same.

She gave him an evil stare as she stepped into the elevator.

"Oh, that," Fred replied. "That was Mr. Jennings getting his just desserts. Nothing to get..."

"My panties in a bunch?"

"I was gonna say all riled up about, but whatever floats your boat."

"And that thing?"

"Dagon? He's a demon," Fred answered as the elevator doors opened.

"How can that be?"

Fred was off to the races again before Lilly could get another word out. All she could do was try to keep up. Fred opened a door leading to a large room containing the hospital's HVAC units. "Didn't they teach you anything in Sunday school?" he asked, reaching a metal ladder leading up to a trap door in the ceiling.

"Yeah, but that doesn't mean any of it's real."

"Oh, it's real," Fred informed her. "Heaven, hell, angels, demons, ghosts, and purgatory." He motioned around them as he said purgatory. "Good people go up, and bad people go down. It's the circle of life."

"But a demon," she said, shaking her head in disbelief.

"What? Dagon? He's a nice guy under the...chain mail and flesh pants. Yeah, now that I say it out loud, I can see where you're coming from," Fred said. "I mean, deep down, he's got a really big heart. Now, don't get me wrong, he is a demon and will flay the skin from your bones without thinking twice about it, but other than that, real solid kinda guy." He pounded his fist against his chest a few times.

Without saying another word, he climbed up the ladder and opened the trap door to the hospital's roof, disappearing from Lilly's sight.

She blew out a sigh of frustration and followed the reaper up the ladder. When she reached the top, she found Fred standing in front of a small wall at the roof's edge.

"What's that?" Lilly asked.

Far off in the distance, a bright dot of golden light illumi-nated the horizon. She had no idea what the bright light was but felt the faint hint of an unfamiliar connection. She looked to the sky and found it the same as it had been when she first appeared in the clearing, but none of that mattered now, as the golden ray of light held her complete attention.

"That is your unfinished business," the reaper answered.

"And what's my unfinished business?"

"How the hell am I supposed to know? It's *your* unfinished business, not mine." Fred took out his watch and checked the time. "Look, everyone's unfinished business is different. Maybe you need to say goodbye to someone special or something else along that line."

She thought about the reaper's words for a moment. She had always had a great relationship with her parents. There hadn't been any secrets or anything she had ever regretted doing or saying to them.

"No?" Fred asked. "Nothing there?"

Lilly shook her head. "I don't think so."

"Ok, what's the one thing that's gnawing at you right now?"

As she pondered on Fred's question, she reached up and played with her hair. It hit her like a ton of bricks. Her hair. "It ticks me off that that guy killed me and buried me in the woods like I was garbage."

"Your killer took a piece of you, didn't he?" Fred asked, touching the area of Lilly's hair where her killer had taken his trophy. "He can't hide what's not his. Follow the light, and you'll find him."

"And what is it I'm supposed to do when I find him?" Lilly asked.

"Bring him to justice. Make him pay for what he did to you," Fred answered.

"But I'm a ghost! No one can see or hear me, remember? How am I supposed to do that?"

"You're a smart girl. I'm sure you'll figure it out, but you need to be quick about it," Fred warned, putting his watch back in his pocket.

"Why?"

"The longer your spirit remains in purgatory, the more frustrated you're sure to become. And with frustration comes anger. Stay angry for too long, and you'll forget what it is you were meant to do," Fred said. "And don't be fooled by the perception of time either. It's not the same as before. Remember your time in the woods?"

"And how am I supposed to get there?"

"Beats me," Fred said, shrugging. "Take the bus, hitch a ride, ask someone who cares. Either way, you need to get moving." Before Lilly could reply, the reaper picked her up from behind and tossed her off the roof. "Clock's a ticking."

Lilly had never screamed so loud in her life. The sensation of falling from eight stories high was like nothing she had ever experienced before. The wind whipped her hair. The adrenaline coursing through her veins filled her head, and the pit of her stomach made its way to her throat. She flailed her arms and legs, the chaotic movement only adding to her current predicament, causing her body to tumble out of control. The only thing missing was the beating of her heart as it threatened to explode from her chest. Then she hit the ground, and the ride ended.

Unbelievably, she got to her feet and brushed herself off. The fall should have killed her, she thought, amazed she had survived the plunge without a single scratch. Then she remembered she was already dead. Gazing up to the roof, she found the reaper gone, leaving her alone once again. It could be worse. She could still be sitting in the forest. The thought of her decaying corpse made her shiver.

So what was she supposed to do now?

According to Fred, she needed to head in the direction of the light toward her unfinished business. That was the only way for her to get out of purgatory, but which way did she need to go? From the roof of the hospital, she had been able to see the bright golden dot of light quite easily, even though it seemed a long way away, but on the ground and surrounded by buildings, her sense of direction had now become distorted. Not having any idea which way was north or south, she turned her attention back to the top of the building. When she had been standing there, the dot of light had been directly ahead of her. She spun one hundred and eighty degrees on her heels and started walking.

Lilly headed in the direction of the nearest street. After a short walk—at least she thought it was a short walk—she found what appeared to be the center of town. There were a handful of businesses, all of which seemed void of life. On the other side of the street sat a rundown-looking bar with loud music and bright lights emanating from its windows. A few blocks farther down the street, she found the sheriff's department.

She stood on the street staring at the old building, wondering if the detective had discovered anything new about her case yet. He had just left her at the morgue, so she didn't expect there to be any new leads. At least, she thought he had just left her. Remembering what Fred had said about the passage of time, she decided to go in and see if there had been any breaks in her case.

Lilly walked up to the glass door of the sheriff's department and reached out to grab the metal door handle, only to have her hand pass right through it. "You're dead, dummy," she said aloud. She stood there for a while, waiting for someone to open the door for her, but no one ever did. The thing Fred had said about being stuck at the bottom of an elevator shaft made her hesitant about walking through the door, but she couldn't stay out here forever. Besides, she could see through this door, and there wasn't an elevator shaft in sight.

Taking several confident steps toward the door, Lilly moved to walk through it but stopped shy of the glass. Reaching out her hand, she pushed it through the solid surface of the door and stared in disbelief. She pulled her hand back through and looked at it, as if inspecting it for damage. "You've done this before," she told herself, trying to boost her confidence. Taking a deep breath and holding the air in her lungs, she slowly pushed her head through the door. She was about halfway through when a sheriff's deputy came out of nowhere, opening the door and walking straight through her as he exited the building.

"Whoa!" Her body rippled out of control for a few seconds before regaining its composure. "Let's not do that again," she said before throwing caution to the wind and walking through the door.

The lobby of the sheriff's department smelled like stale cigarettes and old coffee. There were several chairs lined against the wall to her left. There was a welcome window in the wall to her right, with a sergeant sitting on the other side. On the wall straight ahead were two large maps. One was for the City of Greenville, which she guessed was the city she was in. The other was a map of the state of Ohio.

"I'm in Ohio!"

Cupping her hand over her mouth, she looked around, half-embarrassed at causing such a scene. The sergeant sitting behind the welcome desk window flipped through a stack of paperwork. She stared at him, waiting for him to tell her to quiet down, but he never did. Looking back at the map of Ohio, she discovered that the City of Greenville was on the east side of the state, near the Indiana border.

Wanting to leave the lobby, she made her way to a secured wooden door leading from the front lobby to the actual police department and walked through it without any hesitation.

Lilly wandered aimlessly through the building. Never having been in a police department, she didn't know what to look for. She saw a sign on the wall next to a wooden door, which read DETAIL ROOM. She poked her head through the door and found a long table filled with sheriffs' deputies sitting around it. At the head of the table sat a different sergeant, who was also flipping through some paperwork while the rest of the deputies talked among themselves. Lilly looked around the room but didn't recognize any of them from her crime scene, so she decided to move on.

Eventually, she found the Detective Bureau. She checked each name placard on the doors until she found Brandt's office. The door was closed up tight, making it impossible for her to know if anyone was on the other side or not. Placing an ear as close to the door as she could, she tried her best to eavesdrop on any sounds that might let her know if the detective was inside. Remembering that no one could see her, she shook her head and walked through the door.

A small desk rested against one wall, which sat next to an even smaller window. Off to the side was a tall metal filing cabinet with a more brown than green plant of some kind on top of it. A large stack of paperwork sat in the middle of the desk. On top of the pile was a manila envelope with the name Jane Doe written on it. She instinctively tried to pick up the file, cursing under her breath when her fingers passed through the paperwork. Blowing out a depressing sigh, Lilly's attention turned to a wall of photographs. They were all in black-and-white, eight by ten, and stuck to the wall by small pieces of clear tape. A cold shiver ran down her spine, causing her to turn away when she discovered they were pictures from her crime scene. The images etched themselves into her mind, acting as grizzly reminders of her demise. Laughter echoed from somewhere out in the hallway, pulling her attention from the office.

Stepping out of the office, Lilly stood in the middle of the empty corridor and listened. Had that been laughter, or was she hearing things? After several minutes of silence, she heard it again. It was laughter, but it wasn't any kind of laughter she had ever heard before. It came in short bursts and sounded like it was overflowing with insanity. Probably some crazy drunk lying half-unconscious in a jail cell, laughing incoherently in their sleep. But for some reason, she felt compelled to seek it out.

After searching the entire first floor for the source of the crazy laughter, she came to stand in front of a red metal door leading to the department's basement. The laughter resounded throughout the building once more, filling her ears and virtually pulling her through the door.

On the other side of the door, she found a metal staircase leading to a long hallway. The floor consisted of old, yellowish tiles with near-matching paint on the cinder block walls. Florescent lights hung from the ceiling, casting an eerie glow about the hall. There were several doors on each side of the corridor, but it was the one at the end of the hallway that sent a cold shiver down her spine. The solid metal door was a faded peach color. Before she knew it, she stood in front of the door, speculating as to what lay beyond.

"This is ridiculous," she said out loud, mainly to tell herself that she didn't have to go any farther if she didn't want to.

The demented laugh echoed out from behind the door as the light above her flickered briefly. Blowing out a loud breath, she passed through the door. Before her was another hallway, about twenty feet long. On both sides of the hall were four iron-barred cells. Four old, dimly lit light bulbs hung above her, arranged so that each light bulb illuminated the two cells in front of it. As her gaze moved down the corridor, she noted the last light bulb was burned out, causing the last two cells at the end of the hallway to be cast in heavy, dark shadows.

The first two cells were filled with an assortment of old, dust-covered boxes, as were the next two. Lilly walked down the hall, imagining at some point in the building's history that these cells would have held prisoners. Cells five and six were packed with old desks, chairs, and file cabinets. When she reached the end of the hall, she turned to the cell on her right first. It was almost identical to the others, filled with old things no one deemed useful anymore. Turning to face the cell on her left, she saw only darkness.

Lilly took several small steps toward the cell and stopped inches away from the iron bars. For a brief moment, she thought she had perceived some kind of movement from within the inky blackness, although she knew it was probably just her imagination getting the better of her. But still, the laughter had to have come from somewhere.

"Hello?"

Two large white eyes with bright blue pupils blinked into existence against the black curtain in front of her. They glared at Lilly with an intensity that froze her to the bone. Narrowing and filling with anger and resentment, the eyes surged forth with a loud scream. They belonged to a man with gray, faded skin. A ragged black-and-white-striped jumpsuit hung loosely on his frame, and Lilly could make out a long, wide, black mark stretched across the man's throat, almost like a bruise.

Lilly screamed at the man's sudden outburst and jumped backward. She cried out in pain when her body slammed into the iron bars of the cell behind her. To her disbelief, they were solid, stopping her momentum, but she had no idea why they had burned her. The three light bulbs illuminating the hallway exploded simultaneously, casting the holding area into total darkness. The ghost of the man hooted his craze-filled laugh, his eyes shining brightly in the blackness. Lilly ran from the basement as fast as she could.

Chapter 5

Forbidden Urges

Mark Karle stepped out of the shower. Wrapping the towel around his thick waist, he stood in front of the bathroom sink, where he gazed at his reflection in the medicine cabinet's mirror. His brown hair was thinning in places on the top of his white scalp, and his thick, matching mustache had a few gray hairs, but they were hardly noticeable. He turned sideways and grimaced at his gut. His body was far from perfect, one too many times through the fast food drive-through, though years of working construction jobs had made him dense and solid.

"What's happened to you?" he asked his reflection. "I used to be able to control you."

"You've become weak," his reflection answered back.

"No, I haven't," Mark said defiantly, slamming his fist down on the hard porcelain sink.

"It's not your fault," his reflection pointed out.

A low growl rumbled from Mark's throat. It was his fault, and he knew it. He was losing control, but he had no idea why.

"Marky!" a woman's voice screeched. A voice full of need

and impatience. A voice that pricked at the base of his skull like a thousand tiny needles. "Where are you?"

"I'm in the bathroom," he yelled, breathing out a loud, frustrated sigh while still gazing at his reflection.

"I told you," his reflection said, "it's not your fault you've become weak."

"Marky, I need you NOW!"

Mark grabbed ahold of both sides of the sink and squeezed as hard as he could. He heard his knuckles popping while a vein on the side of his head enlarged and began to throb. He let go of the sink and blew out a calming breath. "Coming," he said, slowing his heart rate.

Mark got dressed, taking as much time as he dared, before walking out of the second-floor bathroom and slowly making his way down the hall to his mother's bedroom. Along both walls of the hallway were pictures of a young blonde woman in varying poses. In each image, she was flashing a brilliant smile, which accentuated her gleaming eyes. Eyes that followed him with each passing step.

Mark entered his mother's room, and the overwhelming scent of shit smacked him hard in the face. "I've been calling for you for half an hour," his mother scolded. "Why didn't you listen to me?"

Norma Karle, who was seventy-three years old, had suffered a massive stroke ten years ago, leaving her bedridden and somewhat delusional. Her long gray hair was greasy and unkempt, and she wore a one-piece nightgown, which was a dingy shade of white and had small red and green flowers printed all over it. Mark's father had died nearly fifteen years earlier from a heart attack, and since he was an only child, the responsibility of caring for his mother fell squarely upon his shoulders.

"I was in the shower."

"Hurry and clean me up," his mother ordered. "I'm going to be late for my big audition."

Mark grabbed an adult diaper from the top of the dresser, closest to the bed, and a box of baby wipes. "There's no audition, Mom," he said, putting on a pair of latex gloves and pulling back her sheets.

"What do you mean there's no audition? Did they choose someone else? Someone...prettier?"

"That was fifty years ago, Mom, remember?" Taking a baby wipe, he began to clean her off. Why didn't he just hire another home health aide to do this? His mother grabbed his hand with enough force to make him wince. An animalistic expression formed on her face as she forced his hand up a few inches toward her vagina.

"Make sure you get it real clean now, son," she said, forcing his hand up and down while a sadistic smile crossed her lips.

That's why, he reminded himself. For the first four years, things had gone well with the aides who had come out and taken care of her, but something changed about six years ago, for reasons Mark couldn't fully explain. After pulling this stunt several times on a certain male aide, who made it abundantly clear he wasn't being paid enough for this kind of fucked up shit, she was put on a list somewhere, and now, every time he called, they told him no one was available. He had toyed with the idea of putting her in a nursing home, but since he couldn't afford it, and because she was blacklisted, Mark had been forced to quit his job so he could tend to his mother's needs full time. The state of Michigan paid him to be her caregiver, but even with her social security and the small pension from his father, he still barely made ends meet.

He pulled his hand away as she cackled at him. "I'm hungry," she said, crossing her arms and pouting like a small child.

He threw the diaper and baby wipes into a plastic bag before removing his gloves and tossing them in with the rest of the garbage. "What do you feel like?" he asked.

"Carrots," she said, her face lighting up. "They're my favorite."

"Carrots it is," he said, tying up the end of the bag and walking out of the room. Once downstairs, he made his way into the kitchen, where he opened the back door leading to the enclosed back porch and tossed the bag onto a mountain-high pile of bags just like it.

Opening a cupboard next to the stove, he found jar after jar of baby food. Peas, apricot, sweet potato, and apple, but no carrot. "How about peas?" he yelled out.

"Carrots!"

"Sweet potato?"

"I said I want fucking carrots!"

"All right!" he yelled back, sighing at the thought of having to venture down into the basement.

The door was in the kitchen, not far from the door leading out to the back porch, but he just didn't want to go down there...not yet anyhow, though he was beginning to think he didn't have much say in the matter. Norma wanted carrots, and he knew she would not eat anything else. No matter how hungry she got, she would carry on with her stubbornness just to spite him.

"I should let you starve," he mumbled, turning on the light and descending into the bowels of his home. He was serious about his statement. The only problem with his plan was that it would probably take close to a week for the old bag to die; a week of him having to listen to her constant yelling and screaming.

The house he shared with his mother was an old, two-story farmhouse situated on ten acres of land roughly fifteen miles from Harrison, Michigan. They were off the beaten path enough that even if his mother screamed for a week straight, no one would ever hear her. No one except for him. He could always leave, he told himself, walking up to a large metal shelving unit full of baby food jars.

The basement was as big as the whole first floor of the house. Back in the day, when the house had been built, it sat on top of a foundation made of large rocks and cement. It was what people of the state referred to as a Michigan basement. When his parents bought the house, they converted the basement the best they could, framing out the walls using two-by-fours and drywall. The original dirt floor and been covered with a layer of cement, all except for one corner, where the water well and a sump pump sat.

On the third shelf, he found four jars of carrot-flavored baby food and thought about the promise he had made his father, Ben Karle, on his deathbed. That was the *real* reason he couldn't muster the courage to leave her to rot in her own shit. Mark was the man of the house now; his father had told him so. And it was his responsibility to watch over his mother. To make sure no harm came to her. His father had made him swear to it, and Mark Karle was a man of his word, if nothing else.

Mark's eyes shifted to the far end of the basement. To the old, wooden door surrounded by unfinished drywall. Taking several tentative steps toward the door, his fingers began to shake, causing the glass jars to clang against one another. "No," he told himself, using a scolding tone. Maybe just for a little while, a voice called out from somewhere in his head. He contemplated giving in to the voice and even went as far as to take another step forward when his mother's voice stabbed him in the base of his skull.

"Marky!"

Mark whirled around on his heels and rushed up the stairs,

making sure to turn off the light before closing the door. He stopped by the sink and grabbed a spoon on his way back to his mother's room. Putting on a brave smile, he twisted off the top of the baby food jar as he made his entrance. "Who wants carrots?"

After his mother's dinner, Mark cleaned her up and made sure to change her diaper for the night. He even went as far as to turn on the little radio on her nightstand, which had been set to a channel that played old show tunes. A slight smile crept across his mother's lips as she closed her eyes and drifted off to a life that had to be better than the one she was living now.

Mark softly closed the door and made his way down to the living room, making another quick stop in the kitchen to grab a few beers before plopping down in his recliner and turning on the TV, which picked up a handful of channels from the large metal antenna on the roof of the house. The living room was straight out of the seventies, with thick shag carpet that at one point had been white but now resembled a stick of butter. Long brown curtains hung from the two windows, while the walls of the room were an exact copy of the upstairs hallway. Everywhere he looked, his mother was always watching.

He must have dozed off because before he knew it, static filled the screen. He moved to turn off the TV when something caught his attention out of the corner of his eye. Turning, he found his reflection staring back at him from a medium mirror with an ornate wooden frame hanging on the wall off to his left.

"Stop taunting me," he said to his reflection, who gave him a "who me?" look. "You know I can't."

"But it would be so easy," his reflection pointed out.

"But I made a promise," Mark argued with himself. "And I don't break my promises."

"Do you think Dad knew this was going to happen? That

he would want his betrothed to suffer like this? You'd be granting her mercy."

"You think?" Mark asked inquisitively.

"I know."

Mark made his way back up to his mother's room. And after tip-toeing down the hallway with the pictures of his mother watching his every step, he stopped in front of her bedroom door, listening to her snoring loudly from the peaceful confines of her bed. He stood there silently for several long minutes before gathering up the courage to open the door. Creeping so softly that he thought he was gliding, he crossed the space between the door and his mother's bed as quickly as he dared. Gently picking up a pillow, he pressed it against his chest, trying to muffle the sound of his beating heart.

"Do it," a voice said. Glancing down at the nightstand, Mark's reflection glared at him from a small hand mirror resting near the radio. "Go on. Do it."

Mark glared at his reflection, a twinge of hatred forming in his eyes. But whose eyes were they? Mark asked, for he truly did not know.

"I told you, you were too fucking weak."

"No, I'm not," Mark whispered, fearing his anger would get the better of him and awaken his mother.

"Then go down into the basement," his reflection suggested, offering an alternative that Mark desperately needed...wanted, but it was too soon. Not enough time had passed since the last time he had ventured down there. Why can't I control you anymore? he questioned, staring at his reflection.

"You know why," his reflection answered.

Mark wanted this conversation to stop. It wasn't healthy, and he knew it, but for some reason, he couldn't. He suddenly noticed the absence of his mother's laborious breathing. Slowly turning his head away from the mirror, he found his mother's fear-filled eyes wide open. "I came up to check on you. You look uncomfortable. Do you need another pillow?"

Norma glared at him for several long, awkward seconds before her expression turned sour. "Leave me the fuck alone," she scolded.

Mark placed the pillow back down and swiftly walked out of the room, making his way back to the living room. He sank back into his chair with a loud sigh. Three minutes later, his mother was yelling his name. He grabbed the TV remote and flicked it on as static filled the screen. After flipping through several channels, the old TV screen came to life with an even older rerun of *Gilligan's Island*. Turning the volume up until he could no longer hear his mother's screeching voice, he closed his eyes and dreamed of finding his way onto a deserted island. Away from everyone in his life. Away from his mother and, more especially, away from *him*. He fought the urge to look at the mirror, for he knew *he* would be there waiting.

Chapter 6

Dead and Buried

Lilly Barnes sat on a metal bus stop bench. The clouds above her continued to move unnaturally fast across the dark sky as the still-present solar eclipse shadow stretched itself across the entire world. She found her thoughts drifting to the thing in the basement of the police department. Had that been another ghost? She recalled the look in its eyes. There hadn't been anything resembling life anymore, only insanity. And what was that mark across its neck? A bruise? Had the man hung himself? Was being trapped in that cell his penance for taking his own life?

She recalled what Fred told her about staying in purgatory for too long. Would she end up that way? The reaper had also told her that in order to pass on, she needed to complete her unfinished business, but how could she do that as a ghost? Follow the golden light?

Lilly's train of thought rapidly shifted to her parents. She could not even imagine what they must be going through. Having no answers for the past six months as to what had happened to their little girl was simply beyond her comprehension, and here she was, stuck in bum fuck Ohio, with no way of reaching out to them or even telling Detective Brandt her true identity and how to contact her parents. The sound of voices pulled her mind back to reality. Three living people now occupied the bench with her.

Within a few minutes, a bus pulled up to the curb. Lilly wearily stood and followed the living onto the bus, which, to her relief, was only half-full. She found an empty seat in the back and sat next to a window. Looking through the dirt-speckled glass, she scanned the sky as the bus pulled away, headed to its next stop. She just hoped she was going in the right direction.

People got on the bus. People got off the bus. Lilly had to change seats several times to avoid being sat on. She did her best to stay near an open window, but being in the city made it hard for her to keep a constant eye on the horizon. She could barely make out the golden glow in the sky, but it seemed like the bus was heading in the right direction until it left its last stop, where it turned around and headed back toward the center of town.

"Shit," Lilly mumbled, watching the glow in the sky get farther and farther away. Reaching up, she tried to grab the cord hanging from the ceiling, so the driver would stop the bus, and screamed in frustration when her hand passed right through it. "Think, think," she said, desperately searching for another exit. Then she remembered what she was and ran at the wall of the bus, not stopping until she had passed right through it. As soon as she cleared the side of the bus, she fell to the ground and rolled several times before coming to a stop on the side of the street. She barely had enough time to jump out of the way of a fast-moving car. Once she made it to the safety of the sidewalk, she looked at the sky to get her bearings before putting one foot in front of the other.

Trying to get out of the city proved to be a harder task than she had thought it would be. The golden glow in the sky would be there one minute before disappearing behind a house or a tall building, and the next time she saw the light, it wouldn't be where she thought it should have been. She stopped at a four-way intersection and gazed upon a large cemetery across the street. It sat behind a small stone block wall, topped with a black wrought iron fence, and ran down the two streets across from her. She had already passed this cemetery once before. "Great. I've been walking in circles."

She made her way across the street and leaned against the cemetery's stone wall. A burning pain shot across her back when she made contact with the iron fence. Screaming out in agony, she jumped away from the wall while trying to see if her back was on fire, because it sure felt like it.

The sound of a young boy laughing hysterically reached her ears.

Lilly's head shot up, her pain forgotten. She peered past the fence and found only tombstones staring back at her. "Who's there?" she asked, making sure to stay away from the fence.

A small boy, maybe around ten years old and dressed in a black suit and tie, shyly peeked out from behind a tombstone not too far from the fence line. His skin was a light shade of gray, and his hair was raven black.

"You can see me?" Lilly asked before noticing the color of the boy's skin.

He nodded.

"Do you know why the fence hurt me?"

Stepping out from behind the stone marker, he pushed his hands deep into his pants pockets. "Because you're a ghost, like me."

That didn't explain anything, she thought, remembering the incident in the basement of the police station. Those bars must have been iron too. Was that why the ghost of the prisoner was still there? Was he trapped? "Ok, mental note, don't touch any iron. You wouldn't happen to know the way out of the city, would you?"

The boy shook his head before his eyes widened. "Lady Annabelle might. She knows a lot of things."

"Can you take me to her?"

The young ghost nodded vigorously. "There's an opening in the gate down that way," he pointed. "Follow me," he added, before taking off like a shot, weaving in and out of the tomb-stones. Lilly did her best to follow the boy and keep him in sight, which was a chore in itself. The cemetery's wall extended for several city blocks, but she found an opening in the gate, about half a block from where she had first laid eyes on the boy, and discovered him sitting on a tombstone waiting for her.

"My name's Sebastian," he said, rushing up to greet her. He took hold of Lilly's hand and shook it hard, catching her by surprise.

"I'm Lilly," she responded. "We can touch each other?"

"We're the same."

"I've got a lot to learn."

"Lady Annabelle can teach you. She taught me when I first arrived," said Sebastian, pulling Lilly by the hand and leading her into the cemetery.

Lilly didn't like the idea of not following her unfinished business, but she could really use the help, and the way Sebastian made it sound, Lady Annabelle might be able to help her in more ways than one. "We have to hurry, ok?" she said to the young ghost.

Deeper and deeper, they ventured into the cemetery. Lilly hadn't noticed it at first, but the air seemed to grow heavier as they walked. It was a sensation she couldn't fully explain, but she soon forgot about it when she caught her first glimpse of other ghosts wandering among the gravestones. Spirits from all eras of time roamed the grounds. Men and women dressed in expensive clothes lined the outer ring of the cemetery. A few rows in, the fashions changed to jeans and tie-dyed shirts. A few rows farther, the fashion changed back to suits and dresses, but this time they had a more elegant design to them. Lilly got the distinct impression that the farther they went, the older the spirits became.

Most of them ignored her. A few made eye contact. One or two nodded, and several waved, but the majority of them acted as if she did not belong. She also noted the ghosts' appearances were not all the same. Some had limbs missing; others had bruising around their necks, like the ghost in the cell. More than a few had the backs of their heads missing. Lilly felt a little relieved when most of them didn't look at her because she couldn't help but stare.

Sebastian pulled her deeper and deeper through the gravestones until they came to a large stone mausoleum. It had a green tarnished bronze door with a small lead glass window. The name *Wilburn* was carved into the stone above the door. "This is Lady Annabelle's mausoleum," he said, reaching out and knocking hard against the metal door, something else Lilly found surprising, given her recent encounters with doors.

The spirit of a beautiful woman glided effortlessly through the solid bronze door. She was a few inches taller than Lilly and about a decade older. Her skin was a dark shade of gray. She had long brown hair adorned with lush, thick curls and wore a blue dress made of lace and silk. It flowed outward and stopped about an inch from the ground. Her hands were covered with a pair of white gloves, with her right hand grasping a large folded-up fan. A piece of blue lace encircled her neck, trying its best to cover up the long black bruise running across her throat.

"And who is this pretty young lass, Sebastian?" she asked. With a quick flick of the wrist, she unfolded the fan and began to move it back and forth.

"My name is Lilly, and you must be Lady Annabelle?"

"That I am," the woman answered. "You are a young soul, now, aren't you? Recently departed, I mean."

"Yes, ma'am. How can you tell?"

"Oh, and she has manners to boot," Lady Annabelle said with a large smile. "Don't get many of your kind here."

"My kind?"

"Spirits that aren't buried here, dear. And to answer your question, the longer we stay in this world, the grayer we become."

"Lady Annabelle, Lilly's lost," Sebastian blurted out.

"Is she now?"

"Yes, ma'am," Lilly answered. "I need to get out of the city. I need to go..."

"Let me guess. Toward your golden ray of light? Toward your unfinished business?"

"Yes. How do you...?"

"Know about the golden ray of light?" Lady Annabelle asked, still fanning her face.

Lilly nodded.

"Mine *was* that way, but it faded a long time ago." Lady Annabelle pointed off to her right without taking her eyes from Lilly. "Show her where yours was, Sebastian."

The young ghost whirled around and pointed up.

Lilly's gaze followed Sebastian's finger up to the sky briefly before returning to the smiling face of Lady Annabelle. "Everyone here had unfinished business, my dear. We are all purgs, like yourself."

"Why are you here then, and...wait, what do you mean by *had*?"

"Why am I not out there trying to undo the chains keeping me bound to this earth? We have all tried and failed miserably. Then one day, you find out your unfinished business has an expiration date. People die. And after that, we become truly trapped in this god-forsaken place, with no hope of escape. Eventually, we make it here, back to where we were eternally laid to rest. Speaking of which, where is yours?"

"The city morgue," Lilly answered.

"You poor dear," Lady Annabelle replied, reaching up and running her fingers through Lilly's hair, right in the spot where the dent in her skull had been. Lilly thought it odd that she would touch her in that spot. Like she knew the cause of her death. "Oh my, where are *my* manners. Won't you come in?" Lady Annabelle whirled about and walked back through the door of her mausoleum.

"Come on," Sebastian said, running through the door and disappearing from sight.

The inside of the mausoleum was not as cold as Lilly had imagined it would be. The wall to her left was white marble, with small copper plaques holding the names of the persons entombed behind them. On the opposite wall was a large stained glass window with the image of a glowing white angel and several red roses. In the center of the room sat a round glass table with a handful of old wooden chairs gathered around it. On the table rested an old pewter hand mirror and an even older hairbrush.

"Take a seat and tell me what brings you here, my dear," Lady Annabelle said, already sitting in one chair, with Sebastian seated beside her. She motioned to one of the chairs with her fan, her gray lips forming a bright smile.

Lilly took a seat and deliberated about where she should begin. "I need to find my way out of the city," she began. "Sebastian said you might be able to help me."

"That I might," Lady Annabelle said. "I have been here for some time and lived here when I was alive...but the city has changed so much over the years. I suppose I could try to draw you a map."

"Can't you take me to the edge of the city or somewhere close to it? If I can get a clear view of the light, I'm sure I can find my way from there."

"I'm afraid no one is allowed to leave the cemetery without permission from the council," Lady Annabelle answered, fanning her face.

"The council?"

"Three of the oldest spirits buried here. They made the rules so the rest of us could live out our so-called afterlives in relative peace instead of wandering around out there in the world all alone. I could summon them for an emergency meeting and ask if they would allow me to help you."

"Could you?" Lilly asked. "I would really appreciate that."

"Sebastian, do be a dear and tell the elders I wish to speak with them."

The young ghost leaped from the chair and raced from the mausoleum. "What kind of unfinished business does he have?" Lilly asked, watching the boy disappear through the door.

"Sebastian came to us in 1970. For the most part, he is quite shy and keeps to himself. I do not believe he has ever told me what keeps his spirit earthbound. What about you, my dear? What unfinished business do you have?" Lady Annabelle asked, picking up the hand mirror and gazing at her reflection.

"I...I was murdered by a man and buried in a forest not far from here," Lilly began. "I guess I have to find a way to bring him to justice. Make him pay for what he did to me. I don't know... Maybe it was my fault or something... Maybe I could have done something or said something differently..."

"Don't you dare blame yourself for what that man did to

you!" Lady Annabelle slammed her fist onto the table. "Look at yourself," she said, turning the mirror around so Lilly could look at her ghostly reflection. "You are a beautiful young woman who strikes me as being fierce and strong."

Lilly looked at her reflection in the mirror and realized that this was the first time she had seen her face since her death. Gazing at her own body on the morgue table was surreal, but that hadn't been her, not really.

Lilly was relieved to find her color had not changed yet. Something red in her hair caught her eye. It was in the spot Lady Annabelle had touched her earlier. Turning her head to the side, she discovered the grim realization of her own death. That was the very spot where he had hit her.

"We all carry the scars of our death with us, my dear, for the whole undead world to see," Lady Annabelle stated, lowering the piece of blue lace tied around her neck, showing Lilly the long black bruise across her throat.

"How can you pick up the mirror?"

"You have much to learn, young one. For starters, iron will not pass through our bodies, and as you have experienced first-hand, will harm us."

Lilly rubbed her shoulder as she thought about the burning pain she had felt when she leaned against the wrought iron fence of the cemetery wall. "Why?"

"The true answer to that question has been lost to the passing of time, but from what I've been told, there are certain minerals in the earth that react with our supernatural form. I believe being laid to rest in the earth has something to do with it. Salt is another one of those minerals. Pour a line of salt on the floor, and we simply cannot cross it."

"How long have you been here?"

Lady Annabelle set the mirror down and began to fan her face again. "I met my demise in 1864. Three years earlier, I had been in love and engaged to be married. His name was Samuel Horn, and his parents were wealthy. Oil, I think. One day Samuel decided he needed to join the war effort and pledged his allegiance to the north. A few months later, he was off to fight the Confederacy. A few weeks after, I found out I was pregnant with his child," she said, crossing her legs and straightening out the wrinkles of her dress.

"At first, I got letters from him on a regular basis. He told me how much he missed me and that he could not wait to return and take me as his bride. I wrote him back and told him he was going to be a father. He had only been gone a few months, but to me, it had felt like an eternity. Then our son was born. I named him Jonathan, after Samuel's father. One year became two. His letters began to grow farther and farther apart until one day, he wrote me to say he had fallen in love with another woman, and they were to be married." The features of Lady Annabelle's face twisted with disgust.

"I went to his parents, who suddenly wanted nothing to do with me or their grandson," she said, her face contorting with anger. "How could he do that to me? To his child? I hated Samuel with every fiber of my being. Not only did he leave me, but he left me undesirable as well. No man wants a woman who's given birth out of wedlock," she said, stiffening her back and lifting her head.

"I found out where the letters had been mailed from and left Jonathan with my parents, so I could travel down south and confront that bastard once and for all. I made it as far as Mississippi. One night, the stagecoach I was traveling in happened upon a group of runaway slaves who had mistaken me for their owner's wife. After killing the driver, they took turns raping me before hanging me from a nearby tree, like their owner had done to many of their friends."

Lilly didn't know how to respond to something like that

and was more than a little thankful when Lady Annabelle continued.

"My body hung from that tree for nearly two weeks before somebody found me and cut me down. They discovered who I was through some of my belongings and made sure my body was returned to my parents, but my spirit pressed on. My golden ray of light led me to Georgia, where I found Samuel living on a cotton plantation with his new wife and new daughter. I tried so many times to speak with him. To ask him why, but he never heard my dead words. I stayed there for several years, trying everything I could think of, but it was no use. I ultimately returned home, and this is where I have been ever since. If you ever have a chance to get out of purgatory, take it," she told Lilly, her face becoming as hard as stone. "Don't end up like me. I'd do anything to be free from this hell."

Lilly was relieved again when Sebastian came rushing back through the door. "The council said they would hear your request."

"Great," Lilly said. "Let's go!"

"The council will only speak with me, my dear. They do not like outsiders." Lady Annabelle got up from the table and smoothed out her dress. "I will go and plead your case to them. Sebastian, give our guest a tour of the grounds? I shouldn't be long."

"Come on," Sebastian said, enthusiastically grabbing Lilly's hand and pulling her through the crypt door. She quickly lost track of time as Sebastian introduced her to the cemetery's entire populace. They eventually made their way down to the iron fence, where Lilly had first met the young ghost.

"This is one of my favorite spots in the whole cemetery," he said, taking a seat on top of an old marble headstone.

"How come?"

"You'll see," Sebastian answered, a devious smile crossing his childish lips.

Lilly gazed through the iron fence. The street and sidewalk were completely void of people. "Is it always like this?"

"No, it's nighttime right now," he answered.

"How can you tell?" Lilly asked. "It always looks the same."

"Because people sleep at night and walk and drive during the day, silly."

"Oh," Lilly answered, taking a seat on a tombstone. They sat there in silence for a while, but before she knew it, people slowly began to appear on the sidewalk, and cars sped past them.

"You've been here a long time, haven't you?" Lilly asked. The thought of such a young boy having some kind of unfinished business kept nagging at her.

Sebastian's cherub-like face grew solemn. His eyes quickly averted Lilly's.

"Why are you here?" Lilly asked.

"Here he comes," the young boy blurted out, jumping down from the headstone and rushing to the fence.

Lilly watched in disbelief as the young ghost picked up an acorn from the ground. "How did you do that?"

Sebastian didn't answer but instead threw the acorn at a slow-moving man walking down the sidewalk in front of the cemetery. He looked somewhere in his early twenties, was over-weight, and had a slight mental impairment. He wore a pair of oversized headphones on his head. In his left hand, a phone was securely held by his tight grip while the fingers of his right hand snapped out of rhythm. The acorn struck the man right in the forehead, causing him to cry out in alarm. Sebastian laughed and picked up another acorn and winged it at the man again, hitting him in the back of the head this time. The man cried out for a second time and waddled off hastily. "Did you see that? I nailed that fat fucker right in the head?" he laughed even harder. "Twice! Every day he walks past here, and every day I wing acorns at him, and he still hasn't learned to walk on the other side of the street. What a dumbass!"

Lilly was taken aback by what she had just witnessed. She knew little boys could be mischievous, but it looked as if Sebastian had taken pleasure out of pestering the poor man, and then the way he talked about him after. It was just nasty. "Why'd you do that?"

"Because I've got nothing better to do," the young boy answered.

She decided to turn her attention toward something else. Something that might even help her in the long run. "How did you pick up the acorn?"

"Oh, that. That's easy," Sebastian said, picking up another one and throwing it at her. He laughed again when Lilly instinctively tried to snatch the acorn out of the air but failed miserably as it sailed right through her hand. "Lady Annabelle taught me."

"Can you show me how?"

"I guess," Sebastian said, sounding unsure. He picked up another acorn and placed it on the headstone where he had been sitting. "You have to concentrate really hard. Think of your finger as being solid, like it was when you were alive."

Lilly stared at the acorn. How was she supposed to make her finger solid? Her finger still felt solid, she thought, as she tried to touch the nut, but sighed loudly when her finger passed through it.

"You're not trying hard enough," Sebastian said.

Lilly stared at the acorn and imagined her finger being as solid as it had been on the last day of her life. She imagined her fingertip pressing against the nut when she pushed it, but again her finger remained ethereal and passed through the acorn.

Sebastian laughed.

Lilly glared at him. She didn't like being laughed at. "This is stupid."

"Put your finger really close to it, but don't try to touch it yet."

Lilly didn't see the point in continuing but decided to humor the young boy one more time.

Sebastian brought her finger to within a few hairbreadths of the acorn and told her to concentrate. "Don't look at anything else," he said. "Don't look at anything in the background. Don't look at the tombstone. Don't look at me. Just the acorn."

"Ok."

"Now, think of something that makes you mad."

"What?"

"Don't lose your concentration," Sebastian scolded. "You have to think of something that makes you mad. Think of whoever it was that did what they did to you. That thing that brought you to this place. Think of their face and what you'd like to do to it."

The image of her killer's face appeared in her mind. His brown hair. His thick-framed glasses. His mustache. The smell of his aftershave. A warming sensation radiated within her cheeks as a bitter hatred for the man manifested in the pit of her stomach.

"That's it," Sebastian said softly. "Now push all that anger into the acorn."

Lilly pushed her finger forward, and for a fraction of a second, the acorn turned solid against the tip of her ethereal flesh. The small nut rocked ever so slightly, but enough that both Lilly and Sebastian registered the movement.

"You did it!" Sebastian cheered. "Man, it took me forever to do that."

"I did it!" Lilly squealed with excitement. "I'm not sure how, though."

"You used your anger," Lady Annabelle said, appearing out of nowhere. "Anger is a powerful force to the dead. It permits us to regain some of our humanity by allowing us to reconnect with the physical world, even if it is only ever so slightly. The council has agreed to meet with you and to hear your plea."

Chapter 7

Anybody Got a Fly Swatter?

Lilly followed Lady Annabelle into a part of the cemetery she didn't recognize from Sebastian's tour. While the rest of the grounds had plush green grass, this area was dry and brown. The tombstones were faded, the trees had no leaves, and the air smelled stale. They continued walking for several more minutes before Lady Annabelle stopped in front of a hillside mausoleum. A cement block entryway stood cracked and crumbling apart. A large set of double wooden doors served as the entrance to the burial vault, their presence partially concealed by a thick blanket of moss and dead climbing vines. A large rusty chain and padlock held the two doors together, while the name carved into the stone header above the door was so faded it could not be read.

"The council's in there?" A cold shiver ran down Lilly's spine.

"Yes, dear," Lady Annabelle answered. Without another word, the woman's apparition walked through the door, disappearing from sight.

Lilly materialized on the other side of the crypt doors and found her path blocked by two ghosts dressed in tattered blue civil war uniforms. Long beards hung from their faces, with the one on her right having half of his face missing. Both held old rifles with rusty bayonets.

Feeling uneasy, Lilly tried to back out of the crypt, but two more union soldiers appeared beside her, each grabbing her by the arms and dragging her to the center of the small tomb.

This mausoleum was the total opposite of Lady Annabelle's. It was cold, dark, and smelled of mold and rot. The walls and floor were littered with large cracks resembling rivers running through a landscape of old concrete. In the center sat a stone sarcophagus. Several long tendril-like cracks stretched across its stone surface. Lilly could make out strange runes carved into its stone skin. She didn't know what any of them were except for the large pentagram in the middle.

"What's going on?" Lilly cried out, desperately trying to break free of the union ghosts. "Where's the council?"

"You poor thing," Lady Annabelle answered, removing one of the bayonets from a rifle barrel. "There is no council. I'm the only one in charge here."

"Why are you doing this?"

Lady Annabelle glided over to the stone tomb and began to scratch some more strange runes into its lid using the tip of the bayonet. "I have been in this hell for over a hundred and fifty years, with no end in sight. Cursed forever to walk the earth in limbo...in purgatory. I can't take it anymore. I yearn for this punishment to be over and am willing to accept whatever waits for me on the other side."

"Even if it means going to hell?" Lilly asked. "Because I'm sure whatever it is you're planning might be frowned upon in heaven."

"Oh, I know there's no way in hell—pardon the pun—I'm getting a halo and a fluffy pair of wings. A few decades ago, I struck a deal with a demon and, in doing so, sealed my fate. You see, the former lady in charge was an old Romani named Marisela Shofranka. Now there was a truly evil bitch. Schooled in the ways of dark magic. She was able to leave this god-forsaken place, but not before showing me how to escape too." She scratched a few more runes into the stone coffin before coming to stand in front of Lilly.

"Now, the demon you're about to meet tasked me with presenting him one hundred fresh souls, and in return, he would end my suffering by allowing me to descend into the fiery depths of hell, where I shall be treated like a queen. And you, my dear, are number one hundred. Take her."

Two ghosts dragged Lilly over to the stone sarcophagus and lifted her into the air, while the other two ghosts grabbed her by the ankles and spread her out on her back over the stone sarcophagus.

Lady Annabelle leaped into the air and landed on top of Lilly, straddling her at the waist. Her beautiful features contorted, revealing a hideous hag of a woman. Her skin turned an even darker shade of gray, with pieces missing around her mouth and nose. Her eyes became as black as night, and her flowing dark hair turned white as ash. "Great and malevolent Merihem," she roared, raising the bayonet high above her head. "Hear my voice! I summon you to the material plane so you may feast upon this young soul. Devour her energy and add it to your ever-growing army."

A loud growl resounded throughout the stone chamber. One which appeared to frighten the soldiers of the dead more than death itself, as they became restless and gazed uneasily about the crypt. The growl continued. Its low, monotone vibration shook the entire tomb. A cockroach crawled out of a large crack in the wall. It sat there motionless for a few seconds before another one crawled out from the same space, joining the first. Then another, and another. Within seconds, an entire army of cockroaches, worms, centipedes, and spiders began to pour from every crack and crevice in the old crypt.

They writhed about, squirming over one another until a human form began to take shape within the crawling chaos. Red eyes, filled with fire and brimstone, came to life and glared intently at the young ghost laid upon the stone sarcophagus. Lilly thought back to the ghost trapped in the cell of the police department and knew there would be nothing to stop this creature from reaching her. She screamed and began to thrash about with all her might. The union soldiers tightened their grips as she saw her fate emerging from the darkness.

The demon approached the stone altar, his insect form continuing to writhe and crawl about, eyeing his prize with a lustful grin. "Oh, Lady Annabelle, you've outdone yourself this time," Merihem hissed, running a finger across Lilly's face.

A large cockroach crawled into her lips, causing her to gag.

He brought his insect-fused face dangerously close to Lilly's quivering lips. "I can smell your fear," he said, sniffing the air. "It's so intoxicating. I can't wait to have a taste," he added as a tongue full of worms and spiders dragged itself across her cheek, causing globs of creepy crawly things to drop onto Lilly's face. The demon grabbed her throat and began to squeeze.

Lilly fought to breathe. Fought to break the grasp of the dead union soldiers. There was a bright flash of light, and Lilly found herself somewhere *else*. She was in a bright room. A dark figure lay on top of her, its features blacked out by the sheer brightness of the background. Their face was as close to hers as the demon's. Something began to tighten around her throat. She tried to fight. The scent of Old Spice overwhelmed her.

"Deliver her to me," the demon ordered, releasing his grasp, allowing Lilly to take a deep breath of ironic life.

"This is number one hundred, Lord Merihem. You do remember our bargain?"

"Have you given me that many already?" the demon asked.

"You know I have," Lady Annabelle hissed. "Time to uphold your end of our agreement."

"But how will I ever replace someone so resourceful?" Merihem asked.

"I'm sure you'll manage just fine."

The demon stared hard into Lady Annabelle's black eyes for several long awkward seconds. "As we agreed."

A crooked smile crossed Lady Annabelle's twisted face as she brought the bayonet down, aiming it for the center of Lilly's chest. The only thing Lilly could do was close her eyes and wait for her death to come again.

The sound of Lady Annabelle screaming, along with the weight of her body being yanked off her, made Lilly's eyes snap open. She couldn't believe what she was now seeing.

Fred stood next to the stone tomb. Lady Annabelle was on her knees in front of him, and he had a fist full of her white hair in his hand. "Drop it!" he shouted, yanking hard on the ghost's hair.

The bayonet slipped from Lady Annabelle's grasp, clanging hard against the stone floor. "Merihem, what brings you to the mortal plane this time of year?" the reaper asked, still holding on tight to Lady Annabelle's hair, keeping the hag on her knees.

The demon's eyes shifted anxiously to Lilly, for only a split second, before returning their gaze to the reaper in front of him.

"Now, Merihem, you know, as well as I, that a soul with unfinished business is to stay in purgatory until their business is complete," Fred said. "You wouldn't be trying to break the rules, now, would you? Maybe I should have a word with your upper management."

An animalistic growl rumbled forth from the back of Merihem's throat.

"If that's your idea of intimidation, you're barking up the wrong tree, pal," Fred scolded.

"Lady Annabelle," shouted a high-pitched voice.

Lilly turned her head to find Sebastian standing in the doorway of the crypt. The young boy ran to Lady Annabelle's side. "What's happening?"

"Sebastian," Lilly called out, struggling against the grip of the soldiers. "Get out of here! It's not safe!"

"You should do what she says," said Fred. "This is grown-up business."

In one quick blur of movement, Sebastian scooped the bayonet up into his tiny hand and stabbed Fred right in the stomach. "You said you were taking me with you," he screamed at Lady Annabelle.

"Oh, you little shit," Fred cried out, pushing Sebastian away from him and pulling the long blade out of his stomach. "What the hell?"

"I was promised a soul," Merihem screamed, bugs frothing from his lips. "And I shall have one!"

"Not this one," Fred said, motioning toward Lilly. "But I'll let you have your pick between this retched hag or the little brat," he added, tossing the bayonet to the floor.

"What about what you just said?" Lady Annabelle asked, the tone of fear raising her voice a few octaves. "I thought all souls were to remain in purgatory until they completed their unfinished business!"

"As I recall, your unfinished business expired about a hundred years ago," Fred answered.

Lady Annabelle swallowed hard.

"The choice is yours," Fred told the demon, letting go of Lady Annabelle's hair and allowing her to stand. "But that's the only choice you're gonna get."

A sour expression etched itself across the demon's face. "Fine, I'll take her," he said, blowing out an exhaustive breath.

Sebastian ran from the mausoleum, disappearing through the front door, followed by the ghosts of the union soldiers and Lady Annabelle.

"Why do they always run?" the demon asked, storming toward the crypt's door. By the time the demon reached the entrance, he was in a full charge. The heavy wooden doors did little to slow his momentum, causing them to explode from their old fragile hinges. The demon exited the mausoleum, his form becoming a massive swarm of black flies.

Lady Annabelle dared a glance over her shoulder as the sound of shattering wood echoed across the area. A terrified scream escaped her throat at the sight that emerged from the old crypt. She tried to run faster but tripped over her long flowing dress, falling hard to the ground. Before she could even stand, Merihem was upon her. Engulfed within the swarm of black flies, she began to swat at the air franticly, another scream fleeing her lips. The swarm saw their opening and poured into Lady Annabelle's open mouth.

The spirit of the woman began to convulse and gag while she tried to scream with all of her might, but her voice was muted. With the last of the swarm disappearing down her throat, Lady Annabelle tore away the lace scarf covering the bruise around her neck.

Her body rose into the air as she desperately ripped at her

own writhing skin in hopes of giving the flies an avenue of escape, but before her fingernails could dig deep enough, Lady Annabelle's body exploded as the black swarm burst forth. The flies buzzed around for several seconds before dissolving from reality, leaving not a trace of either being.

Chapter 8

Back of the Line

"You gotta be careful who you talk to, Purg," Fred scolded. "Especially old spirits. The older they are, the crazier and more unpredictable they become."

"I'll say," Lilly replied softly. By the time they reached the edge of the cemetery, a cold rain had begun to fall. Even though she couldn't feel the rain, or the coldness in the air, an icy chill ran through her body. "Thank you."

"Don't mention it." Fred led her down another street and farther away from the graveyard.

"What are you even doing here?"

"I'm all done with this country bullshit," the reaper responded, his voice full of cheer, and Lilly could hear it even over the sound of the pattering rain. "Headed back to the Big Apple. I felt bad about your situation and thought I'd check in on you before I left. Good thing, huh?"

Lilly didn't have anything to say. How could she have been so foolish? Or such a bad judge of character? Her parents had provided a good life for her, but she hadn't been raised in a bubble. Then again, she had been totally wrong about the man who had killed her. At the time, he had been so nice, so nonthreatening. She didn't have a single concern about talking to him. On the flip side, there was Sebastian. How could a ten-year-old be so evil? She thought about him throwing the acorn at the man walking down the sidewalk. The signs had been there, she thought, looking back, and while what he had done was awful, never in her wildest dreams did she imagine he could have been the same as Lady Annabelle. But there hadn't been any hesitation in his eyes when he stabbed Fred.

"Here we are," Fred said, breaking Lilly's train of thought.

They were standing under the covered pumps of a gas station. Far off in the distance, Lilly could once again make out the faint golden glow in the sky of her unfinished business.

"Like I said, I felt bad about your situation, so I'm going to do you a solid," Fred said, walking over to a pickup truck being refueled by a man in his sixties. "About a hundred miles north of here is a casino. Can't miss it. Word on the undead grapevine is there is someone there that might be able to help you out with your quest. And it just so happens this guy," Fred motioned to the truck driver, "is gonna bite it at the craps table, so you're welcome."

Lilly climbed into the back of the truck's open bed and took a seat near the cab. "Thank you again. For everything."

"Remember what I said," Fred reiterated as the truck pulled off.

Lilly offered him a departing wave, which the reaper half idly returned. She pulled her knees up to her chest and buried her head as the wind and rain howled all around her, and while things like that did not affect the dead, the rain did hide her tears.

∼

WHEN THE MOMENTUM of the truck began to slow, Lilly looked up and saw a large building with even larger neon lights. Her parents had taken her on a trip to Las Vegas a few years back, and while this casino dwarfed in comparison to the size of those, it did have a large, multi-floor hotel attached to it. Lit up in bright red neon letters for the whole world to see was the name THE FOUR WINDS, which flashed every few minutes to break up the monotony of the loud neon.

Lilly climbed out of the truck and followed the driver inside. As soon as the front automatic glass doors parted, the sounds of gambling overwhelmed her. People cheered. Buzzers buzzed. Slot machines dinged. Bright lights flashed, and sirens blared. Everywhere she looked, people moved about with chips in one hand and large colorful drinks in the other. The truck driver made an immediate left and bee-lined straight for the all-you-can-eat buffet.

"Enjoy your last meal," she told him, even though she knew he couldn't hear her.

She moved off to the side of the gaming floor, so she wouldn't be in anybody's way. The last thing she wanted was to have someone walk through her again. This place was a lot bigger on the inside than it first appeared. How was she supposed to find anything in here?

Beginning her search in a wide loop around the outer edge of the gaming floor, she slowly spiraled inward. Loop after loop took her farther and farther into the depths of the casino floor. When she finally reached the center, she found a large ring of red velvet ropes, like the ones in a theater. A crowd had gathered around the ring, but she could still make out the poker table in the center. Three men sat around it, and a large number of chips were stacked in the middle of the table. The first player was black, with a balding head. He had on a purple button-up dress shirt, minus the tie. The second appeared to be

Native American, with long jet-black hair braided into a single strand running down the length of his back. The third man, who was white, had on a black leather biker's jacket, a pair of dark sunglasses to hide his eyes, and a black ball cap pulled down low over his cropped black hair. At first glance, Lilly thought it looked like just a regular poker game, but then she took a second look.

Walking around the table was a tall, lanky, Black man wearing a pair of nice blue jeans and a red polo shirt. On the top of his head sat a ball cap with the Detroit Pistons basketball team logo. Lilly wasn't going to give the man a second thought until she saw the deep lacerations running down each of his forearms. She took several steps toward the entrance of the roped-off area when she found her path blocked by a large woman holding a small Chihuahua, whose neck appeared to have been squeezed too tightly. The dog growled fiercely, though his eyes looked in a different direction. The woman was dressed in a large green flowered muumuu with one of those wicker beach hats.

"Back of the line!" she shouted, holding up a flabby arm. "I'm next."

Lilly stopped and stared at the woman in surprise. "You can see me?"

"Of course I can see you trying to cut in line," the woman bellowed.

Lilly looked past the large woman to find nine people standing in a loosely formed line. There were five women and four men. They were all from different age and social groups, but Lilly could tell they were all dead like her.

Several of them nodded in agreement.

"What's happening here?"

"The guy in the black leather jacket can see us," the man who was second in line said. He stood about six-foot-tall and was somewhere in his thirties. He wore a pair of jeans and a rock and roll T-shirt. The front of his chest was caved in nearly halfway through his body. "Car accident," he said, as Lilly couldn't help but stare. "Don't text and drive," he added with a shrug.

The crowd cheered as the guy in the black biker's jacket pulled the large pile of chips toward him. The man in the purple dress shirt cursed before storming away from the table.

"Why are you guys all here?" Lilly asked, trying to get a better look at the guy in the leather jacket. His glasses and hat made it impossible to make out any of his facial features.

"To have him help us get out of purgatory," snorted the large woman in the muumuu.

"How did you even know he was here?"

"When one of the living can see the dead, the news spreads fast," said the second guy in line. "I'm Carl, by the way, and our boisterous leader is Florence," he said.

"Darnell was here first," the large woman said. "The guy told him he had to help him win big first *before* he would help him with his unfinished business. Therefore, when he's done, I'm next! Everybody understand?"

All the other ghosts nodded and mumbled insults under their breaths.

Lilly turned her attention back to the poker game. The dealer began by dealing the remaining two players two cards, one at a time. Each player peeked at their cards before leaving them on the table facedown. Lilly watched as Darnell, who was standing behind the Native American, peeked over the man's shoulder as he glanced at his cards. He then rushed over to the man in the black leather jacket and whispered something into his ear. The Native American picked up a handful of chips and tossed them out into the center of the table. The man in the leather jacket did the same.

The dealer placed three cards on the table, the king of diamonds, the two of spades, and the ace of diamonds. Both men remained stone-faced, neither showing even the slightest hint of emotion. The Native American picked up an even bigger handful of chips and tossed them out into the center of the table. Without hesitation, the man in the leather jacket did the same.

Lilly watched on as the next card dealt was the four of spades. After another round of betting, the final card was placed on the table. The five of hearts.

"Let's finish this," the man in the leather jacket said.

His opponent squinted at the man in the leather jacket before pushing the remainder of his chips out to the center of the table. A round of whispers passed through the crowd. The man in the jacket did the same. A hush fell across the area. The native man's lips curled into a large smile as he flipped his cards over, the king of clubs and the king of hearts.

"Three of a kind," the dealer announced.

The man in the jacket sat there in silence, staring at his opponent's cards. With a quick flick of the wrist, he tossed his two cards out onto the table. The three of hearts and the five of diamonds.

"Straight wins!" the dealer announced as a cheer came from both the crowd and the ghosts.

The man in the black leather jacket scooped up his winning and briskly left the play area with Darnell in tow. The rest of the ghosts all followed, making sure to keep their place in line as the group made their way to a row of elevators. Lilly hastily followed the line of the dead. About two-thirds of the ghosts had made it onto the elevator before the doors closed. She watched as the remaining spirits all ran through the door leading to the stairwell. Lilly did her best to keep up, but the other ghosts were either in better shape or more motivated than she was.

She found the entire line of spooks on the top floor of the hotel. They were all gathered around room 1203. The woman in the muumuu placed her ear up to the door. "SHHH," she said in a whispered tone. "I can't hear what's going on."

"What's happening?" Lilly asked.

"Darnell's in there right now," Carl answered. "He's so close to crossing over. I hope he makes it."

"Why don't you guys just go in?" Lilly inquired, taking a few steps toward the door.

All of the ghosts gave her a dirty look. "Listen, new girl," Florence said. "The man gave us one rule. He does not want to be disturbed and will take the next spirit in line when he is ready to, and if anyone breaks the rule, he won't talk to any of us, so until then, we wait."

Five more ghosts rushed through the stairwell door. "Is this where the seer is?" asked the first ghost, a good-looking man in his mid-twenties dressed in designer clothes. He also appeared to be soaking wet.

"End of the line is right there," Florence pointed.

The handsome ghost nodded as he and the other four scurried to the end of the line, all while Lilly, who was at a sudden loss for words, watched. "I'm glad we beat the crowd," the good-looking ghost replied. "Every ghost in the tri-state area is headed here."

"Better get in line, girly," the large woman said, with a large condescending smirk on her face. "Looks like you just lost five spaces."

"I don't have time for this," Lilly huffed.

"You think any of us do?" Florence snapped. "I choked on a chicken wing and fell on poor Buster here." The Chihuahua barked aggressively before whimpering softly. "And I need to tell my husband that I slept with his brother. It's been weighing on my conscious for ten years, and I can't get the hell out of purgatory until I confess my sins, and I know there's no way your unfinished business is more important than mine," she added, her body language full of attitude.

"I was murdered and buried in the ground for the last six months, and my parents have no idea where I'm at, *and* I have to bring my killer to justice," Lilly retorted, with more than enough attitude to outdo the woman.

The ghost of Florence gawked at Lilly for a few seconds before opening her mouth in retort. "Like I said, not nearly as important."

Lilly could only stare in disbelief. The nerve of some spirits, she thought. It was almost as if, when you died, you lost your sense of humanity, and everyone was only out for themselves. Lady Annabelle was a prime example. If she wanted to get things done, she was going to have to act the same way, she decided, and with that, she sidestepped Florence and walked through the hotel room door.

She had made it most of the way through when she felt someone grab her wrist and tug. Lilly pulled with all of her might. She gained a few steps as Florence's face passed through the door. "Let go of me!" she screamed, pulling even harder.

"Back of the line!" the ghost of the woman screamed back, pulling Lilly a tad bit closer toward the door.

Lilly knew she only had one option available to her if she wanted to end this tug of war. She balled up her fist and punched Florence square in the nose. The woman cried out in surprise and loosened her grip. Lilly fell backward and landed on her ass as Florence disappeared from sight. Getting to her feet, she turned around and found the man in the black leather jacket and the ghost of Darnell, staring at her.

The man in the jacket had removed his hat and glasses,

giving Lilly her first clear view of his face. Her eyes widened in surprise, as did his. "You!" they both said at the same time. Lilly couldn't believe it. What were the odds that the man who could see ghosts was the same man in the emergency room she had watched die and become a spirit himself?

"You're the girl from the ER," the man declared. "I saw you when I was…"

"Dead," Lilly said.

"Yeah…" the man stammered. "Which would mean that you were dead too."

"Still am," Lilly said.

"I kinda got that impression when you walked *through* my door."

"Sorry," Lilly said, wondering if her cheeks could still get red with embarrassment. "I need to talk to you, but the line keeps getting bigger."

"For fuck's sake," the man said, blowing out an exhaustive breath. "They won't leave me the fuck alone. I don't even know how they found me."

"And more are on the way," Lilly said.

"Excuse me, I don't mean to interrupt."

"Oh, shit. Sorry, Darnell. We had a deal, didn't we?"

"Can we go to the roof?" Darnell asked.

"Yeah, man, whatever you need," the man replied.

"Can I come along?" Lilly asked. "I really need to talk to you."

"Guess I can't really stop you, now, can I? At least the other ghosts listen," he said, opening the door and stepping out into the hall, where he discovered the line of ghosts had now reached the end of the hallway and had extended into the stairwell. "Fuck my life."

"I tried to stop her, sir," the muumuu lady said. "But…"

"Save it," the man snapped, cutting her off and sounding rather annoyed.

"I'm still next, aren't I?"

"I'm dealing with Darnell right now. The rest of you stay here."

The three of them made their way to the roof. Darnell moved dangerously close to the edge of the building, his gaze affixed to the southeastern sky. "There it is," he said with a large smile. "Can you see it?"

Lilly shook her head.

"I forgot only I can see my own unfinished business. Where's yours?"

Far off to the north, she spotted her own faint golden glow. "There," she said, pointing.

Darnell's eyes followed Lilly's finger. "You need to get to it no matter the cost," he told her before staring back at his own. "Make the call."

Lilly watched the man take out his cell phone and dial the number.

After a few rings, a woman answered. "Hello?"

"Hello," the man said. "Is this Laneshia?"

"Yes."

"You don't know me, but I'm a friend of Darnell's. He wanted me to tell you that in the backyard, buried under the garden gnome, the one with the red hat, is a bag full of money. After he got sick and couldn't pay the bills, he robbed a bank and hid the money in the backyard. That was only a couple of months ago, so don't put the money in the bank, but he said there's enough there for you to make a fresh start. He also wanted me to tell you that he loves you with all of his heart."

The man didn't wait for a response before hanging up the phone. "Did it work?"

Darnell, who had not taken his eyes from the southeastern

sky, whooped with joy. The man's spirit began to break apart, dissolving bit by bit into tiny pieces of golden light before being whisked away to his final destination.

"I would say it did," the man said.

Lilly couldn't believe what she had just witnessed. Darnell had been able to accomplish something Lady Annabelle said was all but impossible. And he did it without losing any of his true color, which meant there was still hope for her to do the same. She only had one question. "Who the hell are you?"

Chapter 9

I See Dead People

"The name's Jackson Bowman."

"I'm Lilly. Lilly Barnes."

"Nice to meet you, and let me guess, you need help with your unfinished business?"

"How about telling me how you can see me, for starters."

"Because I'm fucking cursed," Jackson answered, walking to the edge of the roof and staring down at the ground far below.

"No, seriously. What happened to you that night in the ER?"

A sour expression crossed Jackson's face. "I died," he said solemnly. "And when I woke up, I could see dead people. Lucky me."

"Yeah," Lilly said. "Looks like our stories are a little similar, except I didn't wake up," she added with a slight laugh, trying her best to lighten the mood, if only by a little.

Her remark appeared to have worked, as Jackson let out a slight laugh and took several steps away from the edge. "So, what's your unfinished business?" he asked, taking out a pack of cigarettes from the inside pocket of his jacket.

Lilly watched him put a cigarette in his mouth and light it.

He inhaled a deep hit before blowing the smoke out and watching it get caught up in the wind, then it swooshed away.

"I was abducted, murdered, and buried in the woods."

"Oh shit," Jackson said. "Sorry," he quickly added. "I'm new to this whole dead people thing. Darnell was a suicide, if you couldn't tell by the cuts on his forearms. Far as I can tell, the majority of the ones in line died from something somewhat normal, I guess you could say. You're my first...you know, real death. Not like the others didn't die for real, but..."

"I get what you're saying," Lilly said, seeing Jackson's logic starting to unravel. "I'm supposed to bring my killer to justice somehow."

"Really?" Jackson asked. "That sounds like an awful lot of work."

"It certainly is a little more complicated than cheating at cards."

"Ouch," Jackson retorted. "I gotta survive too. The way I see it, it was a win-win for us both. Darnell got to cross over, or whatever he called it, and I got a little spending money to put in my pocket, and all I had to do was make a phone call." He took another drag of his cigarette, then flicked it over the edge. "What you're asking sounds dangerous, and I don't think I want to do dangerous."

"Fine," Lilly said, throwing up her arms. "I didn't ask for your help in the first place. I was just pointed in your direction." She turned away from Jackson.

"Hold on a minute," Jackson said.

Lilly turned her head just in time to see Jackson stumble forward as his hand passed through her arm. "Man, I'm not going to get used to that," he said.

Lilly stepped off to the side to avoid being walked through. "Like I said, I don't need your help. I was pointed in your..."

"And that's another thing. How do you ghosts keep finding me?"

"I guess the others have some kind of ghost network or something, but I was told you would be here."

"By who?" Jackson asked.

"That night in the ER, did you happen to see the guy I was with?"

"You're talking about the odd bald guy, aren't you?"

"That would be him."

"Who was that guy? I got a strange vibe from him."

"His name is Fred, and he is a...decent guy. He saved my ass...and..."

"But who is he, and how did he know I was here?" Jackson asked.

"He's a grim reaper."

Jackson's jaw nearly hit the ground. "No fucking way! That guy was Death?"

"He was and still is."

Jackson swallowed hard. "And why did *he* send *you* to me?"

"He thought you might be able to help me, but I guess he was wrong," Lilly said, making her way back toward the roof door. She only made it a few steps. "Can you at least make a call for me? I can help you cheat at cards or something."

"You ain't gotta do that. Who do you want me to call?"

"My parents. I need you to tell them I've been found, my body anyway, and that it's in Greenville, Ohio. It's been six months, and they have no idea where I am or even if I'm still alive."

"I'm not going to tell someone's parents their daughter is dead," Jackson protested. "That's a pretty heavy thing to lay on someone."

"Then don't tell them I'm dead, just tell them where I am."

"Fine," he said, taking out his cell phone. "What's the number?"

Jackson began to dial but stopped halfway through. "I shouldn't do this," he said, turning the phone off and putting it back in his pocket.

"What do you mean? It's one phone call! How would you feel if you were lying in a city morgue somewhere far from home and your parents had no idea where you were even at?" Lilly was trying her best not to be too pushy with Jackson, fearing if she was, he wouldn't help her, but screw him; he wasn't the one stuck in purgatory.

"Whoa, slow your roll, girl," he told her.

"Sorry."

"I didn't mean I wouldn't call. I just don't think it's a good idea to do it from my cell phone is all. They can track the GPS. I saw some pay phones down in the lobby, ok?"

Lilly nodded in agreement. She thought about apologizing again but decided against it. "Thanks."

"It's the least I can do, I guess." Jackson walked past her and headed down the stairs to the twelfth floor. The line of spirits outside of his room remained, with poor Florence still at the head of the line. "I gotta take care of something," he told her. "You and the others stay right here, got it?"

"Got it," the woman said, giving Lilly a snickering glare.

Jackson and Lilly made their way to the lobby and to the rows of pay phones by the front doors of the casino. "After this, we're done," Jackson told her, picking up a phone and slipping some change into the coin slot.

At least her parents could rest easier knowing where she was, Lilly thought. As far as her unfinished business, she would have to do it on her own. Somehow.

She could hear the phone ringing, followed by the sound of her mother's voice. "Hello?"

"Your daughter is in Greenville, Ohio," Jackson said.

Lilly heard her mother saying, "Wait, what? Who is this?" before Jackson hung up the phone.

"Ok?" he said to her, his expression asking her if they were good.

Lilly nodded.

"Good," Jackson said. "I need to get some rest before the next poker match. Good luck with everything," he said. "I wish I could help, but I gotta look out for myself."

"No, I get it," Lilly said, walking over and taking a seat on a wooden bench by the entrance. "At least my parents can bring me home now." Several tears began to roll down her cheeks.

"And that's my cue." Jackson disappeared into a wave of people.

Lilly felt so tired. The ordeal at the cemetery still had her drained, and now, she had gotten her hopes up so high after finding Jackson, but she now found herself crashing hard after he refused to help her. She couldn't blame him for not wanting to get involved.

More ghosts entered the lobby. One of them noticed Lilly staring at them and gave her a smile.

"Twelfth floor," she said.

They thanked her and ran off into the casino. He was going to have his hands full for a while. Lilly closed her eyes. She needed to rest for a few minutes before hitting the road. Shouldn't be too hard to find another pickup truck heading north. The sounds of the casino grew fainter until they faded from reality. It stayed that way for some time until a familiar voice brought Lilly back to the world of the living.

It was Detective Brandt and a uniformed State Trooper. What was he doing here? "I need to talk to someone in your security department," he said, showing his badge to the woman standing behind the front desk.

A few minutes later, a man appeared and introduced himself to Detective Brandt. "Ray Curshaw, head of security," he said, extending a hand. Once the introductions were out of the way, Curshaw led Brandt to the security center, with Lilly following closely behind, while the trooper stayed in the lobby.

Lilly felt like she would be caught at any moment before remembering what she was.

"What can I do for you, Detective?" the man asked, entering his office and taking a seat behind the desk.

"Two nights ago, a call was made from one of your pay phones in the lobby. I need to find out who made that call. You wouldn't happen to have any surveillance cameras in that area, would ya?"

"We should." Curshaw turned to his computer. "There isn't much in this casino that isn't under our watchful eye. What time was the call made?"

"One o' four a.m."

The man typed away on the keyboard, and within no time, the image of Jackson Bowman appeared on the computer monitor.

"Shit!" Lilly rushed from the small office.

She found the nearest stairwell and discovered the line of the dead waiting to be heard had backed all the way up to the casino floor.

"Excuse me," she said, trying to push her way up the stairs.

Some of the ghosts moved. Most of them grumbled under their breaths. Some shouted for her to get back to the end of the line. This went on until she reached the third floor, when a mountain of a man, or what used to be a mountain of a man, stepped in front of her and crossed his huge tattoo-filled arms. He had a bald head, a long red beard, and a black leather biker's vest with no shirt. A single tire mark ran from his waist to the top of his bald head.

"Excuse me," Lilly said annoyingly.

"Nice try," the large man said. "No cuts."

"I'm not cutting," Lilly tried to explain.

"Looks that way to me."

"Me too," several others said.

"You don't understand," she tried to explain again. "I've already talked to Jackson, but there's something he needs to know."

"Why don't you tell me, and I'll be sure to relay the message," the Mountain said.

"Fine," Lilly huffed. "The cops are on their way up to his room right now, and if he doesn't get out of there, none of you will be able to talk to him."

The large biker ogled Lilly with a blank expression, and she swore she could literally see the gears of the man's dead mind slowly turning. His eyes finally widened at the realization of her message. Spinning around, the large ghost yelled for everyone to get out of his way as he stormed up the stairs. Any ghost that refused to move, or moved too slow for the big biker's liking, found themselves thrown over the railing or, worse, flattened under the force of the charging mountain.

Lilly followed behind in the biker's wake, but by the time she reached the twelfth floor, Jackson was being escorted from his room. Detective Brandt led him onto the elevator, and when the doors were inches from closing, she took a chance and jumped through them.

"This is your fault," Jackson blurted out.

"I had nothing to do with this," Detective Brandt said calmly.

"I wasn't talking to you," Jackson stated.

"What'd I do?" asked Ray.

"You gotta get me out of here," Jackson told Lilly.

"And how am I supposed to do that?" she asked.

"We got some questions for you first, and then, depending on your answers, we'll see," Detective Brandt informed him as the elevator reached the lobby.

Jackson was loaded into the back of Brandt's car. Lilly stepped through the door and sat beside him. "I'm so sorry," she told him. "I didn't know this was going to happen."

"This is because I made that call, isn't it?" Jackson asked.

"So, you admit calling the Barnes's?" Detective Brandt asked.

"I wasn't talking to *you*," Jackson told him again.

"Have it your way," Brandt said as the car pulled out of the casino parking lot.

"Jackson Bowman, do you understand your rights as I have explained them to you?" Detective Brandt asked, taking a seat across from the man and placing a manila folder in front of him.

"Yes."

"And do you wish to waive your rights and talk with me?"

"Yes."

"So, what brings you to the fine state of Ohio?"

"Just gambling at the casino," Jackson answered, staring at the folder.

"Two weeks ago, you paid a little visit to our local hospital in Greenville, didn't you?"

Jackson glanced over to the corner on his left and found Lilly standing there, staring at him. What would she think of him? Why did he suddenly care what she thought? She was dead.

"You were dead," Detective Brandt declared. "Heroin overdose, right?"

The young man's eyes snapped back to the detective. "Cheaper than oxy," he said with a nonchalant shrug.

"Your friends tossed you out of the car like a sack of garbage and left you for dead."

"They weren't my friends," Jackson's voice rose a bit as his cheeks turned a light shade of red.

Detective Brandt took out several pictures from the folder and displayed them in front of him.

Jackson glanced at the pictures but immediately averted his eyes at the sight of the skeletal remains. "Dude, what the fuck!"

"Jackson Bowman, meet Lilly Barnes."

"Who?"

"The dead girl whose parents *you* called and told that their daughter was in Greenville."

"Is that a crime?"

"No, but murder is."

"I didn't kill anybody, especially her," Jackson said, fidgeting with the handcuffs.

"Then how did you know who she was? I didn't even know who she was until her parents came here looking for her."

"Just tell him the truth," Lilly said.

"Are you crazy?" Jackson asked her.

"I would like to think not." Detective Brandt gave him an odd look. "I get it. You're trying to play the mental card, aren't you?"

"I'm not mental," Jackson informed him. "Can I have a cigarette or something to drink?"

"Sure, after you tell me how you knew it was Lilly Barnes that we dug up."

"You won't believe me," Jackson said, staring down at the table, his right leg acting like a piston.

"Try me."

"Do it," Lilly said. "I'll help you convince them."

Jackson laughed. "Helping you is what's gotten me into this."

Detective Brandt's eyes shifted skeptically to his right. "Who do you keep talking to?"

"Her."

"Her who?"

"Her," Jackson said again, this time motioning at the photos spread out before him.

"You're talking to Lilly Barnes?" Detective Brandt asked, practically laughing aloud, the disbelief weighing heavy in his voice.

"Told you you wouldn't believe me."

"Ok, help me understand this. When you say you're talking to Lilly Barnes, you really mean...?"

"Her ghost."

"Hmm." Brandt tapped his fingers on the tabletop. "And she's standing right here?"

Jackson nodded.

"And how long have you been able to see dead people?"

"Ever since I died."

"You are playing the mental card, aren't you?"

"Told you this was a crazy idea," Jackson said to Lilly.

"Tell him I was hit on the left side of my head, and whatever hit me left a small dent in my skull. Oh, and the guy cut off a piece of my hair on the right side of my head."

"I'm not telling him that. Are you crazy?"

"What is she saying?" Detective Brandt asked.

Jackson sighed. "Whoever killed her hit her on the left side of her head, and something about him taking some of her hair."

"Interesting."

"Really?" Jackson said, a glint of hope springing up in his

91

eyes. Maybe he had this cop all wrong. Maybe the cop did believe him.

"Yes. That information was never released to the press. Which means the only person who could possibly know those specific set of details would be the person who killed her."

"Hell no!"

"Tell him there's a ghost of a prisoner in the basement of his department. He's got a bruise around his neck, and he's in the last cell on the left."

"I'm not saying another word."

"Are you now invoking your right to remain silent?"

"Again, I'm not talking to *you*."

A knock at the interrogation room door broke the tension building in the room. Detective Brandt gave the door an annoyed scowl. When he didn't get up to answer the door, his phone rang. "Brandt," he said, answering it. "What? Are you sure? Ok, ok." The detective put his phone away and took out a small key. "You're free to go," he said, undoing the cuffs shackled around Jackson's wrists.

"I am?"

"Yes. Six months ago, you were sitting in a jail cell in McPherson County, South Dakota. You got sixty days for a drunk and disorderly, which means you couldn't have killed Lilly Barnes."

"I told you I didn't," Jackson answered, rubbing his writs.

"Still doesn't explain how you knew she was here, but the higher-ups told me to release you, so you're released." Brandt walked over and opened the door.

"Just like that?" Jackson asked, stepping out into the hallway.

"Just like that."

Jackson went to leave but stopped. He opened his mouth to say something but questioned if he should.

"Do you have something else to add, Mr. Bowman?"

"I'm telling you the truth about Lilly," he said, pushing his hands deep into the pockets of his jacket. "She said you've got the ghost of a prisoner living in the basement of your police department. Something about a bruise around his neck and the last cell on the left, whatever that means."

"Tell him he can't leave because of the iron bars," Lilly pleaded.

"I guess he can't leave because of the iron bars."

"Right," Detective Brandt said, handing Jackson a clear plastic bag containing his things. "Say for shits and giggles, I believe what you're telling me. Does Lilly know who killed her?"

Jackson's eyes searched Lilly's face and instantly knew the answer. "No."

Chapter 10

Play Time

Mark Karle sat in an old lawn chair near the back end of his yard. The chair was straight out of the seventies, with white, orange, and brown nylon straps woven through one another. The entire backyard, nearly an acre, was as brown as the chair he sat in. An assortment of rusted junk littered the drab landscape. The burned-out shell of his old 1987 Buick Grand National sat off to one side near a pile of tires. Three old refrigerators and a dishwasher sat up close to the house, a few feet from the back door. The end of the yard was clearly visible by the transition of roughly cut grass to the waist-high weeds of the large field behind his house. Parked directly behind the house and out of sight from the road was his 1989 Fleetwood Southwind motor home. Next to that, his father's old wood panel station wagon.

Mark twisted the top off his beer and took a long drink before setting the bottle down in the empty stone birdbath he had placed his chair next to. Lost in thought, he unknowingly began to play with his old high school class ring, which he still wore on his right hand. It had a football on one side, the number of his senior year jersey, 33, on the other, and a green gem crowned the top. The last week had been one of the worst he had experienced in a while, for his mother had been extra needy and disruptive. He needed a vacation from his life. No, what he needed was for his mother to die, so he could be rid of her once and for all. Then, and only then, would his life return to normal, but since he couldn't bring himself to do what needed to be done, he was stuck with her.

Picking up the beer bottle, he took another long drink. Even at the back end of the yard, he could still hear her calling his name. She probably shit herself again. He had no idea why she couldn't tell him before she had to go. That would make life so much easier. That's probably why she *didn't* tell him. Mark felt, deep down, his mother enjoyed making his life a living hell. It was her way of getting back at him for leaving her in the first place.

"Marky!"

Mark's mind drifted back to the day he had first laid eyes upon Lilly Barnes jogging in the park. Her long blonde hair, pulled back in a ponytail, gently bobbed up and down while she ran. Skintight black running shorts showed off the curves of her firm little ass. His mouth began to drool at the very sight of her. Driving his old motor home past her ever so slowly, he took in the scenery for as long as he dared, without appearing too creepy, gawking at her from the side mirror.

He drove down the small lane road that wound itself through the park and stopped in a big dirt parking lot right next to a large soccer field. He wrote down the time, three twenty-seven, before making his way to the small bedroom at the back of the motor home, making sure to close all of the curtains and the door behind him. Climbing over the aged mattress, he peeked through a small slit in the rear curtains as he patiently waited.

The front of her looked even better, Mark thought, watching her small breasts bounce up and down. He moved his hand down and rubbed himself. She was exactly his type. Blonde and young. She would do just fine, he thought, just fine.

"Marky!"

"God damn it," he screamed, setting his beer down in the birdbath. He knew there would be no one anywhere near his house to hear him. "Shut the fuck up! For the love of god, die already!"

He shot up out of his chair and roared like a beast. The beer bottle tipped over and spilled out into the stone basin. He gave the beer bottle an odd look before picking it up and throwing it as hard as he could. Slumping back into the chair, he grabbed another beer and guzzled it in a matter of seconds before throwing it out into the field.

It had been six months since he had buried Lilly Barnes in the woods near Greenville, Ohio, and he could feel his hunger building. He had hit her too hard in the head when he took her, and she never fully regained consciousness, he reminded himself, turning his class ring around on his finger. And though he had had his fun, it hadn't lasted long. Mark liked to tease his girls. Toy with them, the way a cat plays with a mouse before killing it.

Sometimes, his games would last for months. His girls were always there for him whenever he needed a release from the reality of his life, but Lilly had only been there for about a week. He was already taking care of one invalid; he didn't need to take care of another. So, he cut ties, so to speak, but doing so had cost him his precious buffer zone.

He made it a point to wait at least one year between his conquests. Enough time for the kidnappings to appear random. Not connected. Blonde girls go missing all the time. After enough time passes, people forget. People move on.

"Marky!"

"Jesus fucking Christ," he muttered. God, he needed a buffer.

After changing his mother's nasty shit-filled diaper, he stuffed several spoonsful of carrot-flavored baby food in her mouth and retired to his bedroom. Turning on the radio, he set the volume loud enough to drown out the sound of his mother's voice. Retrieving a wooden box from underneath his bed, he anxiously placed it on his lap. He felt like a child hiding things under there, but he liked to keep his most prized possessions close to him while he slept. Lifting the lid, he found five locks of hair. They were all blonde, and each had a different piece of silk ribbon tied around it. He gently removed the one tied in purple.

Laying down, he lifted the lock of Lilly's hair up to his nose. Inhaling deeply, he concentrated on her smell, which brought forth a flood of memories. The way she felt, both inside and out. Expelling the breath, he found himself wanting more. Why did he have to hit her so hard? Six more months. Six more months of listening to his mother's mouth. Six more months of cleaning up her shit.

Lilly had been his fifth toy, and he had learned a lot between his first and her. Never shit where you sleep was an old saying his father had been fond of telling him when Mark was a young boy. He had no idea what it meant at the time, but he figured it out on his own later in life. And it was the main rule he now lived by. He would take his girls from somewhere far away. Somewhere he didn't have any connections. Somewhere nobody knew who he was. He would take his motor home and drive around the city he had chosen, scouting his prey with a keen eye for detail. Most times, he would spend several days stalking them from a distance, learning their routines and habits before making his move.

And when he was finished with them, when he had had his fill, he would take them in the opposite direction. His motor home had proved to be an invaluable tool when moving a body from one place to another. It gave him a certain sense of assuredness and allowed him to take his time in finding the perfect location. Somewhere there would be no distractions. Somewhere he wouldn't be rushed. Somewhere he could savor the last few moments he would spend with his girls before hiding them away from the world.

Mark went into the bathroom to get ready for bed. Would six months make that big of a difference?

"You need this," his reflection told him. "We need this."

"I know," Mark answered.

"The last girl barely fed our hunger. She was merely an appetizer, and I'm starving."

"I know."

"And your mother is driving me fucking crazy!"

"I know!"

"If you can hold out for six more months, six long months, one hundred and eighty agonizing days, you're a better man than me. I say you should just go pack your bag and hit the road. It'll only take a few days at the most. She'll never even know we're gone."

Mark stared at his reflection. He knew he was right. Six months seemed like an eternity, and it *would* only take a few days. A week at the most. He had gotten that part down to a science. Find his girl, stalk his girl, take his girl. Easy-peasy, lemon squeezy. Except he had to remember not to hit this one in the head. Not this time. He had used the normal amount of sedative that he had used on the others, but he hadn't expected Lilly to fight the way she did, causing him to drop the needle before he could administer the entire dose.

His mother's doctor had given Mark the sedative he was

using. She had thrown a major tantrum when the doctor said he wasn't going to give her any more Percocet after discovering the last prescription he had given her had already run out when there should have been at least twenty pills left. Mark tried explaining to the doctor that her tantrums were an everyday occurrence and the pills were the only thing that kept the episodes at bay. The doctor told him the sedative would work faster and last longer but to only administer it before bedtime and *only* if she really needed it.

Mark opened the mirrored medicine cabinet and found the small bottle right where he had left it. It was still half-full. He discovered that she would act out on purpose just to get the medication. He also had a sneaking suspicion she had been doing the same with the Percocet, but it kept her quiet, so he didn't care until one day, a few months ago. She threw a major fit when he didn't move fast enough, and she reached into her diaper and threw a handful of shit at him. He decided he would punish her by not giving her any more meds. She could suffer for all he cared.

He snatched the small glass vial and the syringe from the shelf and rushed back to his room. Going through his dresser, he grabbed a few shirts, some socks, and an extra pair of underwear, which he stuffed into a duffle bag, along with the sedative. He made his way downstairs and placed the duffle bag on the kitchen table. Grabbing a handful of baby food jars and a couple of bottles of water, he rushed them up to his mother's room.

Opening the door as quietly as he could, not wanting to wake her, he listened from out in the hall, and only after hearing her labored breath snoring away did he creep into the room. Moving as silently as he could, he went to place the baby jars on the nightstand when his mother's eyes snapped open.

"Oh, Marky. You've come to help me get ready for my audition. You're such a sweet boy," she said with a sincere look. Then she spotted the jars of baby food. "Are you leaving me alone again?"

"Just for a few days."

"You mother fucker," she yelled, trying to spit in his face. "Don't leave me here by myself," she cried, her mood doing a complete one-eighty. "I don't like being alone." A few tears streaked down her cheeks as she began acting like a small child.

"I have to," Mark said, wiping away her tears. "The director called, and they've changed the location of the audition. They also asked for a few more headshots, so I'm going to take them some."

His mother's face lit up with a large smile. "You truly are the best son in the world," she praised. "No matter what your father says about you. I'm going to be a star, you know. And then, I can leave this piece of shit house and move to Hollywood, where I belong. All the stars live in Hollywood. Anybody who's anybody."

"What about me, Mother?" Mark asked.

"Oh, you can come visit me anytime you want," she said before bursting out into a fit of insanity-laced laughter. "Can you even imagine yourself living in Hollywood? I can't. No, you and your loser father can stay here in the sticks where you belong."

Mark knew her words were going to be hurtful. They always were. He hated hearing them. They tore at his heart, what was left of it anyway, but in a way, they made him stronger. Her words of hate and resentment against him helped fuel his own passion. He would become a star, too, someday. When he was ready to reveal himself to the world, his star would burn brighter than any of those before him. Brighter than Bundy. Brighter than Gacy. Even brighter than Ridgway.

"Where did you say you grew up again?"

His mother stopped laughing and gave him the queerest of looks. "Warsaw, Indiana. Why?"

"Just curious is all. I'll be back in a few days."

"You can't leave me here alone! Not again!"

"I don't have a choice." Mark walked toward the door.

His mother began to reach her hand down into her diaper.

"Do that again, and I'll never come back," Mark threatened. The expression etched across his face told her he wasn't lying.

He made his way downstairs and grabbed his duffle bag, a dog leash, and the keys to his motor home. Making his way to the back of his house, he grabbed Gunner. He didn't know if he would need the dog this time, but it was always good to have options. Climbing into the driver's seat of the motor home, he put the key into the ignition. She started up on the first try as a feeling of serenity washed over him. This felt *so* right. This was his true calling. It was what he had been put on this earth to do, and in a strange way, he owed it all to his mother. It was her spitefulness that drove him to do the things he had done. Her hatefulness helped fill the void she had created within him.

Gunner licked his face.

"Good boy," he said, petting the yellow lab on his head.

The dog took his place in the passenger seat, and Mark rolled the window down for him before putting the motor home in drive and giving her some gas.

Chapter 11

Mommy Dearest

Mark had been driving for most of the day, only stopping for gas once he crossed the Indiana border. From there, he kept heading south until he reached Warsaw. A quick Google search on his phone told him everything he needed to discern about the small Midwestern city of about thirteen thousand. And like every great city in the United States, they had a Walmart. He pulled the motor home into the parking lot right before dusk and took up three spaces near the outer edge of the lot.

Mark opened the door, and Gunner made a mad dash for the asphalt. The dog sniffed around for a minute before taking a big shit near the tire of an old red pickup truck. Mark thought about cleaning up after his dog, but he was tired of cleaning up shit, so instead, he hooked the leash to Gunner's collar and took him along on his shopping spree.

After grabbing a shopping cart, he made his way over to the automotive section, where he found some zip ties. Near the paint section, he found an assortment of duct tape. He picked up a roll of hot pink tape and tossed it into the cart. From there, he wheeled his cart down the tool aisle and grabbed a utility knife. Oh, how he loved this store. One stop shopping at its best.

He went through the pet section and picked up some doggy treats for Gunner before making his way to the food section, where he grabbed a case of energy drinks and some beef jerky. The whole time in the store, he mentally examined every young blonde girl he saw. He liked to take his time during this process. No need to be too hasty and grab the first girl he ran into.

After checking out and paying for his items in cash, he climbed back behind the wheel of the motor home and drove lazily around the city. He was somewhere in the southwest part of town when the sound of a marching band came in through his open driver's side window. Mark steered the motor home in the direction of the music and found the local high school, where a football game was nearing halftime. Parking on a nearby side street, he walked Gunner up to the school and took a seat on the home side's bleachers.

On the football field were several long lines of boys and girls dressed in black-and-orange marching band uniforms. Their music boomed out to the crowd, keeping them entertained during the game's halftime, but Mark wasn't listening. He was too busy searching for the one thing he needed most.

There were plenty of young blonde girls seated in the bleachers on both sides. Then there were the cheerleaders in their tiny, leave-nothing-to-the-imagination skirts. There were so many options, but Mark wasn't getting that special feeling from any of them. Some girls were too young, and even though he liked them young, he did have a moral line he would not cross. He was sick, but he wasn't a pervert.

"Go, Norma Jean!" yelled a woman's voice.

Mark's neck cranked around hard upon hearing *that* name. The name of his mother. Where had it come from?

"Norma Jean, you rock!"

Mark followed the sound of the voice and found a middle-aged brunette woman standing up and cheering. He anxiously scanned the marching band, waiting for the next motherly cheer.

"Norma Jean, up here," the woman said, frantically waving and cheering even louder.

Mark's eyes scanned the lines of the marching band, waiting for some type of acknowledgment from one of the girls on the football field. Then he spotted her in the third line, near the middle. Her soft lips were blowing on the reed of a clarinet. Her brown hair was neatly tucked up under her tall hat. A pair of dark-rimmed glasses rested on the bridge of her perky nose, and when she took a breath, Mark saw the glint of her braces. She looked to be about seventeen. His heart beat a little faster. His cheeks flushed with warmth. And while brunettes weren't his preferred cup of tea, she had the right name. He could make an exception this one time.

Never in his wildest dreams did he imagine he would find a girl with his mother's name. It was old-fashioned and out of date. Everybody wanted to name their girls Brittney nowadays. Occasionally he would find a Stella or even an Elena, but never a Norma. This had to be a sign.

When halftime was over, the football teams ran back out onto the field as the marching band filled the seats at the far end of the home side's bleachers. Mark sat where he was for the next quarter, but he barely watched the game. At the start of the fourth quarter, he got up and made his way to the end of the bleachers. A chest-high chain link fence encompassed the field. Mark walked along it after passing the marching band. He didn't wander very far, though, as he leaned heavily against the fence and stared up at his new buffer.

As soon as the game ended, the crowds began to disperse. Mark's eyes followed Norma Jean from a distance, making sure to never stare for too long. She made her way to the woman who had been cheering her on during the halftime show. Mark thought she had to be her mother because they shared some of the same facial features. They hugged tightly before the girl ran off to join a group of other marching band girls who were headed toward the high school.

Mark made his way back to his motor home and moved into the outer edge of the school parking lot. He hastily made his way to the back bedroom and took out a pair of binoculars. From his vantage point, he could keep an eye on both the main door of the high school and the parking lot.

He spotted Norma Jean's mother walking through the parking lot and getting into a blue SUV. With the binoculars, he watched her check her phone for a few minutes before driving off. Good, he thought, this meant Norma Jean had her own car or would be leaving with friends. Either way, most people rarely paid attention to their surroundings like they should, making his job that much easier.

About half an hour later, Norma Jean emerged from the high school with the same group of girls. She had traded in her marching band uniform for a pair of tight blue jeans and an orange shirt with a black tiger on the front of it. They all piled into several cars, with Norma Jean getting behind the wheel of an old red Oldsmobile Alero. Two other girls got in with her. They were all laughing and having a good time. Norma Jean started up her car, and the radio blared out super loud. She didn't even bother to turn down the volume as she sped out of the parking lot, followed by the other two cars.

Mark did his best to keep up with the red Oldsmobile while

keeping a deliberate distance from it. The girls made their way north through town and pulled into a burger place on one of the city's main streets. Mark pulled over before reaching the burger joint and waited. He didn't want to drive by the place and risk Norma Jean spotting his motor home. If she was paying attention, which he was sure she wasn't, given the loud music and her lead foot, he didn't want her to think it odd seeing the same motor home more than once.

Mark glanced at his watch before cracking open an energy drink and guzzling half the can. It was nearly midnight, and he was starting to get drowsy. Gunner sat near the side door and whined. Blowing out a loud annoyed breath, he set his can down and got up from the all too comfy driver's seat.

"You better hurry up," he warned the dog, opening the door and letting Gunner out onto the sidewalk.

The dog walked around in circles for a few seconds before walking over to the nearest lamppost and urinating on it. Mark saw a splash of color within his peripheral vision and looked up to see the red Oldsmobile pulling out of the parking lot and speeding off in a northbound direction.

"Let's go!" Mark ordered as the dog walked back to the motor home as slow as it possibly could. "Come on! Move it!"

Gunner inched forward even slower, causing the large man to snatch a hold of the dog's collar and toss him into the motor home before slamming the door shut and jumping into the driver's seat.

Norma Jean kept heading north, and after passing a small airport, Mark saw her make a right turn and head east. After a while and several more turns, he could tell she was heading out into the country. Mark did his best to keep his distance, especially now, since there were fewer cars on the road to blend in with, and driving a motor home, he needed things to blend in with. About fifteen minutes later, the road turned to dirt, which meant they were getting farther out into the sticks. Off in the distance, Norma Jean's brake light came on as her car approached a stop sign. Mark eased up off the gas, waiting for the car to speed off, but for some reason, it just sat there. Had she realized he had been following her? He began to apply his brakes, trying his best to give the girl some space.

"What is she doing?" Mark tried to lower his head so he could peer into the car. He had literally stopped right on top of her, and she had yet to pull away from the stop sign. Then he saw why. Norma Jean, who was alone in the car, had her phone up to her face and appeared to be texting. "Seriously?"

Gunner barked at the empty front passenger seat and then began to jump about before yelping and jumping right onto Mark's lap, which caused his foot to slip off the brake and onto the accelerator. The next thing he felt was his motor home rear-ending Norma Jean's car.

"What the hell? You stupid dog," he yelled, throwing Gunner off his lap. He peered through the windshield and saw Norma Jean getting out of her car, cell phone in her hand. She held her arms out to the side and gave Mark a "what the fuck?" look.

Sheer panic coursed through his veins. This was not supposed to happen. Not right now. Everything was going to be ruined. He put the motor home in reverse and backed up a few feet, creating enough distance between the two of them so he could drive around her and get the hell out of Indiana.

"Don't even think of driving off," Norma Jean yelled, holding up her cell phone.

"Well, would you look at that," Mark said. "Looks like she's got some bite to her." He put the motor home in park and stepped out onto the dark dirt road.

Norma Jean was already at the back of her car, inspecting the damage, using the dull light from the motor home's headlights to see. "What the hell?" she asked Mark as he slowly approached. "Didn't you see me? You better have insurance on that piece of shit."

Mark had to take a breath. Where was the band girl he had witnessed on the football field? From what he could remember of high school, most band girls were quiet and mouse-like, but not Norma Jean. She acted more like a pit bull. More like his mother. Maybe this truly was a sign.

"I'm so sorry," he said, bending down and examining the small dent in her rear bumper. "I'll pay for whatever needs to be repaired," he added, trying to calm the girl's nerves just a bit. "I had stopped, but for some reason, my dog thought it would be a good idea to jump into my lap." He pointed back to the motor home, where Norma Jean found Gunner staring back at her through the windshield. "He thinks he's a lap dog but doesn't realize he weighs over a hundred pounds."

Norma Jean laughed, and Mark could see her lowering her guard a few more notches.

"I've got the insurance paperwork in the glove box," he said, walking back to the motor home. "You can pet him if you want." Mark opened the side door and let Gunner run out. Opening the glove box to search for the insurance papers, his eyes immediately spotted the glass vial of his mother's sedative, along with the needle. This was not how he did things.

"You're going to have to learn how to adapt," he heard a voice say. Mark looked up at his reflection glaring back at him from the passenger side mirror. "You've got an opportunity here. Seize it. Seize *her*."

"I can still make this work."

"No, you can't! She's seen your face. You've lost the element of surprise, and if you don't do this now, you'll lose her. I want her, and I know you do too. You won't get another chance like this."

Mark took the small glass vial and syringe out of the glove box. He found his hand shaking too much to get the needle in the rubber cap of the vial.

"Get a hold of yourself," his reflection scolded. "Don't fuck this up."

He could hear Norma Jean outside the motor home playing with Gunner. Peeking out the windshield, his anxiety lightened when he saw they were still alone. But for how long? He took a deep breath, inserted the needle into the vial, and drew the amount of sedative the doctor had told him to use on his mother, plus a tad bit more for good measure. From the previous times he had used it, the medication took about a minute before the desired effect became apparent. He hoped the extra amount would speed up the drug's effect. "Sorry I took so long," he said, stepping out of the motor home and handing his insurance information to Norma Jean. "I couldn't find a pen. Do you happen to have one?"

"Yeah, I think so. Back in my car."

Norma Jean began to turn around, and as she did, Mark grabbed a handful of her hair from the back of her head and began to tug her toward him while pulling her head down to throw her off balance. She screamed and tried to get away, but Mark had caught her off guard. The warmth of her body radiated into his as he drew her in close and pressed against her from behind. Wrapping his left arm around her neck, he plunged the needle deep into the right side of her neck.

Norma Jean fought like hell. Mark nearly lost his grip on her when she started to twist about. Mark let out a loud groan when one of her elbows slammed into his testicles. His grip relaxed enough for her to squirm free. Before he could regain his composure, Norma Jean made it back in her car.

Mark fell to his knees in pain. His testicles felt like they were going to explode. A roar of anger burst forth as he watched Norma Jean's red car speeding off, throwing up dirt and rocks in its wake. Within a few seconds, her taillights began to weave back and forth before leaving the road completely. Mark watched in awe as the car struck a tree head-on. The force of the impact crinkled the metal hood and caused the horn to blare loudly into the night.

"Get the fuck up!" Mark staggered to his feet. It took him a few seconds to find the syringe, along with his insurance papers, lying in the darkness. "This whole thing is fucked!" he screamed, jumping into the driver's seat and slamming his fist down on the steering wheel. "I have to get out of here."

"Did she get out of the car?" his reflection asked from the driver's side mirror.

"No."

"Then we still have a chance, but not if you don't get your fucking ass in gear."

Mark knew his reflection was right. There still might be a chance to salvage this whole debacle, but he had to move fast. Scanning the darkened intersection, he miraculously found they were still alone. He pulled up behind the red Oldsmobile and leaped from the driver's seat before it was fully in park. Rushing to Norma Jean's car, he pulled open the driver's side door and found the girl passed out across the front seat.

Mark grabbed one of her ankles and dragged her from the car. Hoisting her up onto one of his broad shoulders, he rushed back to the motor home. Once inside, he tossed the unconscious girl onto a couch that ran alongside the driver's side of the motor home before jumping back into the driver's seat. He took a good look around to make sure no one had witnessed what he had just pulled off. Only when he was satisfied they had yet to be discovered did he shift the motor home into drive and speed off into the night.

The usual amount of sedative his mother had been

prescribed would keep Norma Jean out for several hours, so Mark estimated he had at least four to five hours before she would start to come around. He couldn't take a chance on her waking up early, so he pressed the gas pedal a little closer to the floor as he merged onto the highway and hightailed it north. Back toward Michigan. Back toward his comfort zone.

As soon as he crossed the state line, he pulled into the first rest stop he found. Mark sat there for a few minutes in complete silence while his knuckles turned white from the grip he had on the steering wheel. Norma Jean's breathing was slower than his. He took a deep breath of anticipation before getting up and closing the curtain right behind the driver's seat, cutting off the outside world to the inner area of the motor home. Sitting dangerously close, he watched her sleep for several minutes. She looked so peaceful, he thought. The poor girl had no idea what horrors awaited her.

Mark reached out timidly and gently placed a hand on one of her firm little breasts. From there, he moved his hand down and began to rub her between her legs. When he was certain she was still under the drug's powerful grip, he picked her up and carried her into the back bedroom. Taking out the utility knife, he cut off her clothes and took in the full view of his prize. He had outdone himself this time, he thought. He placed a piece of duct tape over her mouth and zip-tied her hands behind her back. Moving down, he bound her ankles together before rolling her over onto her stomach. "Just a little taste before we get home," he said, taking off his clothes.

Chapter 12

Returning to the Scene of the Crime

Lilly had been wandering around the used car lot for nearly an hour before Jackson pulled up in a newer model silver Kia. "Hop in," he said, opening up the passenger side door.

Lilly made a funny face as she climbed into the car and took in its fake new car smell. "You know I can't close that, right?"

Jackson stared at her with a dumbfounded look before the light bulb went off. Unhooking his seat belt, he stretched all the way across her and closed the door. "Sorry," he said as he pulled out of the parking lot. "So, where we headed?"

"North," she said, looking to the sky and acquiring the golden glow that would lead her to her unfinished business. "Where'd you get the money for this car anyway?"

"Card shark, remember. Thanks to Darnell's help, I netted ten g's on that last poker hand. Any idea how far north?"

"No," Lilly answered solemnly, her eyes glued to the golden glow.

"Where are you from?" Jackson asked.

"Olivet, Michigan."

"Hey, you didn't say anything about driving you all the way to Michigan," Jackson said, his voice rising slightly in protest.

Lilly shot him an angry expression. "You can just drop me off where ever then. The next casino, perhaps?"

"That was uncalled for. Besides, it's my winnings driving you all the way to Michigan," he said with a smile. "I said I would help you for getting me out of that mess back there, even though, technically, my own bad behavior saved my ass. I just thought this was going to be a local thing is all."

"Thanks," Lilly said, returning her gaze back to the sky. "For everything so far, I mean. I'm just happy to know my parents can at least rest easy now, knowing I'm back home."

"Maybe we can stop by so you can see them," Jackson offered.

She didn't answer.

"Yeah, that might be a little weird."

"A little?"

For the next hour or so, they rode in silence. Jackson kept changing the radio station to help pass the time. After crossing the state line, he pulled into the first gas station they came across.

"What are we stopping for?" Lilly asked.

"I gotta take a leak, and I need some road snacks. Want anything?"

"Funny."

"I thought so," Jackson said before disappearing into the station. A few minutes later, he returned with a bag of barbeque pork rinds, an energy drink, a pair of dark sunglasses, and a road map. "Looks like we should make it to Olivet within a couple of hours," he said after unfolding the map.

"You bought a map?"

"How else I'm I going to know how to get anywhere?"

"Why don't you use your phone?"

Jackson shrugged. "Well, it's not actually my phone. My so-called friends," he said, using air quotes, "cleaned me out of all my cash and my cell phone when I overdosed. I swiped this one from an old lady at the slot machines." He took a cell phone out of his jacket pocket and tossed it into one of the cup holders. "It's been turned off. Guess she realized it was missing."

"Ya think?"

"Don't judge me," Jackson scolded. "Besides, the sooner we get there, the sooner we can get your unfinished business done, and you can get out of purgatory."

"Sounds like a plan," Lilly said. "Any idea how we're going to do that?"

"Not in the slightest." Jackson put the car in reverse and backed out of the parking spot. "But I'm pretty good at playing things by ear."

"Just don't forget this guy is a killer."

"Kinda hard to forget, seeing how I'm sitting here talking to a dead girl," he retorted, then opened the energy drink and took a long drink. "Any idea who this guy is or where we can find him?"

"No," Lilly answered. "I got a good look at him when he..."

"We don't have to do this now."

"If not now, when?" She needed to be strong. Stronger than she had ever been before. This was going to be the hardest thing she had ever done in her life, which she found ironic. The emotions that would be coursing through her in a few hours would be gut-wrenching, but she had to pull herself together. Had to push herself further than ever.

Anger swelled within her. Anger at herself for letting her

emotions get the better of her. Anger for being so weak and letting this happen to her in the first place. Anger at the man who had killed her and buried her in the woods. She thought back to Fred's warning about becoming too angry and frustrated and losing herself within those emotions, but then she remembered how anger had affected Lady Annabelle and Sebastian and how they could interact with the physical world. She would have to find that happy medium. Somewhere right in between all the anger and the humanity she had not yet lost.

"When he was burying me."

"Jesus," Jackson replied abruptly. "You had to watch that?"

Lilly nodded.

"Do you remember anything else he did to you?"

"I remember seeing him in the park. I tried to catch his dog for him, and I think he hit me in the side of the head with something. When I came to, I was already dead and in the woods."

"Well, that's something, at least."

"I guess."

A few hours later, and with Jackson bugging her about her parents the whole time, they pulled up in front of Lilly's house.

"I don't get it," she said, looking up to the sky. "The golden light is much brighter, but it still seems so far away."

"Maybe he doesn't live around here," Jackson offered.

"Maybe," Lilly replied. "I don't remember ever seeing him before, so it would make sense that he's not from around here."

"Wanna go in?"

Lilly stared at her house as the flood of emotions she had been holding back crept a few inches forward. She wanted to see her parents more than anything, but without being able to speak to them or hold them in her arms, she didn't see the point. As she continued to stare at her house, she noticed her parent's car missing from the driveway. "What time is it?"

"It's about eleven."

"In the afternoon?"

"Yeah, in the afternoon. Can't you see the sun and blue skies?"

"No, purgatory is quite different," she answered. "Doesn't look like anyone's home. Where could they be?"

"I hate to say it, but it's been a few days since they…brought you back home. They could be having your funeral."

"Head north," Lilly said. "For me, the sky is always filled with fast-moving dark clouds. There's no sun. No moon. It's like an eerie shadow has been cast over the world. Have you ever been outside during a solar eclipse?"

"Yeah, I always thought the sight of the sun disappearing like that was real spooky."

"Welcome to my world."

They continued north out of town for a few miles before pulling up to a small countryside cemetery. Cars lined the narrow road. A large group of people gathered around a gravesite near the rear of the cemetery. Jackson found a parking spot and got out of the car. Leaning against the front fender, he put a cigarette in his mouth and lit it.

"Are your parents there?" he asked.

Lilly spotted them standing in front of a casket being lowered into the ground. Her mother had on dark sunglasses, trying her best to hide the tears. Her father stood beside her, stone-faced, his arm draped around his wife for support.

"You want to head in?"

"You're so lucky I'm dead, or I'd punch you right in the nose." Lilly leaned against the car. "If I thought going into my house was going to be weird, standing next to my parents during *my* own funeral is truly demented."

"Point taken." Jackson took in a long drag from his cigarette. "You'd really punch me in the face?"

"What do you think?" She flashed him a quick smile.

About twenty minutes later, the crowd of people began to leave. Lilly's parents stayed behind for a few extra minutes before making their way back to their car. Jackson gave them a slight wave as they drove past him. Flicking his third cigarette butt off to the side, he began to cross the street.

"What are you doing?" Lilly called out to him, staying by the car. When he didn't answer, Lilly waited for a few seconds before throwing her arms up in annoyance and rushing after him.

When she finally caught up to him, he was standing right where she feared he would be. Placed on top of the fresh earth was a bundle of lilies, her favorite flower. Tears streamed down her cheeks. She didn't think viewing her gravestone would bring about so many emotions, seeing how she already knew she was dead and had been so for some time now.

"I kinda figured you might have needed this," Jackson said, moving a few inches closer toward Lilly. "I'd give you a hug, but you know."

"I know," she replied. "But it's the thought that counts." She wiped her tears away and faked a smile.

Jackson looked around and saw a handful of people milling about the area. "Is it me, or is that guy's color off?" he asked, lowering his sunglasses. An elderly man dressed in a black suit and wearing an old leather pilot's helmet seemed to be wandering aimlessly around the cemetery.

"That's because he's dead," Lilly answered.

"Are you sure?"

"Yes," she said. "That's Mr. Morris. He was a World War II fighter pilot. He died when I was a kid. I remember the town had a parade for him and everything."

"Explains the leather skull cap."

The old man looked in the direction of Lilly and Jackson. "Can you see me?" the old man yelled out.

"Shit," Jackson blurted. "Time to go."

"Hey, he can see us," the old man yelled out to the other spirits.

"Run," Jackson yelled, already sprinting back to his car.

Lilly barely made it through the car door when Jackson stepped on the gas and sped away from the mob of rushing spirits.

They had been driving for nearly an hour. The golden glow in the sky kept them on a northerly course. "It's so bright now," Lilly said, peering up through the windshield.

"What's it like?"

"A giant golden spotlight shining straight up into the sky."

"Like the Bat-Signal?"

Lilly shrugged. "I guess."

"Cool."

"Turn here," she instructed.

Jackson turned the car onto a long dirt road. They passed a large cow farm and an even larger cornfield before an old farmhouse sitting on a large empty parcel of land came into view.

"There!" Lilly said, pointing at the house. "That's it!" The golden beam of bright light shone directly on the farmhouse, encompassing the entirety of it within its glow.

"Are you sure?" Jackson asked, stopping the car in the middle of the road.

"Oh, I'm sure." Lilly followed the bright beam of light all the way up into the clouds.

JACKSON LOOKED into his rearview mirror and saw an old motor home coming down the road behind him. He gave the gas pedal a slight push and pulled into the house's driveway to let the motor home pass by. His throat dropped into his stomach when the motor home pulled in right behind him and honked its horn.

"Fuck," Jackson said, pulling his car ahead a little more so the motor home could make it around him.

The motor home pulled in front of him and stopped abruptly. A man with a mustache and glasses got out and approached his window.

"Hi there," Jackson greeted, rolling down his window.

"Something I can help you with?" the man asked, bending down to take a good look inside the car as the strong scent of Old Spice flooded Jackson's senses.

Jackson glanced over to Lilly, who was visibly trembling, and could only watch helplessly as she pulled her knees up to her chest and shut out the reality of the living.

Jackson knew right away this was the guy who had killed Lilly. Man, he was big. He had hoped she would have had some kind of plan by now, but judging by her current emotional state, he was going to have to come up with something on his own and fast. He really needed to stop doing things on the fly.

"What are you doing in my driveway?"

Jackson grabbed the road map and began to unfold it. "Sorry, sir," he began, his eyes scanning the map and trying to find something close by. "Trying to find my way back to the highway. US 127. Had to take a piss, so I got off, and then, you know, had to find a secluded spot, but I must have made a wrong turn somewhere."

"Why don't you use your cell phone?" the big man asked, motioning toward the phone resting in the cup holder.

"Forgot to pay my bill, so it's been shut off," Jackson lied, looking at Lilly, whose demeanor had not changed. "Can you help a brother out?"

The man eyed Jackson hard for a few awkward moments before telling him how to get to the highway. "And don't pull into my driveway again," he warned. "I don't care too much for trespassers."

"No problem-o." Jackson put his car into reverse and backed out of the driveway.

As he drove off, Jackson kept an eye on the guy, who was still standing at the end of his driveway, until they were no longer in sight of each other. A few miles down the road, and when he was sure he wasn't being followed, he pulled the car over. "So that was him, huh?"

Lilly didn't answer. She just stared through the windshield, her gaze a million miles away as her body shivered ever so slightly.

"Lilly," Jackson said, snapping his fingers in front of her face.

Lilly's eyes blinked a few times as she appeared to be coming out of her trance. "I'm sorry," she managed as her breathing began to slow. "I don't know what happened. I didn't think it was going to be...like that."

"What'd you think it was going to be like?" Jackson asked, taking out a cigarette and lighting it. "The guy killed you and buried you in the woods for Christ's sake. I think you acted the way any normal person would have, given the situation."

"But I'm not normal, remember. I'm a ghost."

"Exactly, and *you* need to remember that. He can't hurt you anymore, so you don't have anything to be afraid of," he told her, flicking some ashes out of the window. "Now, me, on the other hand."

"We need to do something before he kills another girl," Lilly said.

"I agree, but what can we do?"

"We should go to the cops," she said.

"No way in fucking hell," Jackson said. "I'm not going through that again. Besides, we don't know anything about this guy other than he killed you, and I'm not telling anybody that I can see ghosts again. Sorry, but I can't. That last cop was this close to throwing me in the looney bin," he said, showing Lilly a small space between his thumb and pointer finger.

"Then you need to take care of him."

"Take care of him? Did you not see how big that guy was?"

"Can't you get a gun or something?"

Jackson's expression turned to one of shock. "I'm not going to do *that*. I don't care what he did. I'm not going to kill someone."

"You don't have to kill him. Just shoot him in the leg or something and *then* call the cops."

"And they're going to do what? Unless you've got some physical evidence or something else the police can actually use, all you've got is me shooting a guy for no good reason, which ends with me going to prison."

"No good reason?" she asked.

"Don't do that," Jackson retorted. "You know what I mean."

"I know," Lilly said. "I'm just so...frustrated right now. I mean, he's right there!"

"I get it, really, I do, but unless we do this the smart way, we got nothing, and he'll skate if we go in half-cocked."

"If you've got any suggestions, I'm all ears," she said.

Jackson flicked his cigarette out the window. "We need to find out this guy's name, for starters. You said he took some of your hair, right?"

"Yeah, what about it?"

"That's called physical evidence. That's the one thing linking him to you," Jackson told her. "He would have a lot of explaining to do if the cops could find that anywhere near his house."

"And how are we supposed to find it?"

"Not we, *you*," Jackson said.

"Me! Why me?"

"Because you're the ghost, not me. He can't see you or hurt you."

Lilly let out a loud breath as her left leg bounced up and down. "I don't know..."

"Hey, you got this."

"And if I don't?"

"You're going to end up like old man Morris back there. Turning all gray and shit and hanging out in your graveyard."

LILLY WALKED the few miles back to the house alone. She followed the road, deliberately taking the long way instead of cutting through the fields and small wooded area surrounding the old two-story farmhouse. She needed time to think. Was she really going to go into *that* house? The house of the man who had killed her. The man who had probably done other things to her that she didn't want to think about. For the first time, she was thankful she had never woken up.

She concentrated on the words Jackson had spoken to her back in the car. Words that resonated through her undead mind. *You're dead. He can't see you. He can't hurt you.* She knew what he said made sense, but it didn't make this walk any easier.

She slowly made her way up the driveway but didn't see the motor home anywhere. Maybe he left? Then she saw the tire tracks going around to the back of the house. Following them, she found the old RV parked out of sight. She heard a strange whining noise coming from underneath it. The yellow lab she had seen in the park came charging out of the darkness. When it reached the end of its chain, the dog growled and barked aggressively at Lilly, causing her to fall backward.

"You can't hurt me," she told the dog, swiping her hand out at it. The dog stopped barking and gave Lilly a curious look when her hand passed right through him.

"Marky," a woman's voice bellowed.

Lilly's attention was drawn to the second floor of the house. She made her way to the farmhouse's back door. The dog continued to bark at her, but she ignored him. "You can do this," she reassured herself, standing in front of the old wooden door. "He's like the dog. He can't hurt you." She took a deep breath and walked through the door.

The horrid smell of shit greeted her as soon as she materialized on a small, enclosed back porch. The confined space was overflowing with trash bags. Lilly saw another door on the other side of the porch and ran through it as fast as she could. The inside of the house didn't smell much better. The scent of feces wasn't as bad, but it still lingered about. There were other smells, too, though she wasn't sure what they were. Judging by the pile of unwashed dishes in the sink and stacked up on the counters around it and the over flowing trash can, she had a good hunch where the other smells were coming from.

"Marky! God damn it! I heard you come home."

Lilly made her way through the kitchen and into the living room, where she found the walls filled with pictures of a pretty young blonde girl. The golden beam of light shined through all of the windows, blinding her when she turned at certain angles, while streams of dust could be seen floating about from others. She found the stairs leading up to the second floor, and the same girl's face stared at her as she passed picture after picture. It became suddenly apparent why her killer had chosen her.

"Marky!"

She made her way down the long hallway, past more pictures of the same girl, until she came to the door where the voice had come from. She swore she could feel her heart threatening to beat out of her chest, but she knew that wasn't going to be happening anytime soon.

"Marky!"

"Just a minute," came the man's deep voice from somewhere downstairs. The sound made her jump, and her breathing rapidly increased.

"You can do this," she said, using the most confident tone she could muster. "You have to do this."

She took several steps forward, walked through the door, and found Norma Karle lying in her bed. A shit-filled diaper lay on the floor, mingled in between shit-smeared blankets and sheets. Her hair was unkempt and full of knots, and her eyes had a wild-like glare to them.

"You shouldn't be here," a voice said from behind her. Lilly slowly turned and found a girl about her own age staring back at her. They were virtually identical in both height and weight. She had on an extra-large black T-shirt and a pair of dark gray underwear, which was the same color as her skin.

Lilly swallowed hard and took a step back. Judging by her color, she had been stuck here for a while.

"You need to leave now."

"I...I can't," Lilly answered.

"You have to," the ghost argued. "You must go and bring back help. He...he has a new girl in the basement."

"Another one?"

The ghost nodded.

"Show me."

The ghost led Lilly to the basement. As soon as they set foot upon the cold concrete floor, the door at the far end of the basement opened, and the man who had taken her life came rushing out toward them. Lilly moved out of the way as the big man passed through the ghost of the other girl and raced up the stairs. The ghost stared at Lilly and pointed at the door. Lilly took several deep breaths to calm her nerves and walked through it.

The room on the other side of the door measured about ten feet by ten feet. A long, bright, fluorescent shop light hung from the ceiling. A small metal drain cover sat embedded in the middle of the concrete floor. The walls and ceiling were hidden behind thick white foam panels, making the room virtually soundproof. A large ornate chair rested in the closest corner to Lilly's right. It reminded her of one of those big wooden chairs a priest might sit in during a Catholic Mass. In the far corner to her left, she found her killer's newest toy lying motionless on an old piss-stained mattress. She was naked as the day she was born. Around her right ankle was a large metal shackle. A large black chain ran from one end of the shackle to a large metal hoop set into the concrete floor.

"Her name is Norma Jean."

"He brought her here today, didn't he?" Lilly asked, remembering when the RV had pulled up behind Jackson's car in the driveway earlier. "I have to help her." Lilly rushed to Norma Jean's side. She tried to grab the chain but grew frustrated when her hands passed through the metal.

"You can't," the ghost told her.

"But I have to," Lilly cried.

"You know *you* can't."

"Wait," Lilly said, getting to her feet and rushing to the door. "I've got a friend waiting for me outside. He's alive and can see spirits like us. He can call the police. We *can* save her! And with her safe and him in jail, we can leave purgatory!"

"But what about the others?"

"What others?" Lilly asked.

"There are five of us trapped in this hell because of him. If your friend can do what you're saying he can, then only the two of us will witness his downfall, which means the others won't be able to complete their unfinished business."

"What will happen to them?"

"They'll be forced to stay in purgatory until the End of Days. But, if you can find them and bring them back with you, they can cross over too."

"What about her?" Lilly asked, fearing all the things her killer would do to her.

"He will keep her alive for at least a couple of months, maybe longer, if she's strong."

"How do you know this?"

"Because I watched him do it to four other girls," the ghost said, walking through the door and disappearing from sight.

Lilly glanced back at the unconscious girl as tears streamed down her face. She didn't want to leave her here. She didn't want to leave her with him, but if the ghost was right, she had some time before he decided to bury her somewhere like he had done with Lilly.

Her thoughts drifted back to Lady Annabelle and to how long she had been forced to stay in purgatory and to the lengths she had gone to just to be able to leave. She didn't want to wish that fate on anyone, so if there was a chance for all of this bastard's victims to cross over and be free from this hell, she owed it to them to at least try.

Lilly ran out of the room and followed the ghost, who led her upstairs to *his* room. When she walked through the door, she found the other ghost standing in front of a small wooden desk. The contents laid upon its surface were neat and orderly. A dispenser of clear tape. A stapler. An old laptop. A simple black photo album.

The spirit of the girl reached out and flipped the photo album open to its first page. There, sandwiched between two sheets of clear plastic, was *her* missing poster. Her name was Tracy Lafond. The date on the missing poster: July 17, 1998.

"He's been killing girls for that long?" Lilly asked.

"No," Tracy answered. "I was his first and his last for a while. I tried my best during those first few years to bring him to justice for what he did, but I couldn't figure out a way to do it. He had so much rage built up within him. I figured it wouldn't be long before he killed again, and maybe I could do something then, but he never did. I believe whatever anger he had was released onto me, allowing him to move on and live a regular life, for the most part. He moved around a bit, and I followed him everywhere. Phoenix, Houston, Atlanta. He never hurt anyone else. Then his father died, and he had to come home and take care of his mother. She can be a real handful. It wasn't until she began acting out that he started killing again."

"How long did it take them to find you?" Lilly asked. "It took them six months to find me."

Tracy didn't say anything as she moved to the bedroom window. A single tear ran down the dead girl's gray cheek.

"They never found you, did they?"

Tracy solemnly shook her head, wiping away the tear.

"Do you know where you're buried?"

Tracy pointed out the window. Lilly followed Tracy's finger and saw a stone birdbath near the end of the yard.

"Jesus."

"I tried to stop him. I made his dog get all riled up and jump on his lap when he was behind the new girl in his RV. He crashed into the back of her car by accident. I thought that might have scared him off, but he..."

"You did the best you could, given the circumstances," Lilly said, trying to comfort the girl. "Did you feel compelled to stay with...you know...your body?"

Tracy didn't answer. Moving away from the window, she returned to the scrapbook. "Remember their names," she said, flipping to the next page. Lilly saw a missing person's flyer for a girl named Jessica Watkins. Her resemblance to the two girls looking at her picture was uncanny. She lived in Sault Ste. Marie, Michigan, and went missing on December 6, 2016.

Allison Murphey graced the third page. She was seventeen when she went missing. She had long blonde hair, like the rest of them, and hailed from Boonville, Indiana. She went missing on November 15, 2017.

The last girl she would have to find, Laura Elliott, lived in Oak Hill, Ohio, and disappeared on October 3, 2018.

"Flip the page," Lilly said after watching Tracy remove her fingers from the book. She knew whose picture was next, but she still needed to see it for herself.

Tracy flipped the page.

As Lilly gazed upon her own picture, heavy footsteps approached before her killer burst through the door. Lilly froze, fear's grip tightening around her. The smell of Old Spice filled the room, and Lilly found herself fighting to breathe.

"He can't hurt you," Tracy told her, but Lilly wasn't listening.

The man reached under his bed and pulled out the wooden box. His fingers were visibly shaking as he lifted the lid and peered inside. A bright golden light emanated from inside the box, making it impossible for Lilly to see its contents, but she had a notion of what it contained. He closed the lid and returned the box to its hiding place. Turning to leave, he stopped when he saw the open scrapbook on his desk. He stared at it with questioning eyes before closing it and rushing back out of the room.

Doubt crept into Lilly's mind as the thought of going out and trying to find the ghosts of the other girls brought with it that feeling of dread she had experienced when trying to leave her gravesite. Maybe it was because she wanted this to end now. Once and for all. Or maybe it had something to do with the new girl in the basement and the things she knew Mark would do to her. She just wanted to cross over and put this whole ordeal behind her. She then wondered what the other girls must have gone through before Mark had lost interest in them. What they had gone through in trying to complete their own unfinished business. Did she deserve to cross over any more than they did? No. They all deserved to be free of this place, and she needed to do everything in her power to make sure they all got their happily ever afterlife.

"Let's bring this mother fucker down. How do I find them?"

"I'm not sure," Tracy confessed. "They all made their way here eventually. Guided by their light. It didn't take long before their frustration got the better of them and they moved on from this place. You might want to start where they were taken from."

"Do you know his name?" Lilly asked.

"Mark Karle."

July 17th, 1998

The door chime went off, telling Tracy a customer had entered the gas station. Glancing up from her magazine, she saw a man in his early thirties perusing the candy aisle. He was a big guy, kind of muscular, with brown hair and a matching mustache. She looked out to the gas pumps and spotted his shiny black Buick Grand National sports car. The man had been in the store a few times before, and Tracy would always catch him staring at her.

The man picked up a candy bar before making his way to the beer cooler, where he grabbed a case of Budweiser. He gave Tracy a flashy smile when he reached the counter.

"Hey," Tracy said. "Is that your car?"

"Yeah," the man answered, taking out his wallet. "Like it?"

"Hell yeah," Tracy answered. "I bet it's fast."

"Sure is," the man said, placing a twenty-dollar bill on the counter. "Are you?"

Tracy gave him a coy smile. She didn't have any real friends. Everyone thought she was a little weird. "Sometimes."

"My name's Mark." The man extended a hand.

"Tracy." She shook his hand and felt a small electric shock when their fingers touched.

"I can take you for a ride whenever you'd like." Mark motioned toward his car.

"You gonna drink all of those beers by yourself?" she asked.

"Was planning on it, unless you want me to save you some," Mark said with an inviting smile.

"I get off work at eight," Tracy told him, handing him his change.

Mark picked up the change and slid it into his pocket. "Pick you up then," he said.

He began to walk away but stopped when Tracy called out to him.

"Don't forget your beer," she said. "And pick me up around the corner."

TRACY HOWLED *as the wind whipped her face. The speedometer of Mark's Grand National topped out as the car raced down a*

long country road. Tracy opened her fifth beer and took a long drink before howling again. She loved the sensation of adrenaline that a rush like this always brought her, though things like this were rare, and she could honestly say she had never done anything as adventurous as this before. Fucking dumb high school boys in the woods out behind her house was one thing, but offering herself to a grown man was something completely different, and she liked it.

Mark turned the car down a small two-track trail leading into the woods and put it into park when they were out of sight of the road. He had barely put the car in park when Tracy took her pants off and climbed onto his lap. She stuck her tongue in his mouth as his hands wandered all over her body.

"I want you to fuck me," Tracy whispered into his ear as she slid her hand down to his crotch. Finding that Mark wasn't quite hard yet, she undid his jeans and began to stroke him off, but after a few minutes, nothing had changed. "What the fuck?" She took her hand out of his pants and straightening up.

"Sorry," Mark said, his cheeks turning a little red. "Not sure why this is happening."

Tracy moved off his lap and placed his manhood into her mouth, causing his cock to stiffen up. Tracy kept sucking for a few more minutes before climbing back onto his lap. She pulled her underwear off to the side and slipped him inside her.

"What the fuck!" she said again as Mark went soft. "Are you gay or something?"

"What?"

"Are you gay?" she asked again, this time in a slow, mocking voice.

"NO!"

"Then why won't you fuck me? Why can't you get it up, you little bitch?" She burst into a fit of uncontrollable laughter.

Tracy's head snapped back when Mark punched her in the

face. Warm blood poured from her nose, running across her lips. The taste of iron saturated her mouth. Her world began to spin out of control. She tried to climb back to the passenger seat, but Mark grabbed a hand full of her hair and pulled her head backward. She saw the reflection of light on the steel blade of a knife.

A piercing pain erupted from her chest as Mark plunged the knife into her. She screamed. He pulled the blade out, only to stab her over and over again.

Tracy saw her blood spraying against Mark's face, but it did little to discourage him. His face twisted with anger.

Tracy felt her life force leaving her. She closed her eyes, and the darkness took her.

Then she was standing behind Mark in the backyard of some old farmhouse. He stood at the lip of a deep hole near the end of the property. Mark picked up a shovel and began to fill the hole in.

"What the fuck are you doing?" Tracy asked, but Mark ignored her. "Hey! I'm talking to you," she yelled, stepping up to Mark and giving him a hard shove. "What the..." She watched her hands pass right through him. She glared at her hands in disbelief before looking into the hole. Tracy screamed and fell to her knees when she saw her own face staring up at her.

Mark finished filling in the hole and smoothed the dirt out around the area.

Tracy, still sitting where she had fallen, watched through tearful eyes as Mark disappeared into the garage, reappearing a few minutes later carrying a red gas can. He crossed the backyard and entered the field behind his house. The field where his car was now parked. Opening the doors, he poured the contents of the gas can all over the interior of the car. Reaching into his pocket, Mark pulled out a book of matches. Striking the red top of the match against the rough black strip on the back of the book, he brought the match to life and ignited the entire pack. He watched it burn for a few seconds before tossing it into the car.

Tracy watched Mark stand there for several hours, hypnotized by the flames.

She could still see her blood smeared all across his face and hands in the reflection of the fire's light. After a while, he walked into the house as if nothing had ever happened.

Chapter 13

Road Trip

Lilly ran all the way back to Jackson's car. Bypassing the road this time, she sprinted blindly through the cornfield until she emerged onto the dirt road and spotted the silver Kia. Jackson jumped out of the driver's seat and banged his knee hard on the bottom of the steering wheel when Lilly passed through the passenger side door.

"Fuck!" Jackson screamed, grabbing his knee. "You gotta give me a heads-up or something. You can't pop in like that!"

"Drive," was all she said.

"Where to?"

"Just drive!"

Jackson put the car in gear and stepped on the gas. After several silent miles, he let his foot up on the accelerator. "So?"

"He's got another girl in the basement."

Jackson slammed on the brakes, causing the Kia to stop abruptly in the middle of the road. "So why are we driving away?"

"Because things just became complicated."

"Complicated? Like how? Like he's gonna kill that girl if we don't do something complicated?"

"No, complicated like the ghost of his first victim, Tracy Lafond, was in the house complicated," said Lilly, dropping yet another bombshell onto Jackson's lap.

"We can't just drive away and do nothing," Jackson insisted. "I can call the cops and tell them what's going on. Get them out here and stop him."

"Because that worked out so well for you the last time the cops got involved?" Lilly reminded him. "And we don't have any hard evidence, remember? Besides, there's another problem."

"Great, just what I need, more problems. Now what?"

"If we stop him right now, Tracy and I will be the only ones who can cross over."

"Wait a minute, the only ones? There's more victims out there?" Jackson asked.

"Three more."

"This guy's a real piece of work, isn't he?"

"Tracy said he'll keep this new girl alive for a while, which gives us some time. She wants us to find the others and bring them back here. That way, all of us will be able to get out of purgatory. We all have to be here when he's brought to justice. Otherwise, they'll be trapped here forever."

"I don't like the idea of leaving that girl in there with that monster," Jackson said. "I can only imagine the things he'll do to her."

"I don't like it any more than you do, but I can't fathom spending eternity in purgatory. From what I have been learning, it's rare for a ghost to complete their unfinished business. Remember how many spirits were lined up outside your door? And now I have a chance to help four other girls get out of this hell."

"You gotta take it. I can't blame you for wanting to at least try. Doesn't mean I have to like it."

"I know," Lilly replied. "And I also know I can't do this without you, so if you want to save the girl now and then bail, I can't blame you for that either."

"Did you at least get his name?"

"Mark Karle."

"Where are we headed?"

"North," she answered. "Sault Ste. Marie."

"The fucking U.P."

"The others are in Ohio and Indiana."

"The U.P. it is," Jackson said, stepping on the gas and putting as much distance between them and Mark Karle's house as he could.

THEY HAD BEEN DRIVING in silence for nearly one hundred miles. The sun was setting and a heavy rain poured from the sky as they passed a sign showing the Mackinac Bridge was still forty miles away. The Kia's windshield wipers were on high, but Jackson could barely make out the road in front of him. "I need to get off the highway," he said. "My eyes are bugging out, and we need some gas."

Jackson took the next exit ramp, and they found themselves in the small town of Indian River. It wasn't hard to find the only gas station in town. After a quick fill up, an even quicker piss, followed by a slow relaxing smoke, Jackson headed back toward the highway. The rain had yet to relent even a bit, so when he saw a guy hitchhiking, he felt obligated to stop. He had been in this man's shoes a number of times. The number of cars that sped past him, not giving him a second thought, always amazed him.

"Hop in the back," he told Lilly, pulling the car over in front of the hitchhiker.

"What?" she protested.

"You don't want the guy sitting on you, do you?"

"Why are we even picking him up?" Lilly asked. "We don't have time for this."

"Listen, I've spent the last week having my entire life filled with dead people. No offense, but I just want to talk to someone who's alive for a change."

Lilly started to climb over the seat, but before she could move, the hitchhiker passed through the back door and took a seat.

"Dude! What the fuck," Jackson said.

"What?" the hitchhiker asked. "Didn't you stop to pick me up?"

"Yeah, but I thought you were..."

"Alive?" The ghost's expression indicated he was rather offended.

"Yes."

"Hey! Wait a minute, you can see me, can't you? Of course you can see me. You stopped for me, and now we're having this conversation. You're the seer everyone's talking about, aren't you?" He leaned forward and pointed at Jackson.

Jackson let out a loud sigh and put the car in gear before pulling back out on the road.

"I'm Lilly," Lilly said, offering her hand.

"Joshua," the dead man replied, reaching out and shaking Lilly's hand.

The ghost appeared to be somewhere in his early thirties, with light brown hair and green eyes. He had on a pair of jeans and a black hooded sweatshirt. The color of his skin hadn't faded much, so Jackson knew he was a fresh purg. His appearance also looked normal, so he couldn't tell what his cause of death had been.

"This is Jackson," Lilly said, motioning toward the only living person in the car. "Where are you headed?"

"Sault Ste. Marie."

"No way!" Lilly exclaimed. "Same here."

"Were you summoned too?" Joshua asked.

"I'm not sure what that means," she said, looking to Jackson for the answer.

"Don't look at me."

"Do you mean your unfinished business?" Lilly asked.

"I've been trying for some time now to complete that, but I have no idea how I can when nobody even knows I'm here, except for people like you," Joshua said, directing the last part of his comment toward Jackson. "No offense."

"Am I supposed to be offended?" Jackson asked. "Cursed... maybe," he said with a shrug, "but offended?"

"Well, that's all about to change," Joshua said with a big smile.

"Because you've been summoned?" Lilly inquired.

"Right."

"Dude, what the hell are you talking about?" Jackson asked. "We're a couple of newbies up here."

"Oh, my bad. I mean, I've been summoned for a séance."

"Good luck with that." Jackson laughed. "Make sure to get your palm read too. Those things are all fake."

"Says the person *talking* to a ghost," Lilly pointed out.

"No, I don't blame you for being skeptical," Joshua said. "I never believed in any of that mumbo jumbo either, but then I received this letter." He pulled out an envelope from his pants pocket and handed it to Lilly. His name was scrawled across the front in a fancy looping font.

"Dear Joshua," Lilly read. "Your presence is being

requested by Lilith Rogers at Madam Denesha's House of Spiritual Healing in Sault Ste. Marie. The séance will take place in seven days at exactly one hour before midnight. This will be your only chance to communicate with the living, so please do your best to attend. Sincerely, Madam Denesha."

"See," Joshua said.

"How do you even know this is legit?" Jackson asked, trying his best to read the letter in Lilly's hands and stay on the road at the same time.

"I asked around," Joshua answered. "All the other ghosts I talked to said this is the standard procedure for being summoned to one of these things."

"Who's Lilith Rogers?" Lilly asked.

"That's my mom. I died kinda suddenly," Joshua replied. "Brain aneurysm. I had just gotten a good-paying job with great benefits. I took the company's life insurance and listed her as my beneficiary. I didn't have time to tell her, though, and she could really use the money. She's been on a fixed income ever since my dad died."

"I'll make sure you get there," Jackson promised.

"Thanks, man."

"You know, maybe you can talk to this Madam Denesha," Lilly said.

"I was thinking the same thing." Jackson flashed a quick smirk. "If we can get her to summon all three of the girls, that would save us a whole lot of time and hassle."

"And the quicker we can find them, the quicker we can get back and save Norma Jean," Lilly added as the momentum of the car surged forward.

Chapter 14

A Coin for the Ferryman

It was a little after nine o'clock at night when Jackson pulled up in front of a small brick building on the main drag running through Sault Ste. Marie. There was a large picture window in the front of the building, but a heavy white lace curtain blocked the view into the interior of the structure. In front of the curtain hung a bright red neon OPEN sign.

"This must be the place," Joshua said, looking through the car window. "I can't believe my time in purgatory is almost up. I had lost hope a while back, you know." He turned his gaze to Lilly. "Never thought I'd make it to the other side."

"I'm happy for you," she lied, facing the ghost. She *was* happy for Joshua, but deep down, she felt a twinge of jealousy. Like someone getting to eat the dessert you wanted right in front of you type of jealousy.

"Promise me you won't give up hope." Joshua placed a hand on Lilly's arm. "With him helping you, I'm sure you'll make it out of here in no time."

Lilly nodded.

"Well, what are we waiting for?" Jackson asked, getting out of the car.

A small bell above the door rang as Jackson entered the building. The smell of incense and vanilla filled the air as a large black woman wearing a long, one-piece dress made from vibrant red and yellow cloth greeted him. Her long, braided hair reached halfway down her back, and she wore a necklace and two bracelets, one on each wrist, made from small bones and seashells.

"Welcome to Madam Denesha's House of Spiritual Healing," she said. "Here to have your palm read or your future gleaned?"

"No, just giving Joshua a ride," Jackson said, motioning to the dead man on his right.

"He's here?" Madam Denesha asked, her eyes widening in surprise.

"Can't you see him?" Jackson sensed he was right about this whole thing being a sham.

"Heavens no. I am but a humble portal for the deceased," Madam Denesha explained. "My gift is not as great as your own. Please, follow me."

The medium led Jackson, Lilly, and Joshua to another room with a large round table in the center. A white lace tablecloth covered its surface, and four chairs were placed around it. A large crystal ball sat in front of one of the chairs. Lit candles cast their brilliance throughout the room, giving the area an air of ambiance. A large grandfather clock sat in one of the corners, ticking away. "The séance isn't scheduled to begin until eleven o'clock, and I do have a nine thirty about to begin. Will you be staying?"

"Can I?" Jackson asked.

"Normally, uninvited guests are not permitted to attend, but given your talent and that you played a role in bringing

Joshua to me, I'm willing to make an exception. You can tell me when the other spirit arrives."

"You should know there is another ghost here too," Jackson pointed out. "Don't worry though, she's with me. We'd like to talk to you about having a séance of our own."

"Wonderful," Madam Denesha said. "I can always use more business."

"So, how does this whole thing work?"

"When a client comes to me," the medium directed Jackson to the chair across from the crystal ball, "I first call out to the spirit world, signaling the deceased of my intentions. I do this by writing a formal letter of invitation, which is then burned using a candle made from human fat, ensuring that it finds its way to the realm of the dead and is delivered to the spirit in question. I give them a week to respond, making sure they have ample time to make their way here. Once the ceremony begins, I allow the spirit to enter my body and use me as a vessel of communication with their loved ones."

"And in doing so, you let them complete their unfinished business and move on?" Jackson asked.

"Precisely. For a small fee, of course."

"Of course."

The bell above the door sounded out, drawing Madam Denesha out of the room. "If you're not cool with us being here, we can leave," Jackson said to Joshua, who paced anxiously about the room.

"No, you guys are fine. You helped me get here, so it's only fitting you see me off to...whatever lies beyond. I'll wait in another room until this séance is done."

Madam Denesha returned with a peculiar-looking man dressed in a black suit. If Jackson had to guess, he would have said the man had to be somewhere in his mid-sixties. His thinning black hair was greasy and combed over the top of his balding head. He stood nearly as tall as Jackson, and his skin was as pale as the snow.

"Barry Finton, this is an associate of mine," Madam Denesha said, introducing Jackson and motioning the man to a chair next to hers. "He'll be assisting me in tonight's séance."

"Hello," the man said, taking a seat. "You're sure that my brother will be here?"

"As I stated before, I cannot make any promises. But the message has been delivered."

"How do you know he even got the message?"

"They always get the message. I have another spirit already here waiting for his séance later tonight."

"He's here now? In here with us?"

"He's waiting in another room," she said.

The grandfather clock chimed, causing everyone in the room, including the dead, but not Madam Denesha, who was as cool as a cucumber, to jump.

"Shall we begin?"

"Fine," Barry huffed. "Let's get this over with."

"First, you must tell me why we are summoning the spirit of your brother here tonight?" Madam Denesha inquired.

"Why do you need to know that?" Mr. Finton asked, crossing his arms across his chest and turning slightly in his chair. "It's a private matter."

"I can assure you that even when your brother's spirit is inside of me, I have complete control and am fully aware of what's going on, so there won't be any secrets here tonight," Madam Denesha said, which only irritated the man more. "The longer a spirit walks the earth, the more forgetful they become. The angrier they become. I may need to help him focus and stay on track if you wish to have a tangible conversation with him."

"Larry was my twin brother," Barry began. "We were very

close for most of our lives. Our mother died when we were young, and our father filled his grief with his work and never really had any time for us. When our father died, Larry didn't take it well. I mean, neither of us did, but for some reason, it affected him harder. Caused him to sink into a deep depression."

"How long has it been since your father departed this world?" Madam Denesha asked.

"Oh, it has to be close to twenty years now," Barry answered. "When our father died, he left us a substantial inheritance, but together, my brother and I had our own successful business, so we didn't need the money. We transferred the paper money into precious metals and jewels and placed them into a safety deposit box, which required two keys to open. I have one," he said, showing the medium a skeleton key dangling from a thin gold chain hanging around his neck. "And my brother had the other."

"Go on."

"Larry killed himself on this very day ten years ago, and his key disappeared. Our business has been failing ever since his death, and I'm afraid I'm going to have to file for bankruptcy next month. I desperately need him to tell me where he hid that key."

The medium placed both of her hands on the large crystal ball in front of her. "Larry Finton, I invite you to come forth and converse with us. Your brother is here and wishes to speak with you. If your spirit is present, come forth and use this vessel freely."

A dark shadow materialized near the back of the room. Jackson noticed it right away, as the hairs on the back of his neck stood on end. From the darkness came a man who looked exactly like Barry Finton, only a little younger. His skin was a dark gray, while his suit was as black as the shadow from which he had emerged. The spirit appeared confused and disoriented, but when his eyes locked on to his brother, his confusion vanished. The ghost stepped into Madam Denesha, disappearing from sight.

Madam Denesha's pupils rolled back into her head, showing only the whites of her eyes. She let out a hard, exhaling breath of visible arctic air. "Hello, dear brother," she said in a low, masculine voice.

"Larry? Is that you?"

"In the flesh, so to speak," Larry answered, his voice still visible in the cold air surrounding him. "Why have you summoned me here?"

"Why did you kill yourself? Why did you leave me?"

"I couldn't stand the man I had become," the spirit answered.

"After our father died, I needed you more than ever."

"Do not speak of our father," Larry warned, his voice becoming even colder.

"Why not? He might not have always been there for us, but he loved us."

"He loved you, don't you mean, dear brother?"

"What are you talking about?"

"You were always his favorite," Larry hissed, his cold voice casting a layer of frost upon the crystal ball. "Don't deny it."

"I don't know why you would say such a thing," Barry said, shaking his head in disbelief.

"Why did you call me here?"

"The key," Barry said, lifting his own into the air between them. "I need to know where you hid yours."

"I knew you didn't summon me because you missed me. There is always an alternative motive in everything you do, isn't there? Just like father."

"Where is this hate coming from? You are not the brother I knew. The brother I loved."

Larry began to laugh. "Do you really want to know why I took my own life, dear brother? The night father passed, he called me into his room and told me how disappointed he had been with me. Asked me why I could not have been more like you. Everything I did was to garner his approval, but all he ever saw was my failure. In my marriage. In *our* business. He called me weak. Threatened to cut me out of the will. Something in me snapped, and I found myself shoving a pillow in his face, but the old bastard had a heart attack before I could finish what I had started.

"Fuck," Jackson said softly, shifting uneasily in his chair.

"Do you want to know where your precious key is? It's in the inside pocket of my suit jacket, which is now six feet under. The thought of you getting your hands on any of that money made me sick to my stomach. He was right, you know. Father, that is. I was weak. After I tried to murder him, the guilt began to devour me from the inside until I couldn't take it any longer. But in my death, I found the strength I needed, and now, thanks to your own greed, I can do what I should have done all those years ago."

Razor-sharp teeth appeared in Madam Denesha's mouth. Long and pointy. The large woman leaped from her chair and crashed down upon the unsuspecting Barry. Saliva-drenched fangs ripped into the poor man's throat, tearing through his flesh with ease and unleashing an unstoppable flow of blood when his jugular was ripped from his throat. Barry's dead body fell to the floor as Madam Denesha turned her attention to Jackson, who was frozen with disbelief.

"Run!" Lilly screamed, snapping Jackson back to reality.

He tripped over his own feet as he tried to back away from

the possessed medium, who came to stand over him with snarling blood-soaked fangs.

Lilly sprang into action. She charged straight at Madam Denesha and punched her as hard as she could square in the face. The spirit of Larry Finton flew backward as the ghost's essence began to emerge from the rear of Madam Denesha's body. Larry reached out and grabbed the medium by her shoulders, stopping his momentum. Using her body as an anchor, he pulled his ethereal form back into her body and, in doing so, threw a punch of his own, hitting Lilly right in the forehead, sending the spirit of the dead girl tumbling across the floor.

Jackson tried to get to his feet, but before he could, the possessed medium was on him. She picked his body up with ease and slammed him hard onto the table. Jackson couldn't believe the amount of strength the woman had. She easily held him down as he flailed about. He tried with all his might to get up, but it was no use, for she had him pinned securely in place. Bloody fangs moved in for the kill. A rapid clicking sound erupted from nowhere as Jackson saw two-pronged wires from a Taser sticking out of the medium's chest. Madam Denesha's body seized up and became as stiff as a board before falling off to the side, leaving Larry's ghost in its place. Sparks danced about the prongs, which were now protruding from his chest.

Jackson followed the Taser wires and found a red-headed woman standing behind him, holding a strange device. She was a little taller than Lilly and had an athletic build. Her long red hair was pulled back in a ponytail, and she had on a pair of blue jeans and a black leather jacket, much like Jackson's. Around her waist hung a black leather duty belt. There was a holster on the right side of the belt, and several small black plastic cartridges clung to the left side.

The red-haired woman released the trigger, and the clicking

sound stopped. The device in her hand resembled something like a sci-fi pistol. It was black with blue flashing lights. It had a large square front, which was where the wires had shot out from. She pushed a button on the side of the gun, and the sound of pressurized air hissed into being for a split second as the plastic cartridge holding the wires ejected itself from the front of the gun. The woman swiftly replaced it with a fresh cartridge as she rushed over to Larry Finton and placed his wrists into a pair of weird handcuffs.

"Been after you for a long time, Larry Finton," the woman said, slamming the spirit onto the table. "Consider yourself retrieved."

"Who the hell are you?" Jackson asked, helping Lilly to her feet.

"You can see me?" the woman asked.

"Yeah," Jackson said, sarcasm oozing from his lips.

"And you can see him?" She pointed to Larry.

Jackson nodded.

"Can someone tell me what just happened?" Joshua asked, rushing back into the room and discovering all the carnage.

"What about him?" the woman asked, pointing to Joshua.

"And her," Jackson replied, pointing at Lilly. "Now you gonna answer my question?"

"Interesting," the woman said, grabbing Larry by the arm and walking him out of the room.

"Hey!" Jackson yelled, chasing after the woman, followed by Lilly and Joshua. The woman opened the front door of the building and dragged Larry through it and over to a black van with no windows. She opened the two back doors, revealing a cage made from thick silver bars. Fishing a key out of her jacket pocket and unlocking the cage, she shoved Larry into it head first and slammed the back doors closed. Without saying another word, she began to make her way to the front of the van.

"Hey!" Jackson said again, not liking the cold shoulder. He grabbed the woman by her arm, but before he could do anything else, she spun around, and Jackson found his arm locked in place as the woman raised her fist. Jackson looked up and saw a large red ruby ring about to hit him hard in the face.

"You're a reaper, aren't you?" Lilly asked.

The woman gave Lilly an odd stare but still held her fist cocked and ready to fire.

"It's your ring," Lilly began to explain. "It's like the ring of a reaper I know. Fred?"

The woman let out a short burst of laughter. "Fred *is* a reaper, but who knows for how much longer. You should steer clear of him."

"I'm just trying to complete my unfinished business," Lilly said.

"I know," the woman said. "You're not on my list, so that means you're a purg, which also means you're none of *my* business. What about you?" she asked Jackson, still holding his arm locked in place. "What's your story?"

"I see dead people."

"A seer? Very rare. What about him?" She motioned to Joshua.

"His séance was next," said Lilly, looking back to the front door of Madam Denesha's House of Spiritual Healing. "He was hoping to pass over tonight. Will she be ok?"

"She'll be out for most of the night and have one hell of a hangover in the morning. Then there's the little matter of the dead body in her parlor," the woman stated, letting up her grip on Jackson's arm.

"So what am I supposed to do?" Joshua asked.

"Beats me," the woman answered. "Not my problem. Now if you'll excuse me..." She cut her words off as her face became illuminated in the headlights of a car pulling up a short distance behind her van.

"Mom!" Joshua rushed over to the car.

An elderly woman, barely able to see over the steering wheel, got out of the car and began to walk up to the front door of the building.

"Mom! Don't go in there!" Joshua yelled, stepping in front of his mother to block her path, but the old woman walked through him.

"Jackson, stop her! You have to do something," Joshua pleaded.

"Don't you move," Jackson told the reaper. "Ma'am," he called out, running up to the old woman and blocking her path to the front door.

Lilly and the reaper watched as Jackson talked with Joshua's mother for a few moments. The old woman reached out and gave Jackson a heartfelt embrace as Joshua dissolved into tiny pieces of golden light, disappearing from sight. Jackson helped the woman back to her car, where they hugged one more time before she drove off.

"It's a nice thing your friend's doing," the reaper said. "You do this job long enough you forget about good moments like this. Is he helping you too?"

Lilly nodded as Jackson rushed back over to them.

"All right, time to talk," Jackson said.

"Fine," the reaper sighed. "But only because of what you did for that purg, but not here. The police are going to be arriving soon. Get in your car and follow me. I have to take care of this bouncer anyway."

"Bouncer?" Jackson asked, more confused than ever.

"Just follow me," the reaper said, getting into her van and driving off.

"Another reaper," Lilly said. "What are the odds?"

"I always thought there was one grim reaper," Jackson said, doing his best to catch up to the blacked-out van.

"Fred, the reaper you saw in the hospital, said he was one of many."

"How many are there?" Jackson wondered.

They followed the van for about fifteen minutes before it pulled into the parking lot of a small marina, where a variety of boats were tethered to a number of docks.

The black van backed into a parking spot. Jackson and Lilly met the reaper there, as she opened the rear doors. "The name's Carol, by the way," she said, opening the cage and grabbing Larry Finton by his shirt and giving him a hard yank. "Move it, Bouncer."

"I'm Jackson."

"Lilly."

"Where are we?" Jackson asked.

"On the shore of Lake Superior," Carol answered. "I need to get him to our substation." The reaper pushed her prisoner down one of the docks, then took out her cell phone and sent a quick text.

"I'm still at a loss," Jackson confessed.

"Just give her a minute," Lilly insisted.

"Listen to the purg," Carol told him, walking down the dock, where to Jackson's and Lilly's surprise, they found a small boat waiting for them. A lone man sat in the back of the boat with a hand resting on the boat's motor. "Hey, Dan," Carol called out to the man. "Got a couple of guests this run," she said, flipping a gold coin to the boat's captain, who snatched it out of the air with ease. "Take a seat up front," she directed as she and Larry sat in the middle of the boat.

The small boat surged forward and began to head out toward open water.

"Where are we going?" Jackson yelled out over the sound of the engine and crashing waves.

"I said we're going to a substation. We have them strategically placed all over the country. This one patrols the Great Lakes."

The small boat zipped through the water, maneuvering easily through the choppy waves. Jackson, who had never been on a boat of any kind before, started to get a little woozy and a little concerned, but the reaper and the boat driver both appeared unfazed, so he tried not to worry. After about ten minutes, a large shipping freighter came into sight. The driver changed course, and the small boat entered an intercept course. The boat ran up alongside the large ship, and the driver cut off the motor. The reaper got to her feet and directed Larry to a ladder hanging over the side of the ship. "Welcome to the *Azreal*."

Chapter 15

The Weight of One's Soul

The *Azreal* wasn't one of those large super freighters commonly witnessed chugging across Michigan's Great Lakes, but it was big enough. Her forward deck, where Jackson and Lilly had boarded the ship, was packed with large metal shipping containers stacked three high. They followed Carol through the maze of containers until they reached an open area. The cold night air blasted across the bow of the ship, and Jackson could feel the mist of Lake Superior washing across his face.

The reaper led them to a metal hatchway door with a large metal wheel in its center and a small circular window above it. On the other side of the door, a grated metal floor led them into the bowels of the ship. Stairs took them below to another deck. Large pipes lined the narrow hallway's ceiling, and the air became thick with moisture. They went through another door and down several more flights of stairs before coming to yet another metal door. Lilly noted this door appeared different from the others. While solid in construction, there were no visible knobs or windows. It resembled a single piece of shiny stainless steel, except for an odd-looking indented hole where the keyhole should have been.

Carol placed the blood-red ruby of her ring into the hole, and the door slid open, revealing a large room. On one side of the room sat three desks occupied by two men and one woman. They all looked "ordinary" for it being a reaper substation. They sat behind archaic computers with large boxy monitors, their faces bathed in the eerie green light of the past. Old phones with rotary dials sat next to the computers and were constantly ringing.

On the other side of the room, an old phone switchboard hung on the wall. Two women and one man sat in front of the switchboard with headsets on. There were numerous small holes in the switchboard, and each hole had a small light above it. When a light flashed, the operator would plug in a wire, with a large headphone jack at the end, into the hole, answer the call, and then plug another wire into another hole.

Carol pushed Larry toward a lone door at the far end of the room. Everyone stopped what they were doing and gawked at the group as they made their way across the room. After several long, uncomfortable seconds, they all returned to what they were doing and paid them no further attention.

The door at the far end of the room opened to a short, dead-ended hall with two doors on each side. Carol directed Larry to the door on the left. The small room measured twenty feet by twenty feet and was divided in half by a wall with a large bay window in the middle of it. The room on the other side of the glass was all white and blindingly bright.

Carol took off Larry's handcuffs and pushed him *through* the wall into the second room. Larry immediately went crazy as he desperately searched for an avenue of escape, but for some reason, he could not pass back through the wall—or any of the other walls, for that matter. Even the large glass window proved solid to the spirit, who began pounding on it.

"What are you going to do with him?" Lilly asked.

Stepping up to the window, she watched in her own horror-fueled anxiety as the trapped ghost continued to search for a way out. Could this be her future? If Jackson couldn't help her complete her unfinished business, would she end up as insane as Larry Finton?

"Don't worry, Purg. You won't end up in there like ole Larry here," Carol said, as if she could read the ghost's mind.

The reaper walked over to a small desk positioned in front of the window and took a seat in the only chair. A microphone stand with a small red button on its base was positioned within arm's reach of the chair. Next to the microphone stand was a small control panel with two buttons. One black, the other white.

"How do you know?" Lilly wondered.

"Because you're a purg, not a bouncer," the reaper said.

"You need to pretend like we don't understand anything you're talking about," Jackson butted in. "We both know what a purg is, but other than that, this shit is all new to us."

"Where would you like me to start?"

"How about with the whole grim reaper thing? How many of you are there?" Jackson asked, taking out a cigarette and lighting it.

"Jackson!" Lilly said. "You can't smoke that in here."

"Why not? You don't have to worry about secondhand smoke anymore, and I'm pretty sure neither does Death."

"He's right," Carol said. "The title of Death is held by many," she began. "So many that we have our own union. The rate the human race kills itself is so vast that having one Angel of Death," she said, emphasizing the words Angel of Death with finger quotes, "is impossible. Even in the beginning. So, the business of Death was incorporated shortly after the cruci-fixion of Christ. Today, we have over ten thousand members, serving all Christian-based countries."

"Wow," Jackson and Lilly said at the same time.

"Yeah, and we're still understaffed, but management keeps threatening us with budget cuts and furlough time. Go figure, right?"

"Wait, the crucifixion of Christ?" Jackson asked.

"And?" Carol replied.

"So, that means that God and the Devil are real? Heaven and hell? Angels and demons?"

"Yeah, demons are real," Lilly answered. "I've met two already."

"Everything you learned in Sunday school is real. For the most part. Even though the majority of things aren't actually depicted as they truly are, but we don't have time for that discussion, and by that, I mean I really don't want to have *that* discussion. Besides, I thought you would have figured all of this out by now, with you being able to see the dead and all."

"That means I seriously need to re-evaluate...everything..."

"You told me I wasn't on your list. What does that mean?" Lilly asked.

"Like any large corporation, there are a plethora of depart-ments that are needed to fulfill all the demands of the business. I'm in the retrieval department and one of the senior reapers on the SRT."

"SRT?" Jackson asked.

"Soul Retrieval Team. Let me try to explain this in a way you will understand. There are five categories for a newly departed soul. You have those who automatically go up and those who automatically go down. Those who need to have their souls weighed. And the purgs." Carol motioned at Lilly. "Purgs, for the most part, led a good life but never did anything exceptional during their time on earth that would guarantee them automatic entrance through the pearly gates. So, Heaven gives them one final test."

"My unfinished business?" Lilly asked, although she already knew the answer.

"A nearly impossible task, but a task that will allow you to prove your worth and ascend to paradise once completed. Then you have the bouncers, like Larry here. Technically, they're souls that need to be weighed. People like him live right on the edge. Picture a circle. Half of the circle is white, while the other half is red. Now, right where the two colors touch is a thin, practically invisible gray line. The people who live their lives there are the souls that need to be properly weighed before they can be sent off to their final destination. Standard operating procedures dictate a reaper must be present at the soul's TOD to ensure the weighing is properly carried out, but sometimes reapers can get behind schedule and don't show up on time like they're supposed to."

"When I died, I couldn't go more than twenty feet from my body," Lilly said, remembering the six months she spent tethered to her corporeal shell.

"You could have if you *really* wanted to," Carol said. "That heavy sense of impending doom you felt is a built-in fail-safe. Designed to keep the spirit from wandering off until they've been greeted by their Designated Afterlife Representative."

"Which does what, exactly?" Jackson asked.

"They inform the purg of their situation and go over the ground rules before pointing them in the general direction of their test."

"I sat in the woods for six months. Six fucking months," Lilly exclaimed, her voice rising with her temper. "Where was my representative?" The lights in the room flickered for a brief second. It happened so fast, it went undetected by nearly everyone in the room.

"I don't know," was the only thing Carol could offer, glancing up at the lights. "Sometimes shit happens. Spirits get overlooked. The system is far from perfect, but we do the best we can."

"Yeah, well, that's not good enough," Lilly said, her voice still filled with anger.

"The same sense of foreboding is there for those who need to be weighed, as well, but every once in a while, a spirit will run, especially if they're desperate enough or scared enough, before the reaper can arrive. We call those bouncers. Because they bounce before we can weigh them, and that's where I come in."

"This is crazy," Jackson said, taking the last drag from his cigarette. He dropped the butt onto the ground and put it out with the tip of his shoe. Carol glared at Jackson until he got the hint and picked up the cigarette butt and put it into his jacket pocket. "How did those handcuffs work on a ghost?"

"They are constructed from two layers of metal. The inner is iron, which is solid to the spirit world and causes immense pain upon contact. The outer layer is silver, which has certain spiritual properties," the reaper answered, taking out her pair of handcuffs and tossing them to Jackson. "The cage in the back of my van is constructed in the same design."

Jackson caught the cuffs, and Lilly saw that they had weird runes carved into the metal surface. "What are these?" he asked, turning the handcuffs over and examining the other side.

"They're runes of incantations," Carol said.

"Incantations?" Lilly asked. "You mean magic?" she said the word magic with a heavy question mark.

"Exactly," the reaper answered.

"Hold the phone," Jackson said. "Magic is real too? I'm finding all of this a little too hard to believe."

"Says the human hanging out with ghosts and reapers," Carol said. "Anything else?"

"What was that thing you used on Larry? It looked like a Taser," Jackson asked.

"That's exactly what it was," Carol replied. "But ours are specifically designed to work on the ethereal. The barbed prongs that shoot out of the cartridge are iron, and instead of an electrical current, our Tasers emit an electromagnetic pulse, which, as you saw firsthand, immobilizes the ghost. I'm not sure of the exact science behind it. Our R&D branch designs the toys; I just play with them. Enough of the gab session," she said, turning to face the microphone. "Gotta get back to work."

Lilly peered into the room on the other side of the glass and saw Larry clawing at one of the corners in a desperate attempt to free himself. Carol adjusted the microphone in front of her and pushed the red button. "Mr. Finton, can you hear me? Please step into the center of the room."

If Larry could, he didn't acknowledge the reaper as he continued to claw at the wall and moan as if he was in tremendous pain.

"Mr. Finton, it's time to weigh your soul."

The ghost snapped his head around at an impossible angle for anyone living and glared at Carol with red eyes and wickedly sharp teeth.

"Is that normal?" Jackson asked, stepping up to the window to get a better look.

"Unfortunately," the reaper answered. "Ever hear of a poltergeist? That's what happens to some spirits the longer they stay behind. They get angry and develop a real hatred for the living, which can lead to what happened back at the séance."

"Will those kinds of things affect his overall outcome?" Lilly asked.

"No, he will only be weighed on the things he did when he was alive," Carol answered. "If the scales are in his favor, his... condition will be rectified before his transition takes place."

"How do the actions of one's afterlife affect someone like me?" Lilly asked, thinking of Sebastian. The things she witnessed him do were truly disturbing, given the fact they were done by such a young child.

"To a purg, completing your unfinished business is your greatest test. And, like any test, you will be graded on your performance, as well as other factors. The way you pass the test is just as important as the test itself. It can make the difference in if you go up or down."

Carol had given Lilly a lot to ponder.

"Mr. Finton, this is your last warning. Please move to the center of the room." Carol pressed the black button on the control panel. The outline of a small black circle appeared in the center of the white floor.

Larry spun around with an unnatural speed and launched himself at the window.

Lilly screamed as the ghost slammed into the glass before rebounding harmlessly off it.

"Fuck you, bitch," he screamed, slamming into the window again, hoping the outcome would be different from the first. It wasn't.

"Fine," Carol said, pushing the button on the microphone. "Have it your way." She pressed the black button on the control panel again. The entire room turned black, except for the black circle, which turned white. Larry screamed in pain and began to run frantically around the room. "Please step into the center of the room," the reaper said again.

Larry eyeballed the white circle in the middle of the black

floor. He shook his head violently back and forth. "NO! NEVER!"

"Is this absolutely necessary?" Jackson asked. "You're hurting him. Can't you put the cuffs back on him or something? He seemed to be under control when he had them on."

"The incantations on the cuffs do keep them docile, but he has to be weighed, and only him. The handcuffs could be perceived as added weight, which could sway the outcome," Carol said. "And once the handcuffs come off, you get this," she added, pointing to Larry, who was now standing in front of the glass and slamming his head into it over and over. "So, unless you want to go in there and put him inside of the circle...?"

Lilly was about to interject but decided against it. She didn't like the idea of the ghost being tortured like he was, but she didn't have the experience in matters like this to tell the reaper how to do her job.

Carol pushed the black button a third time, and the blackness of the room increased, if such of thing was even possible, while the white circle became blinding. Larry screamed at the top of his lungs. He grabbed at his head and tried to pull the hair from his skull. He glared at the white circle of light in the center of the room, and after several long, agonizing moments, he began to stagger toward it. The ghost of Larry Finton was finally ready to have his soul weighed.

As SOON AS Larry stepped into the light, his horrifying screams ceased. The maddening noise that had filled his head for so many years faded. The insanity fogging his vision cleared, bringing his mind back from the outer fringes of madness. "What have I done?" he asked, lowering his head. But the statement wasn't a question meant for those who could hear him.

Larry could remember everything he had done, though he could not explain why he did some of them. "Barry..."

~

Carol pushed the white button on the control panel. At first, nothing happened. Larry surveyed the room in anticipation, as did Lilly and Jackson. The white circle of light began to blink in and out of existence. Slowly at first, but the longer Larry stood within the circle, the faster the cycle became. Flashing over and over. This continued for several minutes before the white circle became as red as the blood that had sprayed from his brother's throat.

The spirit of Larry Finton burst into flames, but before a single scream could escape his fiery lips, his body exploded into tiny embers. The glowing remnants of the ghost flickered ever so briefly before fading from existence.

"The scales have spoken," Carol said, pressing the black button one last time, casting the room on the other side of the glass into total darkness.

"So...he went..." Jackson began to say.

"Yep," the reaper answered. "Why were you two even at that séance to begin with? I know you took that other purg there, but the living and the dead don't usually hang out together."

"Like I said before, Jackson's helping me with my unfinished business," Lilly said.

"Like he did with the other purg?"

"His name was Joshua," Lilly said. The word "purg" sounded more and more offensive to her the more she heard it. "But yes. Only...my situation is a little more..."

"Fucked up," Jackson said.

"How's that?" Carol asked.

"I didn't die from natural causes," Lilly told the reaper. "I was murdered and buried in the woods, and in order for me to pass over, I have to bring my killer to justice. I have to make him pay for what he did to me and the others."

"The others?"

"That's why we're here in Sault Ste. Marie," Jackson explained. "Lilly is this guy's fifth victim."

"His first victim was still at his house when I got there, and she said all five of us share the same unfinished business and that we *all* needed to be there because those who weren't wouldn't be able to cross over when the time comes," Lilly said.

"Technically, I guess that would be accurate. If you complete your unfinished business and the others don't, *they* would be trapped in purgatory forever," Carol said. "Talk about an impossible task."

"Why is that?" Jackson asked.

"Because the spirit world is not meant to interact with the living world. That's why hardly any purgs ever cross over."

"But I can see and hear her," Jackson pointed out.

"I guess you can," the reaper said.

"I've also already helped two pur...spirits cross over. One that *you* were a witness to."

"That you did," Carol agreed. "And I must say I'm impressed."

"Not so impossible now, huh?" Lilly asked, with a smug look.

"So what's your plan?" the reaper asked.

Jackson and Lilly looked at each other with blank expressions as the reaper began to laugh. "I admire your guys' gumption, but for something like this to work, you need to have some kind of plan."

"And we'll have one when the time comes," Jackson promised.

"Yeah," Lilly argued, still wearing her smug expression. "We just need to find the others first."

"Well, I wish you both the best of luck," Carol offered, getting up from the desk. "And just so you know," she said, her words directed at Jackson, "you can't walk up to him and put a bullet in his head and expect everyone to live happily ever after."

"I...I wasn't planning on it," Jackson said.

Lilly wondered if the reaper somehow knew about the conversation she and Jackson had had back at Mark Karle's house.

"Good, because killing him will only hurt *your* soul in the end, if you know what I mean," Carol said.

"What about self-defense?" Lilly asked.

"Self-defense is one of those tricky gray areas," Carol warned. "If it happens naturally, you're golden. But, if you go into the situation with a gun, thinking that if you get into a fight, you can pull it out and *bang*, you're technically trying to use the act of self-defense to justify murder, and our scales will know. And if you're truly Jackson's friend, which I believe you two have become, I don't think you would want him to jeopardize his eternal ever after on such a technicality, now do you?"

"No, I would never," Lilly answered.

"I just wanna make sure we're all on the same page," Carol said. "It's not my place to be giving advice like this. I'm supposed to remain impartial, but I hate seeing good people do stupid things and having their souls damned when they didn't have to."

"We appreciate the advice," Jackson said, extending his hand to the reaper, who stared at it until Jackson retracted it.

"Follow me," Carol told them, leaving the room. After returning to the large command center, she walked over to one of the antique computer stations. "Kenny, say hello to Jackson and Lilly."

"Hello," the man said nervously. He was a scrawny fellow with dark greasy hair and thick glasses.

"Kenny here is one of our locators and a damn good one at that. He's the one who gave me the tip on Larry," Carol said, giving the scrawny man a fist bump. "What's the name of the purg you're looking for?"

"Jessica Watkins," Lilly said.

She watched Kenny type out the name on his keyboard. The green monitor hummed to life as the girl's name appeared on the screen in yellow, followed by a long list of information.

Carol grabbed a small piece of paper from the desk and scribbled something down on it. "Here," she said, handing the piece of paper to Jackson.

"What's this?"

"The last known address for your purg," the reaper answered. "Here, take this too." She handed him one of her business cards. There was a phone number printed on one side and nothing else.

"Thanks, but I don't have a phone at the moment."

"Jesus Christ," Carol said, snatching the piece of paper out of Jackson's hand. "Give me a burner," she told Kenny, who began to rummage through one of his desk drawers.

Kenny pulled out a brand new cell phone and handed it to Carol, who activated one of the preloaded apps. "Here," she said, handing the phone to Jackson. "I inputted the purg's location. Just follow the directions."

Chapter 16

Awakenings Part Two

Norma Jean opened her eyes, and all she could see was a big bright blur. Her head felt like it weighed a hundred pounds, and the right side of her neck hurt like hell. Her entire body felt sore and stiff. She tried to sit up and, in doing so, heard something metal echo softly as it clanged against a hard surface. The memories in her head were as fuzzy as her vision but slowly began to reform.

She remembered some weird man rear-ending her, and... Oh my god, she thought, he had attacked her! Had stabbed something into her neck. She had fought the best she could and remembered making it back to her car and speeding down the dark country road. Her heart raced out of control as she began to shake her head, desperately trying to clear the cobwebs. She didn't remember anything past getting behind the wheel of her car.

That soft echoing sound of metal reached her ears again as she moved her body.

The sensation of something heavy around her right ankle made it through the fog in her head. Shaky fingers made their way down her leg and stopped when they felt a cold piece of metal. Her vision began to clear. An iron shackle was padlocked around her left ankle. The soft echoing sound of metal came from the three-foot chain running from the shackle to a large metal eyelet embedded into a concrete floor.

"No...no...no," she cried, pulling at the chain.

Tears streamed down her cheeks. She screamed for help as loud as she could. She screamed until her throat was on fire, but no one came rushing to her rescue. Desperation began to consume her. Frantically, she looked around to get a bearing on where she was and how she could escape.

She sat in the corner of a small room, ten foot by ten foot, if that, and was lying on an old stained mattress. A long, bright light hung from the ceiling. The concrete floor had a small metal drain cover in the middle of the room. The walls and ceiling were covered with large thick foam panels, and there was an old wooden chair, much like the one her priest sat in during church service, in the opposite corner of the room. Next to her mattress was one of those portable toilet chairs. The kind one might find in a hospital.

She scanned the room, searching for anything she could use. Then she saw it, the outline of a door within the foam panels on the wall in front of her. She struggled to her feet and, with all the strength she could find, made a mad dash for the door. Norma Jean fell hard against the concrete floor when the length of the chain ended abruptly.

"Help me!" she screamed. "Somebody! Anybody! Please..." she cried, tears continuing to run freely down her cheeks.

The door, a few teasing feet in front of her, swung open. Norma Jean's heart raised with relief but fell with despair as the man who had attacked her now stood between her and her freedom. A wicked grin stretched across his lips as Norma Jean suddenly realized she was as naked and as helpless as the day she had been born.

She scampered backward as fast as she could until she had nowhere left to go. "Please, mister..." she begged. "Just let me go... I...I won't tell anyone. I swear..."

~

MARK cockily strode into the room, closing the door behind him, and squatted near the metal loop keeping Norma Jean his captive. He grabbed the chain and shook it violently as he made some menacing noises. Norma jean screamed and tried to back away. Mark laughed at her before walking over to the big chair in the corner and taking a seat.

"Are...are you going to rape me?"

"Already did that," Mark answered, getting a sense of arousal from the look on Norma Jean's face at the realization that her innocence had been stolen. "But yes, I do plan on doing *that* quite a bit more," he promised. "And from now on, you'll be wide awake, so you can enjoy every minute of it."

Norma Jean let out another scream. Mark rose from the chair and screamed at the top of his lungs, right alongside her, before mocking her cries for help. "Scream all you want, little one. There's no one near to hear you."

"Are...are you going to kill me?"

"You know, you're the first girl to ever ask me that," Mark said. "Yes," he answered coldly. "Yes, I'm going to kill you and then bury you somewhere you'll never be found. However, *when* I do depends entirely on you. The longer I stay amused, the longer you stay alive."

Norma Jean started to cry uncontrollably again, her breath coming in gasps. Mark stood and began to remove his clothes, making sure to take off his class ring. No need for a repeat of the last girl, the thought, before sitting back in the chair. Grabbing his penis, he began to masturbate. The whole time not taking his eyes off his prize. When he was ready for the real thing, he made his way to the edge of the mattress and got down onto his knees.

"Come here," he ordered.

Mark knew she wouldn't listen. They never did at first. He liked it when they didn't listen. God, he thought, she looked just like his mother did in all the pictures hanging on the walls of the house, minus the blonde hair. The idea of killing his mother consumed him. He wanted nothing more than to ruin her life, as she had ruined his, but he had made a promise to his father, and Mark Karle was a man of his word, if nothing else. Therefore, Norma Jean would have to scratch his itch for now.

Mark grabbed the chain and pulled Norma Jean toward him.

She screamed and kicked at him.

Mark snatched her leg out of the air, and with one quick yank, Norma Jean was underneath him. Her muscles strained as she tried to pull away from him, but try as she might, she couldn't break free from his iron-like grip. She tried to turn onto her side and struck out at his face with her hands.

Mark swatted her hand away easily. "That's it," he said to her. "Fight."

Norma Jean screamed and punched him as hard as she could in the chest.

Mark took the punch and slapped her across the face as hard as he could. He wanted to punch her, to show her who was boss, but he remembered what had happened to the last girl he had hit too hard.

~

A BURNING SENSATION flashed across the skin on the left side of Norma Jean's face. Her vision blurred again. Her head spun. Before she knew what was happening, she was on her stomach, with Mark fully on top of her, his hot, sour breath caressing her right ear. He grunted several times as he painfully entered her from behind. Tears flowed down her face as she screamed in agony.

She lost all concept of time and eventually blacked out from the shock. When she came to, she was alone once again. Dried blood smeared across her left inner thigh. Her insides still hurt, and she felt so filthy. The smell of Old Spice lingered in her nose, making her nauseated. She looked over and saw a plastic bucket of water and a washcloth next to her now, as well as a jar of pea-flavored baby food. Grabbing the washcloth, she scrubbed her body clean, trying her best to wash any feeling of *him* from her.

She pressed the damp washcloth against the left side of her face. The cool water took away some of the sting that still remained. He had told her to fight, and she did. That seemed to get him off, she thought. Maybe he would only keep her alive as long as she fought him. Didn't he say the longer she kept him amused, the longer he would keep her alive? If he wanted a fight, she was going to give him one, she vowed, opening the jar of baby food. She would need to keep her strength up.

MARK STOOD in front of the mirror in the upstairs bathroom, smugly staring at his reflection. The sound of the water running into the sink was just an echo in his thoughts. Norma Jean had had a little more fight in her than the others, he thought, rubbing the spot on his chest where she had punched him. It made the whole experience much more thrilling. He had broken the spirits of the others so quickly that they were no longer as appealing to him as when he had first taken them. He would have to take his time with Norma Jean. He would have to control his urges and space out the precious time they would spend with each other.

"You feel like a big man now, don't you?" his reflection said.

Mark puffed out his chest and nodded.

"Marky," the shrill voice of his mother cut through his thoughts like fingernails running down a chalkboard, causing him to wince and giving him an instant headache.

"Not big enough to do what really needs to be done, though," his reflection pointed out pompously.

Mark hung his head low and exhaled a hard breath at the same time. His reflection was right, and he knew it. With all the horrible and violent things he had done—and was currently doing—and he couldn't take care of one old, bedridden bitch, who constantly made his life a living hell. He cupped his hands under the running water and brought it up to his face, letting the cold liquid wash away his temper.

He walked into his mother's room before she could call his name again. The all-too-familiar smell of shit greeted him as he made his way to his mother's side.

"About fucking time," she said. "I smell like shit."

"If you'd call me before you went, I could get you over to the portable toilet, and you wouldn't have to shit yourself," Mark scolded.

His mother cackled in his face. "Then you couldn't prove to me how much you love me."

Mark's face turned red. It would be so easy. One hand wrapped around her scrawny neck. He could even bury her right beside Tracy, and no one would be the wiser. The thought of visiting Norma Jean again entered his mind as he took off his mother's diaper. He had just told himself he would have to control his urges so as not to break her spirit too hastily.

"Don't forget to give mama her bath," his mother said in a seductive voice.

He did his best to finish as quickly as possible before retiring to his room. He lay there on his bed, staring at the popcorn ceiling, while his mind relived his latest encounter with Norma Jean.

He was getting hard picturing her helpless, naked body underneath his.

"Do it," he heard his voice say.

Mark got up and stood before the mirror on his dresser.

"Just do it," his reflection said.

"I thought we agreed to take our time with this one?"

"We did, but a little extra indulgence from time to time can't hurt anything...can it? Besides, you've earned it after all you just had to put up with."

"Maybe..." Mark said, his voice trailing off. The thoughts of a second session with Norma Jean made his pulse quicken.

"You know you want to. It's been too long since you had a plaything in the house. And what good is having a plaything if you can't play with it whenever you want? And the more time you spend down there means the less time you have to be up here. With her. That's all you ever do now. Hang around the house, waiting for dear old mom to summon you to clean up her shit. If she really loved you, she'd use the portable toilet like you said."

"I know she does it on purpose," Mark insisted. "You know when you have to go."

"Any minute now, she's gonna be calling your name again. You know I'm right," his reflection said. "You just have to man up and do what needs to be done."

"I want to," Mark said, balling up his hands and squeezing

so hard his knuckles cracked. "But I can't—you know that! I made Father a promise, and..."

"And Mark Karle is a man of his word," his reflection said in a whiney tone. "Dad's not here anymore, and the way it looks, Mommy Dearest is going to be here for a long time. You need to put her out of her misery. That way, she and Dad can be together again."

"Shut up," Mark roared, slamming a heavy fist on the top of the dresser with enough force to crack the wood. "You need to shut your fucking mouth!"

"*You* need to shut *your* fucking mouth before you wake *her* up."

"Marky!"

"Now you've done it," his reflection scolded.

"Marky, I've shit myself again!"

Mark's reflection began to laugh.

Mark slammed his fist down again and again, causing several more cracks to appear.

"If you just listen to me, we could be done with this shit detail and hit the open road. Have I ever steered you wrong before?"

Mark lowered his head and took a deep breath. After holding it for several seconds, he exhaled it loudly, trying his best to slow his heart rate and lower his blood pressure. "I can't," he whispered in a low, defeated voice.

"Then go and have some fun and deal with Mommy Dearest later."

Mark stared at his reflection and slowly nodded. It was what he needed right now. It was the only time he ever felt truly free.

"Marky!"

Mark walked out of his room and strode past his mother's doorway as he made his way to the basement. He came to stand before the door leading to his safe space, his pulse quickening with anticipation. Norma Jean had fought him before. He hoped she still had some fight left in her.

Mark entered the one place in the entire world where he felt truly happy. Truly in control. He found Norma Jean curled up in a ball in the corner right where he had left her, sobbing uncontrollably, her body visibly shaking. Her brown hair had become a tangled mess, and there were streaks of dirt running up and down her legs. Mark slammed the door shut as he entered the room and took great pleasure in witnessing Norma Jean's body flinch at the sound.

He crossed the distance between him and his new toy with only a few strides, confidently entering the inner space of the chain's distance. Squatting next to the mattress, he ran a lone finger up one of Norma Jean's legs, starting at the ankle and ending at her thigh. "I'm sorry for what's happened to you," he said, in a sincere voice, leaning in even closer. "It's not like I want to do the things I do. I have to. There's this...compulsion from somewhere deep within me. It's like a voice screaming in my head. Over and over, and it will only silence itself when... Well, you know when. I don't even enjoy it."

Norma Jean let out a primal scream as she moved with an unexpected speed, catching Mark completely off guard. He tried to back away from her. Tried to make it back outside the chain's range, but she got to him first. She punched him hard in the chest, and Mark felt a searing pain followed by a warm sensation. He scooted backward across the floor and watched in dismay as his blood began to soak through the cloth of his shirt right above his heart. His eyes flashed to Norma Jean as she crouched in a defensive posture. In her right hand was a blood-soaked piece of glass from the jar of baby food he had left her.

Mark slowly got to his feet and walked over to his throne-like chair. Keeping his back to Norma Jean, he took off his shirt and inspected the wound. It was deep but not deep enough to have done any real damage. He took his pants off, folded them, and placed them on the seat of the chair. Next, he slid his class ring from his right ring finger and gently placed it on top of his pants.

"I was trying to be sincere before," he said, his back still to the girl.

"Fuck you!" Norma screamed.

"Though I did lie about one thing," Mark said, turning to face Norma Jean with his manhood fully engorged. "I truly am going to enjoy this.

Chapter 17

The House Leonard Built

"This is the place," Lilly declared.

There had been no sign of Jessica at the address Carol had given them, but shortly after leaving the house empty-handed, Lilly felt a gentle tug pulling her toward the other side of the city. The longer they traveled, the stronger the tug pulled at her.

Jackson put the car in park and double-checked the map on his new phone. "How can you be sure?" he asked, staring at a dilapidated building.

The building was roughly twelve miles south of Sault Ste. Marie. The two of them sat quietly in Jackson's car, staring at what, at one point in time, sixty years ago perhaps, must have been an extravagant mansion. The sun had a few hours before it was due to rise, but both doubted that even the light of day would do little to change the building's overall appearance.

"I'm not sure," Lilly answered.

The remnants of a tall wrought iron fence still encircled the property. The weeds and underbrush of the severely neglected yard had tangled themselves in between and up the fence, making the metal barrier nearly invisible. Crossing the driveway was a large iron gate. One-half laid on the thick weed-covered driveway, while the other was hanging on for dear life by only its top hinge.

"You think it's safe to go in there?" Jackson asked, stepping out of the car and lighting a cigarette.

"I'm sure it's safe for me," Lilly said, stepping *through* the car door and walking up to the large gate. "But then again, I'm dead."

"Lucky you," Jackson said, blowing out a lungful of smoke and turning on the flashlight app on his cell phone.

After taking a couple of quick drags from the cigarette, he flicked it away and walked through the gate, making his way up to the house. Looking back, he watched Lilly carefully tiptoe through the fence's iron bars, causing him to chuckle at the sight. "Man, this must have been some place back in the day."

The building was huge. Three stories high, with a large pitched roof covered in clay tiles. Large windows with heavy wooden shutters stretched across the front of the mansion. Half were missing. The other half lay hidden behind old, faded pieces of plywood. Large vines stretched themselves up the walls and onto the roof. The exterior of the building was made from wood planks, but Jackson had no idea what their original color had been. Now, the entire building had become a dull shade of gray, except for some sporadic splashes of color made from the numerous spots of graffiti left upon the walls over the years.

"There's something off about this place," Jackson said, stepping up to a large set of ornate wooden doors.

"What do you mean?" Lilly asked.

"It's like the air is heavier here or something, if that makes any sense. Like we stepped into a magic bubble," he added, reading an old cardboard condemned sign nailed to one of the doors. "Probably just my nerves," he said with a quick shrug. "Do you want to stay out here?"

"No," Lilly answered. "The quicker we find Jessica, the better."

Jackson pushed open one of the doors and disappeared into the darkness. Lilly quickly stepped through the other door and found Jackson standing in a large open foyer. The inside of the house looked as bad as, if not worse than, the outside. Numerous holes dotted many of the visible walls, along with more graffiti. Small heaps of trash lay strewn about the area, and bits of broken glass, scattered about the floors, reflected the light of Jackson's phone, reminding him of the stars shining in the night sky.

Straight ahead of them stood a massive staircase of dark-stained mahogany. It split in two about halfway up, with each end going to opposite sides of the second floor, while three large hallways were visible from their vantage point. One to each side of the room, with the third being visible off to the side of the ascending staircase.

"Should we split up?" Lilly asked.

"Are you fucking crazy?" Jackson asked. "Have you never watched a horror movie?"

"Is this your idea of a horror movie?"

"Old creepy abandoned house? Check. Ghosts?" Jackson motioned toward Lilly. "Check. Living guy going into the house to look for more ghosts? Check."

"Touché. Any idea where we should start?"

"Jessica Watkins," Jackson called out. "Why should we go looking for her when we can bring her to us?"

"Not bad," Lilly said with an approving nod.

Whispering voices filled the foyer. Neither Jackson nor Lilly could see the source of the voices, but they seemed to be coming from all around them.

"Did he say Jessica?"

"I think so."

"Why does he want to speak to her?"

"Where is she?"

"She's with him."

"She's doomed."

"Is he one of the living?"

"Who's the girl with him?"

"I think she's like us."

"We should warn her."

"We should give her to him."

"Then he'll leave us alone."

Jackson and Lilly turned their heads from side to side, trying to follow the conversation taking place around them, though they still couldn't see who was speaking. There were three distinct male voices and one female voice. "Maybe we should leave?" Jackson suggested, taking a few steps backward.

"For once, I wholeheartedly agree with you," Lilly said, glancing up to the second floor of the house.

Jackson noticed Lilly's eyes shifting upward. "Did you see something?" Jackson directed the light from his phone to where she was looking. He saw only cobwebs and the word BEES spray-painted in yellow on the wall in large balloon-like letters. Before Jackson could say anything else, four ghosts materialized, surrounding them.

The ghost in front of them was in his late twenties. The shade of his skin was that of ash, and he wore a soldier's uniform. Half of his face had been blown off. The ghost to their left was of a man as well, but older, maybe in his forties. His skin, which at one point had been black, now matched that of the soldier, while his clothes were from the disco era. A large bloodstain graced the front of his shirt.

The ghost to the right of them was in her thirties and gray

like the rest of them. Her face showed signs of Asian heritage, while her long, straight black hair hung freely past her shoulders. She had on a pair of bell-bottom jeans, along with a short-sleeved shirt and a leather vest. Dark circles were visible under her eyes, and her lips were as black as her hair.

Jackson dared a glance over his shoulder and saw the last ghost still had some color to him. He was somewhere in his twenties, with dark tanned skin, and was dressed in what Jackson considered regular clothes. A pair of jeans and a Metallica T-shirt.

"You shouldn't have come here," the soldier said, the lines of his face stern and unmoving.

"We're looking for someone," Jackson answered.

"I wasn't talking to you," the soldier responded.

"Hey, man, he can see us," the ghost in the disco outfit said in disbelief.

"Maybe he can help us," said the spirit of the woman.

"It's too late for that," the soldier argued. "Grab her!"

The disco ghost and the ghost of the man behind them surged forward, each grabbing one of Lilly's arms.

"Hey!" she screamed. "Get off me!"

"Hey!" Jackson yelled. "Get the fuck off her!" He tried to tackle the disco ghost but shot through the spirit and hit the floor hard. Before he could get back to his feet, the ghosts had dragged Lilly through a solid door and disappeared from sight.

"Lilly!" Jackson screamed, rushing to the door only to find it locked. "What can I do? What can I do? What hurts ghosts? Iron!" Running back outside, he kicked at the rusted iron gate. After knocking the bottom of one of the iron rods free, he began to bend and twist it until he was walking back to the house with a three-foot piece of iron rod in his hands.

Jackson ran through the foyer and up to the door the ghosts had disappeared through. He gave the handle a hard turn and pushed his shoulder against the door at the same time, but it still wouldn't budge. Taking a few steps back, he rushed forward, slamming his body into the door, hoping he could force it open. A searing pain shot through his shoulder as he bounced off the solid wood door and fell to the floor. He pushed himself to his feet and fought through the pain. He hit the door several times with the iron bar, but even that assault failed miserably. He had to do something. But what? There was no telling what the spirits were going to do to Lilly or where they had even taken her. He ran back into the foyer, trying several more doors, before charging up the stairs toward the unknown.

"Let go of me!" Lilly screamed, kicking and twisting her body, but it was no use. The ghosts of the disco man and the regular guy held on tight while they followed the soldier through the hallway of the first floor. In every doorway they passed, ghosts from all eras watched as the group passed by quickly.

"Help me!" Lilly screamed in desperation.

The ghost of an older woman wearing a black dress reached out a gray hand but pulled it back when the soldier gave her a disapproving stare.

"No one here's going to help you," the soldier said, rounding one corner and heading off down another hallway.

"Why not?" asked Lilly.

"Because they don't want to end up like you."

"Wait!" Lilly exclaimed. "My friend can help you if you let me go. You're all purgs like me, right? He's alive and can help you with your unfinished business. Just let me go, and I'll talk to him."

"This place is like a roach motel for ghosts, sweet thing," the disco ghost said. "Spooks check-in, but they don't check out."

"Dan," the woman ghost spoke up. "This is wrong. There has to be another way."

"Not now, Melinda," the soldier said, stopping in front of a heavy metal door. "You know this has to happen. If not, one of us could be next."

"At least let me talk to her and tell her what's happening," Melinda pleaded.

"Fine, but make it quick," Dan ordered, pounding a fist on the door three times. His face contorted in pain with each strike, giving Lilly the impression the door was constructed out of iron and impassible by those of the spirit world.

"Listen," Melinda said. "I've only got time to say this once. There's a demon down there who feeds on our essence. He's trapped within this place, so he set a trap of his own. You felt it, didn't you? Something drawing you here?"

Lilly nodded.

"That was him. Once a ghost enters this place, we can't leave. We become trapped like him. The girl you're looking for, Jessica, she's down there," Melinda said, leaning close and lowering her voice to a whispered tone. "I'll find your friend and tell him where you are. Maybe he can find a way to help you."

The door swung open on its own, revealing a darkened enclosed stairway leading to the house's basement. "Times up," Dan shouted. He came up behind Lilly and gave her a hard shove, causing her to topple forward and tumble down the stairs.

JACKSON MADE his way to the top of the stairs and found a darkened hallway filled with open doorways. Lifting his phone into the air, he found the eyes of the dead glaring back at him like animal eyes caught in the headlights of a car. Keep looking straight ahead, he thought. He wasn't sure if these spirits had the same intentions as the ones who had taken Lilly, and while he was sure they couldn't hurt him, he didn't want to take any unnecessary chances.

On the low end of the spectrum, he figured they would act like the ghosts at the casino, lining up to get his attention and wanting his help with their unfinished business. On the high end, the memories of what had happened at Madam Denesha's flooded into his head. Suddenly he became very worried.

"He's one of the living," said the ghost of a young woman, her face and body mangled from a car accident.

"Can he see us?" asked the spirit of man, the back of his head blown out from an apparent suicide.

"The living can't see us," said another man, whose appearance looked normal enough.

"But he was here with that other purg," said the ghost of the woman, who started following Jackson after he had passed her doorway.

"One way to find out," said the man with the bullet hole in his head. The spirit stepped out of his doorway and stood directly in Jackson's path. Jackson wasn't sure what to do. Would he simply pass right through the ghost, like Lilly did with doors, or would passing through the spirit allow his body to be possessed? At the last possible second, Jackson decided he couldn't risk it and stopped within inches of the dead man's nose.

"Screw this," he jumped backward and raised the iron rod up in a defensive position.

"He *can* see us," the man said as all the ghosts in the hall surrounded Jackson.

"Back off," Jackson yelled, swinging the rod out in front of him in a wide sweeping arc. The tip of the iron rod skimmed the arm of the man with the bullet hole in his head, causing him to howl in pain as he scurried back into the darkness of his room. "I mean it! Back off!"

"We need your help," pleaded the ghost of the mangled woman.

"I just want to find my friend and get the hell out of this crazy-ass place. I don't have time to help you purgs with your unfinished business."

"We're way beyond that," said the ghost of the man with the bullet hole, sticking his head back out into the hallway to check if it was safe or not. "We'd all settle for being able to leave this place too."

"Then why don't you?"

"Because we're trapped here," answered the woman, whose appearance was making Jackson a little woozy. "Just like your friend is now."

"Do you know where she is? How can I get to her?"

"She's in the basement," came a voice from the darkness behind Jackson. He and the other ghosts turned as the spirit of Melinda materialized before them.

"Because you helped take her," Jackson shouted, pointing the iron rod at the woman's head.

"Only because I didn't have a choice, but maybe you can save her before it's too late."

"I'm listening."

"In the basement lives a demon named Leonard, and he's the one responsible for all of this."

"Leonard? The demon's name is Leonard?" Jackson asked skeptically.

"Rumor has it he was summoned here over twenty years ago by the house's original owner and has been trapped here ever since. He cast some kind of spell, drawing any spirits within the area here. And once we step inside, the spell acts like a powerful ward, trapping all who enter."

"Why? What's he get out of trapping all of you here?" Jackson asked.

"He feeds on us," Melinda told him. "He keeps three ghosts imprisoned with him at a time. When one gets used up, he tasks the others and me with finding him a replacement. In return, he leaves us alone."

"And all you have to do is sell out your own kind," Jackson said, his words bringing murmurs from the other ghosts, signaling they shared the same sentiment.

"Don't judge me," Melinda hissed. "I don't want to die like that. None of us do, but better them than me."

"I hate to break it to you, but you do know you're already dead, don't you?"

"Of course I know," Melinda retorted. "Still doesn't mean I want to be slowly eaten by a demon."

"Enough of this bullshit," Jackson huffed, shaking the iron rod at Melinda. Her eyes followed the piece of metal. "You said I could save my friend, so spill it."

"I'll take you to the basement," Melinda promised. "But the others won't be too happy about it."

"And what do I do when I find her?"

"Beats the hell out of me," Melinda said with a shrug.

Jackson let out a loud, exhausted breath and lowered the iron rod. Ghosts? Ok, he was getting used to the whole idea of communicating with the spirit world. The thought of grim reapers running around Sault Ste. Marie and tasing bouncers? A little harder to swallow, but demons? He wasn't in the kiddy pool anymore and had a feeling he was about to sink like a rock.

Melinda led him back to the first floor, down a different set of stairs, and before he knew it, he was standing in front of the basement door. He tried the handle and found it locked up tight. "Shit!" he cursed, giving the door a hard kick, causing a wave of pain to shoot through his foot. Reaching into his jacket pocket, he pulled out the business card Carol had given him. Maybe she could come help him or at least give him some insight on what to do. He cursed again when he saw his cell phone didn't have any reception.

"You told him?" Dan asked, appearing before them.

"I had to," Melinda tried to explain. "This has gone on for far too long. I...I can't be responsible for sending anyone else down there."

"You want out? Fine, you're out," Dan said with a smug expression on his ghostly face. "Grab her!"

The disco man and the regular man appeared out of nowhere and grabbed Melinda by the arms. "Let go of me," she screamed.

"Hey! Let her go," Jackson ordered, taking a swing at the spirit of the disco man, who shrieked in pain as the iron rod made contact with his face. The ghost released his grip and faded out of sight. He returned after a few seconds but kept his distance from Jackson. "You too," he said, pointing the iron rod at the other ghost, who let go of Melinda's arm and ran through the nearest wall.

Dan made a quick move toward Jackson but stopped when Jackson spun around, iron rod first. "How do I get down there?" Jackson asked. "How do I open the door?"

"You can't," Dan said, running through the wall to his left and disappearing from sight.

Jackson lowered his guard as Dan appeared from his right side, materializing through the wall, fist first. The ghost landed a solid right hook, knocking Jackson to the ground. The iron bar slipped from his grasp and clanked hard against the floor.

Dan came to stand over Jackson with an evil look etched upon his gray face. "I bet Leonard will reward us handsomely for him."

"Dan, you need to stop this," Melinda begged. "He can help us! He can stop Leonard and free us all!"

The soldier looked into the eyes of the woman, his face full of doubt. "If he can't beat me, how's he going to beat a demon?"

Jackson's mind was clouded with a hazy fog, but he knew one thing for certain. The ghost had actually hit him. He didn't know how that was possible, but the ghost's ethereal fist had made contact with his very living jaw. His head cleared a little more, and he saw Dan was still distracted. He reached out toward the piece of iron and found it laid a mere few inches out of his reach. Stretching his arm as far as he could, a wave of relief washed over him when the touch of the cold iron reached his fingertips. With a quick flick of his finger, he rolled the iron rod toward him, snatched it up, and thrust it out toward the soldier's chest.

Dan winced in pain as he faded from sight. Jackson sprang to his feet and looked all about the hall, waiting for the ghost to return.

"Quickly," Melinda said, pounding her fist upon the metal surface of the door three times. Within seconds, the door swung open. "Hurry before he returns with reinforcements," she said, directing Jackson toward the stairs.

"How am I supposed to stop a demon?"

"You wanted to know where your friend was, so I'm showing you," Melinda told him. "I put my ass on the line for you. So, it's either go down there and try to save us all or go out the front door and only save yourself."

Chapter 18

Renegotiations

Jackson took the first couple of steps as slowly as possible, but the sound of the door slamming shut behind him made him freeze in his tracks. It took a few seconds for his eyes to adjust to the new level of darkness. The flashlight on his phone could only shed so much light on the area.

He stood there on the stairs, frozen, listening to his own heartbeat. After what felt like an eternity, he resumed his trek and entered a long hallway. Several doorways lined both sides of the corridor. Jackson peeked into each room he passed and found not all of the rooms were empty. Some had garbage, while others contained miscellaneous items scattered about.

He had made it about halfway down the hallway when he heard his heart beating louder than ever. He took a deep breath to try to steel his nerves. The smell of moisture and mildew filled his nose. The sound of metal clanking together made him stop as he tried to determine where the noise had originated. He walked into the first room on his right and found another open doorway leading to another room. He heard the clanking sound again, closer this time.

Jackson glanced over his shoulder and could barely make out the doorway he had walked through. When he turned his head back in the direction of the other doorway, he saw a light, one which hadn't been there a second ago, emanating from the other side of the entrance. It took him longer than he had thought it would to cross the room, but when he reached the doorway, he cautiously peered into the room on the other side.

Lit candles were placed all about the floor of the area, their flickering flames casting weird shadows across the gray cinder block walls. Three sets of iron shackles, all bolted into the mortar of the far wall, were occupied by Lilly and two other ghosts. Lilly was sitting on the floor to his far right, with her arms raised above her head, her wrist bound by the shackles.

In the far left set of shackles, in the same position, was the ghost of a middle-aged man. In the middle was the ghost of a young blonde girl who bore a striking resemblance to Lilly. She was dressed in a puffy pink skirt with a white short-sleeved button-up shirt. Both of the other ghosts were dull gray in color, and all three appeared to be unconscious.

"Lilly!" Jackson exclaimed as loud as he dared, rushing to her aid. He tried to touch her shoulder, but his finger passed right through her. "Lilly, wake up," he said, grabbing the iron shackles and giving them a shake, but she didn't stir. Neither did the others. Grabbing the chains that held the shackles, he tried to pull them from the wall, but they refused to give even the slightest.

"I'm afraid she's not going anywhere," came a deep voice from somewhere behind him.

"Shit," Jackson cursed under his breath, turning around.

A figure appeared from the darkness. He had the body of a man dressed in an expensive three-piece suit, but his head was that of a black-furred goat with three horns and a set of very human eyes.

"Leonard, I presume? What are you doing to my friend?" Jackson asked.

"And you are not what I was expecting," the goat-headed demon confessed. "Now I really am going to have to reward that pain-in-the-ass spirit."

"Let her go."

"And why would I do that?" Leonard asked, walking over to Lilly and kneeling next to her. He gracefully waved his hand in front of her face before waving it back toward his own, pulling with it glowing white trails of the dead girl's essence, which he inhaled through his black nostrils. "Nothing tastes as good as a fresh soul."

Jackson tried to punch Leonard in the face, but the demon turned his head, blocking the strike with one of his horns. Jackson felt a sharp twinge of pain in his hand. An animalistic growl came forth from the demon's throat. In one quick move, Leonard lunged forward and grabbed Jackson up by his jacket, lifting him off the ground with one hand and pinning him against the cinder block wall.

"I'm going to take great pleasure in tearing your still-beating heart from your chest," the demon said, his breath smelling of sulfur.

"You're trapped here like them, aren't you?" Jackson asked, needing to buy some time as he tried to remember what Melinda had told him about the demon.

Leonard growled louder.

"What's it been? Twenty years?"

"Thirty-three, but who's counting?"

"Maybe we can help each other out?" Jackson suggested. He still hadn't come up with anything resembling a plan, so he needed to stall.

"I'm listening," the demon said, his human eyes narrowing at Jackson.

"Why don't you tell me how you got trapped here?"

"Hmm, sounds like you're trying to stall for time, if you ask me," Leonard replied, scratching one of his three horns. "Desperately trying to delay the inevitable?"

"No...that's not it. If I knew how you got trapped here, maybe I could undo the trap and set you free."

"Just like that?" Leonard inquired.

"Well, there would be a few stipulations, of course."

"Of course."

"You let me, my friend, and the rest of the spirits you've trapped here go unharmed."

"Oh, is that all?"

"Once you're free, you won't need to feed off them anymore, right? You'll have no further use for them," Jackson tried to reason.

"I suppose you've got a point there," Leonard mused, setting Jackson back on the ground. "The original owner was an old bastard named Harold Woodruff. An underachiever in the worst of ways. Scrawny, ugly, and not gifted in other departments, if you know what I mean. I'm sure you've known someone like that in your lifetime. Everyone does. When Harold was a boy, he came upon a group of teenagers in the woods who had a book they should not have had. They were so on edge that the sound of Harold stepping on a stick caused one of the boys to drop the book, and they all scattered like the cockroaches they were.

"The book was a tome on the occult and magic. Young Harold devoured the words between its covers, and while most of it was nothing more than made-up gibberish, there lay enough scattered information upon the pages to give the boy ideas. He was twenty-five when he summoned me to his room upstairs in this very house. We made a deal that night. Signed in blood and unbreakable."

"What did he sell his soul for?" Jackson asked.

"What do all men sell their souls for? Money and power, of course," the demon answered. "Thanks to me, he made a fortune in the shipping industry, but when his time came, he thought he could renegotiate the terms of our original agreement. In his old age, Harold Woodruff, having lived on the finer side of life, did not want to spend an eternity in hell anymore. He had become civilized and thought himself too good to associate with the likes of demons.

"So, on his deathbed, which I do mean literally, because he was bedridden and dying, he summoned me for a second time to plead his case. Oh, he was quite upset when I would not renegotiate and proceeded to tell me that if he was going to be trapped, then so was I. He then put a gun to his head and blew his brains out. I was immediately expelled from the room, with the door slamming shut behind me, and now here we are."

"Here we are."

"I suppose I could be inclined to leave this dreaded place, and all that remains with it, for my freedom," the demon said, extending his hand.

Jackson sealed the deal with a handshake and got the queerest notion upon touching Leonard's hand, as if he had just signed his life on the dotted line. "Any idea where I should start looking?"

"The main bedroom on the third floor," Leonard said without a sound of doubt in his voice. "It's the only room I cannot gain entry to, and it's heavily warded."

"I'll see what I can do," Jackson told him.

"You don't even have a clue as to what you should be searching for, do you?"

Jackson answered with silence.

"There are several types of devil's traps," Leonard explained.

"A large pentagram inside a circle on the floor accompanied by runic letters inside the symbol is usually a summoning ward. That is what Harold used to summon me. That one is at the foot of his bed, drawn upon the wood floor in black paint. Once summoned, the demon is confined to the inside of the pentagram until the circle is broken. It's effective, but not enough to keep me prisoner."

"What is powerful enough to keep you trapped here?"

"There is only one spell I know of. It needs five separate items, each marked with its own devil's trap. By themselves, they are all but worthless, but when all five are within close proximity to one another, they will trap any demon within whatever structure he has been summoned to. Find them and destroy the symbols the best you can. It only takes a slight disruption of the overall appearance to render them harmless, but all five will need to be deactivated in order to break the spell."

"Got it," Jackson said, taking one last look at Lilly. "Is she in pain?"

"She has no idea what is happening to her," Leonard promised. "To her, it's as if she were asleep."

"Make sure it stays that way," Jackson stated, not caring if he insulted the demon. Nobody hurt his friends and got away with it. He thought it odd to refer to a ghost as his friend, but Lilly had proven to be a better friend to him than any of the living ones he'd had over the years.

"Oh, I would not be worrying about that if I were you," Leonard replied. "If you fail me, you'll be sitting right next to her," he promised.

MELINDA MET Jackson as he came up from the basement and became quite excited upon hearing about the deal he had made with Leonard.

Dan appeared from out of the darkness, and Jackson felt a sudden sting of pain where the ghost had hit him before. He kept his distance and glared at Jackson. "Why would you make a deal with Leonard for people you don't even know?" he asked.

"I didn't do it for you," Jackson said. "I did it for my friend. You know, the one *you* gave to him."

"I'm not proud of what I did, but I've got friends here too," Dan said before disappearing.

"How'd your boyfriend hit me like that?"

"He's not my boyfriend," Melinda responded sharply. "And he's got a lot of anger within him."

"I need to get to the main bedroom."

"I'll take you," Melinda offered. "I know exactly where it is. It's the only room in the house no one can enter. Well, at least no one who's dead."

They made their way to the third floor and to a solid wooden door at the end of a long hallway. The door had an ornate iron doorknob with a keyhole requiring an old skeleton key. Jackson gave the doorknob a twist and found it locked up tight. He had figured as much; nothing was ever easy for him. Kneeling down and peeking into the keyhole, he found something in the hole blocking his view into the room.

He flashed the light from his phone into the keyhole. It looked as if the key was still in the lock but on the other side of the door. "You wouldn't happen to know where I could find a metal coat hanger?" Jackson asked.

"There are some in the closet of that room," Melinda answered, pointing to one of the other doors in the hallway.

Jackson retrieved the coat hanger and untwisted the bent

end, making it as straight as he could. He inserted it into the keyhole and, after giving it a hard push, heard the metal key clang against the hardwood floor on the other side of the door. Jackson put the side of his head to the floor and peered into the room from under the door. The smell of stale air and dust blasted him in the face, causing him to blink a few times, but when the sensation passed, he could see the skeleton key lying about a foot from the door. He re-bent the end of the coat hanger, putting the hook back into place. Once he was satisfied with the overall shape of the hook, he slid it under the door. It took him several tries, but he finally managed to get the hook around the key in just the right position.

"Wallah," Jackson said, pulling the key out and proudly displaying it to Melinda. He stuck it in the keyhole and gave it a sharp twist. A clicking sound signaled the lock had been disengaged. The door's old hinges cried out in protest as the door swung open. "You coming?" he asked.

Melinda reached a hand out toward the open doorway and found an invisible barrier blocking her hand from passing through the threshold. "Be careful," she told Jackson. "The old man was powerful enough to trap Leonard here. Who knows what other traps he's got lying about."

"He's dead," Jackson said with a hint of amusement crossing his face. "I don't think he's got any traps in there that can hurt me."

"Magic works on the living just as it does the dead," Melinda warned.

Jackson's face became deathly serious as he gazed into the dark room. Magic was something he had never considered a viable threat until now. "What kind of traps are we talking about here?"

Melinda shrugged. "I said who knows what kind of traps, meaning I have no idea."

"I knew that," Jackson said, taking a deep breath and puffing out his chest a bit before stepping into the room.

The main bedroom was larger than his last apartment. It had three separate rooms and a main bathroom. Fancy furniture was staged about the room, covered in a thick layer of dust and cobwebs. Horrific images captured in oil paintings hung on the walls. Piles of once-expensive clothes were scattered about the floor.

Jackson wandered aimlessly through the first two rooms, not sure what he was even supposed to be looking for. He stepped through a doorway and entered the third room. Against the wall to his left was a large king, four-post bed. One of those fancy ones made out of dark wood and covered with a canopy. A thick blanket stretched across the bed, with a large human lump in the middle. Jackson's heart beat faster at the thought of what might be lying under the covers. Surely Harold Woodruff's body had been buried a long time ago, he thought, inching closer to the bed.

With a trembling hand, Jackson grabbed the edge of the heavy blanket and pulled it back. The empty-eyed skull of Harold Woodruff's pajama-dressed skeleton stared up at him, causing the young man's heart to skip a beat. "Jesus fucking Christ!" he yelled, jumping several feet backward.

The skeleton was dressed in dark red silk pajamas, with the letters H W embroidered in a decorative gold font right where the man's heart had once been. Strands of white hair still clung to the sides of the skull, and Jackson could see a small hole in the right side of it.

The light on his cell phone dimmed by half its power. "Shit," Jackson cursed, staring at the battery indicator on the screen and finding it in the red. Glancing around the room, he spotted an old oil lamp on the nightstand on the other side of the bed. Its base was made of clear crystal, and it had a tall glass cylinder. Jackson made his way around the bed but stopped at its foot, where he saw a large black pentagram, filled with runic lettering, painted on the wood floor.

Along the outer area of the pentagram, a runic symbol was drawn in between each point, for a total of five runes. The pentagram itself was drawn in a fashion ensuring that there was an empty space on the inside of each star tip, and an extra space in the middle, for a total of six empty spaces, with each containing its own rune, for a total of eleven runes within the pentagram. Jackson snapped a quick picture of the symbol with his cell phone before moving over to the nightstand.

Picking up the lamp, he saw it was still nearly full, giving him a slight sense of relief. He lifted up the clear glass top, exposing the wick, and used his cigarette lighter to ignite the still oil-soaked wick, bathing the room in its bright light. Jackson turned off the flashlight app and stuck the cell phone into his jacket pocket.

"Where to begin?" Bending down, he took a quick peek under the bed, and his eyes widened in surprise when he found himself staring down the barrel of a small, black revolver resting on the dust-covered floor.

Jackson picked the revolver up, which felt extra heavy in his hand, given the gun's size. Placing the lamp back down on the nightstand, he turned the gun over in his hands. He didn't know the first thing about guns other than to pull the trigger to fire them. He searched for a way to open the cylinder, so he could check if it was still loaded, but he gave up after a few minutes. Turning the revolver around, he peered into the front of the open-faced cylinder, making sure not to point the barrel of the gun at his face. He could see the tops of four bullets, two on each side of the cylinder, telling him the gun was indeed still loaded. He wasn't sure what to do with it, but putting it back where he had found it didn't seem like an option, so he slipped it into the inside pocket of his jacket, right next to his pack of cigarettes.

Aided by the light of the oil lamp, Jackson began to scour the large suite for any signs of the devil's traps. The way Leonard had described them, it sounded like they could be on virtually anything in the room, so that's where he began looking, under rugs, underneath chair cushions, and inside dresser drawers. He came upon a large painting on one of the walls of the second room. The scene drawn upon the old canvas depicted a medieval setting, for several of the characters were wearing armor and carrying swords. They stood atop a large wooden hangman's gallows. A crowd of men, women, and children were gathered in front of the structure as five men hung at the end of long ropes. What parent in their right mind would take their children to watch five men swinging from the gallows? It seemed downright morbid and would surely give any child witnessing the horrific event years upon years of trauma.

"Five men," Jackson thought aloud. "Like the five points of a pentagram." Lifting the lamp up to the oil painting, his eyes scoured every inch of the painting, but the satanic symbol was nowhere to be found. When he was sure he hadn't missed anything, he set the lamp down and lifted the painting up from the wall. To his surprise, he had found the first devil's trap scrawled on the back of the canvas.

The symbol looked a lot like the one drawn on the floor, but after closer examination, Jackson could tell that the runic letters were different, although their placement within the symbol was identical to the large one on the floor. Jackson took out his phone and snapped a picture before taking the painting back to the third room and placing it down within the large pentagram on the floor.

He found the second devil's trap carved into the bottom of

a foot-tall bronze statue of a nude woman buried under a large pile of clothes in the bedroom's massive walk-in closet.

While rifling through the third drawer of a tall dresser in the first room, he found the third trap located on page 450 in a book entitled *Complete Stories and Poems of Edgar Allan Poe.*

The fourth trap was in the bathroom, scrawled upon the thick brown paper lining the back of the large mirror hanging above a gold-plated sink.

After taking a picture of the other three traps, Jackson piled all four traps on top of one another inside the large pentagram at the foot of the bed. "One more to go," he thought, leaning against a small table holding a single glass vase with dried flower stems. He set the oil lamp down and took out a cigarette. Inhaling a much-needed drag of nicotine, the gears in his mind still turned. After searching everywhere he could think of, the last devil's trap still eluded him.

"If I were a bat shit crazy old man, no offense"—he waved his cigarette at Harold Woodruff's body—"where would I have put the last devil's trap? I'd probably keep it someplace close."

He took one last drag of his cigarette before tossing it into the empty vase. Walking over to the bed, he lifted each side of the mattress, careful not to disturb the dead body on top. When Jackson didn't find anything under the mattress, he turned his attention to Harold. The red silk pajama shirt didn't have any pockets, but the pants did. He reached his hand into the pocket closest to him and came up empty. Leaning over Harold, he slipped his hand into the second pocket, and his fingers brushed against something cold and metallic.

Nestled in the pocket, Jackson found a large coin made from dark metal. One side of the coin held the last devil's trap. His cell phone had enough power left for one last photo, as the screen went dark after the flash went off. He flipped the coin over and stared at the side profile of a man, who he thought had to be Harold Woodruff.

"Now, how do I destroy these?" he began to retrace his steps through the rooms, looking for something, anything he could use. He knew he didn't have to deface the entire trap, but he needed something hard enough or sharp enough to do the trick. He found a small desk in the corner of the middle room. A pile of old envelopes, their paper had turned yellow from a thick layer of dust, lay scattered across its surface. He rummaged through the top drawer and found a gold letter opener.

Jackson placed the tip of the letter opener against the side of the coin containing the devil's trap and began to scratch vigorously. The soft metal deformed easily as he scratched several deep lines through the symbol. When he was satisfied with his work, he walked back to the pile of remaining devil's traps. "One down, four to go," he said, his eyes widening in wonder as his breath became visible in the light of the oil lamp. The temperature in the room plummeted rapidly. Goose bumps raised across his skin as a cold shiver cascaded down his spine.

Jackson reached the pentagram on the floor and went to toss the coin onto the pile, but when he looked down, something seemed off. In his hand was a syringe full of heroin instead of the dark coin.

"Here, let me," a female's voice said, the words echoing through the air.

Jackson recognized the voice; at least, he thought he did. It sounded a lot like Lexi Robinson, but it had been years since... His eyelids felt so heavy. He fought to keep them open. Just for a few seconds, he thought, letting his eyelids slide shut, but when he finally found the strength to open them again, he was sitting on a bed with his back resting against a wall.

"What the fuck?"

"You asked me to help you, remember?" Lexi said.

Jackson peered to his right and found Lexi sitting on the bed beside him. Lexi had been his girlfriend in college. She was into the whole Goth scene and had long, dyed, jet-black hair. Her lipstick matched the color of her hair, and a silver loop dangled from her nose. Looking around, he found himself back in his freshman dorm room at Northern State University in South Dakota. How was this possible?

The lamp on his nightstand had a red piece of cloth over it, giving the room a red hue. Not having much money in college, his room had only the bare necessities. There were two beds, each one pushed into a separate corner of the room. One was for his roommate, who was never there. There was also a table with two chairs, two dressers—his had a mirror on top of it—a mini fridge, and an old TV.

Jackson felt something tightening around his right bicep. Lexi was tying a rubber tourniquet around his arm. He had just turned nineteen, and she had been his first real girlfriend. She had also been his first love, for she was the one who had taken his virginity.

For their first date, he had taken her to this cheap Chinese restaurant that served the best egg rolls he had ever had. After, they went to the movies. The movie they picked had been out for nearly a month, so the theater was practically deserted. They sat in the back, and all Jackson could remember about the movie was Lexi's tongue in his mouth and her hand down his pants. After the movie, they went back to his dorm room and had sex, and he swore he had never cum so hard in his life, and that was the only thing he could think about when she took him to the tattoo parlor on their second date. He got his nipple pierced to match hers.

The needle punctured his skin, causing a slight stinging

sensation, as Lexi pushed the heroin into his vein. Euphoria washed over him. Every care in the world faded out of existence. He leaned hard against the wall as Lexi undid his pants and began to give him a blowjob. He never wanted this night to end. He never wanted this feeling to end. The euphoria soon began to fade, replaced with an urgency of something important he needed to do, but he couldn't remember what. Something tightened around his arm. He watched with confusion as Lexi tied a rubber tourniquet around his right bicep. "What's going on?" he asked. A slight twinge of pain pricked him in his forearm, and then there was only pleasure.

Jackson's head felt heavy, like it was underwater. The image of a young woman flashed through his mind. She had a spot of dried red blood matted in her blonde hair on the left side of her head.

"Lilly," he mumbled.

"Who?" Lexi asked, tying a rubber tourniquet around his bicep. There was a slight prick in his forearm, and ecstasy was all he could feel. "Forget about her," she said, undoing his pants.

God, he loved her. Which was the only reason he had agreed to try heroin in the first place. He had never considered himself a hard-core drug user, though he had smoked a lot of weed. He remembered being totally caught off guard when Lexi confided in him about her drug of choice. She told him they would have the best sex ever if they were both high at the same time. It was at that very moment in time Jackson discovered he could not say no to her. They started spending every waking minute with each other. He began skipping classes, and before he knew it, his GPA had taken a hard nosedive, but he was in love.

The ecstasy faded.

"I need to do something," Jackson said, his mind still covered by a thick blanket of fog.

"You need to relax," Lexi said, tying the rubber tourniquet around his arm.

Jackson shook his head, trying his best to clear the fog. There was something important he had been tasked with. "No," he said, jumping off the bed. "I have to do something."

"You *have* to sit back down, silly," Lexi said, grabbing Jackson by the hand and pulling him back toward the bed. Back toward her. He stood there on the edge of the bed and watched as Lexi pushed the needle into his arm. The ecstasy returned, and it only multiplied when Lexi undid his pants.

The fog began to lift, and Jackson found himself sitting on his bed, leaning heavily against the wall. Lexi was tying a rubber tourniquet around his arm. "Wait," he said, reaching down and undoing the tourniquet while getting out of bed. "This isn't right."

"What isn't?" Lexi reached out to grab his hand.

Jackson took a few steps back and bumped into his dresser. "This," Jackson declared, waving his hands about the room.

He turned around and found his reflection staring back at him from the mirror. His eyes met Lexi's in the same reflection, and he could see the tears welling up. He had made her cry a couple of times during their relationship, and he hated himself for it every time. His gaze drifted down to the syringe in her hand as a feeling of dread washed over him. Scenes began to flash through his mind, and he couldn't tell if they were real or not, but the emotional response he was experiencing sure felt real. Then everything changed. He was sitting in the back seat of a car and had, only a few seconds earlier, pushed a syringe full of heroin into his vein, bringing with it the all-too-familiar feeling of euphoria.

He had gone and gotten kicked out of school, and when

Lexi told him she wasn't going with him, it nearly destroyed him. She said her parents would kill her if she dropped out of school. With no other options, he moved back in with his parents. It did not take long for them to discover his new addiction and the real reason he had gotten expelled. After they kicked him out, he surfed from couch to couch, friend to friend, city to city. It took a few years, but he had finally been able to get clean and back on the right track again. Then he got the news that Lexi had died from a heroin overdose. While at her funeral, he met up with some old friends from school and now found himself in the back seat of one of their cars.

His head drooped when the car hit a large pothole, and he saw a single french fry on the floor between his feet. He thought about how great hot, fresh french fries tasted. A long string of drool stretched from the corner of his mouth down to the blue carpet of the car. His head felt *so* dense. All he wanted to do was sleep. A heavy weight pressed on his chest, and his lungs refused to expand. He could hear his throat gasping for air. Hard and fast at first, then slow and low, like a deep rumbling gurgle coming from somewhere in the back of his throat.

Next came flashes of bright light and a lot of distorted noise. He thought he could hear voices all around him, but he couldn't make out what they were saying. Then he was standing at the foot of a bed, staring at his own body. For some reason, he had the strongest urge to look out into the hallway, where he saw a young blonde girl standing next to a short, white, bald man who gave him the heebie-jeebies.

Jackson shook his head again, and the images disappeared. He gazed back upon his reflection and saw the gray, ghostly image of an elderly man standing behind him. At first, he had no idea who the ghost was until his eyes fell on the red silk pajamas. Harold Woodruff's ethereal hands were touching both sides of Jackson's head.

"Get out of my head," Jackson struggled to say, spinning around to face Harold. As he spun, the coin in his left hand passed right through the ghost when he brought up his arms to push Harold away from him.

The ghost screamed in pain and flickered out of existence, as did his college dorm room. Jackson knew the spirit wouldn't be gone for long and needed a way to destroy all of the devil's traps quickly. He tossed the defaced coin onto the pile as Harold Woodruff reappeared on the other side of the pentagram.

"I can't let you release him," hissed the ghost. "Not until he gives me more life."

"Yeah, not going to happen," Jackson replied.

"Then we'll both rot here for an eternity."

"Listen, it's only a matter of time before this rundown house of yours is turned into a parking lot or a Dollar General, and he's got one of *my* friends tied up in the basement, so you'll have to forgive me if I don't share your sentiment."

"I will not let you release him."

"You're kind of forgetting one important piece of information in all of this," Jackson said.

"And what would that be?"

"You're dead, and I'm not." Jackson smashed the oil lamp down upon the pile of devil's traps. The glass lamp shattered into a thousand pieces, causing the oil to ignite instantly. The canvas of the painting of the gallows melted without hesitation. The *Complete Stories and Poems of Edgar Allan Poe* turned to ash. The brown paper on the back of the mirror didn't put up much of a fight either, which left the bronze statue of the naked lady.

The oil stuck to her metal skin and burned uncontrollably.

Jackson didn't know what the melting point of bronze was but prayed the fire would be hot enough. Embers of burning paper floated about the room as the bed containing the remains of Harold Woodruff erupted in flames.

Harold's ghost screamed, as the glass of the mirror, warping from the heat of the fire, shattered. More flaming embers lifted into the air, and before Jackson knew what was happening, the entire room was engulfed in flames.

Jackson rushed out of the room, making a beeline for the basement, but found Lilly waiting for him in the foyer area of the first floor. "Jackson!"

Smoke filled the first floor of the large house. Jackson's eyes began to burn, and his throat became scratchy, causing him to cough violently. "How do we get out of here? I can't see where I'm going."

"Over here," Lilly cried out. "Follow the sound of my voice."

Jackson honed in on Lilly's cries and soon found the door. Bright sunlight poured into the abandoned house, making it even harder to see. He was only a few steps away from being free of this seriously haunted house when a spectral hand shot out from the smoke and grabbed his right forearm. An intense cold began to burn its way through the leather of his jacket and into his arm. The ghostly hand started to drag him back into the smoke-filled foyer.

Jackson screamed in agony at the pain searing his skin. The smoke around him began to clear as the form of Harold Woodruff materialized in front of him. "You will pay for this boy," the ghost hissed.

"I believe your tab needs to be cleared first," came a voice from within the smoke.

"No!" Harold screamed. "You owe me more life! We were in the middle of a renegotiation!"

Leonard, the three-horned goat demon, walked out of the smoke, coming to stand between Jackson and the angry spirit. "You can't negotiate with what you don't have," the demon responded, giving Jackson a quick wink.

Jackson backpedaled as fast as he could as a ring of hell fire sprang up around the demon and the vengeful ghost. The flames grew in intensity until they reached the ceiling. Jackson heard Harold scream one last time.

The smoke began to blind him again, but he kept moving backward until he broke through the wall of smoke and out into the clear air of the new day. He stumbled a few times before falling flat on his ass. "We need to get the hell out of here," he yelled, picking himself up and high tailing it toward his car.

Lilly got into the passenger seat as Jackson put the key into the ignition. Jackson looked into the rearview mirror and saw the reflection of the blonde girl from the basement get into the back seat.

"Jackson, this is Jessica."

"Buckle your seat belt," he responded, stomping on the accelerator, the sound of sirens wailing in the distance.

Chapter 19

Looking for Buried Treasure

Jackson had been riding in relative silence for several hours, with the only sound coming from the radio. The sun had crossed its apex by a few hours when he drove over the Michigan-Indiana border. He needed a little alone time. Lilly had told him the next girl on their list was Allison Murphey and that she had lived in Boonville, Indiana, so he just drove.

He kept glancing in his rearview mirror for any signs of the police, and although he hadn't seen anyone outside of the old Woodruff mansion when they had fled, he had lost track of how much time they had spent in the house and didn't know if anyone had noticed his car parked outside. But that wasn't the only reason. Lilly and Jessica had not said much to each other for the majority of the long drive, but now, Lilly had made her way to the back seat, and they were having a hushed conversation. The problem was he couldn't make out what they were saying because of the loud music, but whatever it was, Jessica did not look happy about it.

"You EXPECT me to go back to that house?" Jessica's body trembled.

"It's the only way to guarantee we all pass over together, and you won't have to do it alone," Lilly promised.

"You have no idea what *he* did to me," Jessica said with fear in her voice as she rubbed the dark bruises around her throat. It took her a couple of seconds, but she finally made the connection. "Sorry, I forget I'm not the only one."

"I know *exactly* what you're going through," Lilly said, trying to be as comforting as she could. "But time is of the essence right now. He has another girl locked in his basement. Her name is Norma Jean, and we're her only hope of surviving if it isn't already too late."

"What do you need me to do," Jessica said, trying her best to sound brave.

"Honestly, I'm not sure. Tracy said to find all of his... victims and bring them back to the house. She said together, we would be stronger."

"You mean the girl that stays there with *him*? I got the weirdest vibe from her," Jessica confessed. "She tried to get me to stay there with her too, but I needed to get as far from that house as possible. I know I was supposed to try to complete my unfinished business, but I couldn't stay there." She broke down, crying softly.

"Don't you dare do that to yourself," Lilly said defiantly. "I wouldn't want to stay there either, and if there wasn't a chance for us to cross over, I wouldn't be going anywhere near that house." Her words of encouragement brought a slight smile to Jessica's face. "Why don't you tell me what he did to you? Sometimes sharing helps you cope with things better."

"Did it work for you?"

"Not really," Lilly answered honestly. "But if it helps, I'll go first."

After Lilly shared her story, Jessica took a deep breath and held it for several long moments.

August 7ᵗʰ, 2015

"I can't believe you liked that movie," Brittney said, laughing loudly before taking a hit of a joint and then passing it around.

"I guess I'm just a hopeless romantic." Jessica grabbed the joint from her best friend and took a long hit. She had finished working an eight-hour shift at the local ice cream parlor before meeting her friends for a late-night movie. They had been especially busy this particular night, and she was extremely grateful for some quality relaxation, even though she was still dressed in her work uniform.

"That movie was so predictable," said her other friend Jenny, taking the joint from her. "At least it had some good eye candy," she added, causing all three of the girls to burst out laughing.

Jessica took a nervous look around the parking lot. She didn't like smoking weed out in the open like they were, but they had waited until all the other cars had cleared out. They were sitting on the hood of Brittney's car, and the only other things she could see were her own car and an old motor home tucked away in the lot's far corner. It was completely dark and looked like it might have been there for the past few days.

She took the joint from Brittney and inhaled deeply. "You guys wanna get something to eat?"

"Ohhh, I could go for some pancakes right now," Jenny said, taking the joint.

"That sounds really good," Brittney agreed. "I'll drive."

"I'll meet you guys there," Jessica said. "It's getting late, and I don't want to have to come back here and then drive all the way home."

"Ok, meet you there, bitch," Jenny said with a laugh as she and Brittney piled into Brittney's car.

Jessica made her way across the parking lot and gave her friends a wave as they drove past her. Brittney honked her horn a couple of times. The blare sounded extra loud in the middle of the night as it echoed off the theater walls. She unlocked her doors, using her key fob, and climbed behind the wheel. The engine made a winding sound when she turned the ignition. It turned over several times but refused to start. She tried again and got the same response. "Shit," she cursed, hitting the steering wheel with the palm of her hand. Reaching down under the dashboard, she pulled the hood release and got out of the car.

Jessica opened her hood and, using the flashlight on her phone, stared obliviously at the car's engine. She didn't know the first thing about cars and began to wonder why she had even popped the hood. She thumbed through her contacts, wondering if she should call her parents, who would find out she was stoned, or Brittney and have her and Jenny come back and get her. The car could wait until later. Right now, she just wanted to eat pancakes.

A strong arm reached across her neck, and Jessica felt herself being yanked backward hard, causing her to lose her balance. She tried to cry out, but a large hand covered her mouth. The scent of oil and grease filled her nose. There came a sharp pain in the right side of her neck as her vision blurred. Her movements became labored and lethargic...and then there was only darkness.

"I woke up in his basement, chained to the floor. I lost count of how many times that sick bastard raped me. He told me to fight back, and I did at first, but after a while, I didn't see the point anymore. He had broken my spirit. Had stolen my reason for living, so I let him do whatever he wanted and didn't offer any resistance. It wasn't long after that..." She rubbed the bruises on her throat again.

"How long ago was that?" Lilly asked.

"Five years ago, maybe," Jessica answered with a shrug.

"Did they find your body, at least?"

Jessica shook her head. "No one will ever find us. He's good at hiding his conquests."

"They found me," Lilly said. "It took six months and a dog named Wrigley, but someone eventually found me, and thanks to Jackson, my parents were able to bring me home and have a bit of closure."

"That would be nice. I went home after I left that horror house and watched my parents fall apart. I couldn't take it anymore and was headed out of town when I felt that place calling to me. It was ok at first. I thought I might have found a new place to live. You know, with others like us."

"Do you know where your body is?"

Jessica nodded.

"Where?"

"Climax, Michigan."

"Jackson, we need to turn around."

JACKSON PULLED his car into the Walmart parking lot in Coldwater, Michigan. "You got the list?" Lilly asked.

"Got it," Jackson answered, heading into the store. He had suggested the two girls stay in the car. That way, he wouldn't have any distractions and could get in and out of the store as quickly as possible. He wasn't too keen on making this unexpected detour, but he understood the importance of letting someone know where they could find Jessica's burial site.

"Why can't he call them again?" Jessica asked once they were alone.

"Because he's still sore about what happened the last time he called the cops," Lilly answered. "It's best if we don't mention it."

Jackson headed to the electronics aisle and picked up a handheld GPS unit that would allow him to get Jessica's exact location, which in turn, could be used by the authorities to find her. Next, he went to the automotive section and grabbed one reflective driveway marker. A pack of self-sealing envelopes, a pad of paper, a pen, a book of stamps, and a box of latex gloves completed the list. He was thankful he still had a large chunk of his poker winnings because doing the right thing was starting to add up.

Once they reached the Village of Climax, Jessica directed them down South Main Street until they reached a cemetery sitting right next to the high school. Across the street from the school's large chain link gate was a worn dirt footpath that lay between the property lines of two houses. Jackson slowed and gazed down the small trail. On the left side of the path, a small wooded area obstructed the view of the path from the house on the left. The house on the right had a large privacy fence that stretched about halfway down the length of the path. The two-track led to a large field and a small forest farther down on the left side of the open field. There wasn't any place to park without being too conspicuous.

Jackson pulled the car into the graveyard and began to circle through it, searching for a good place to stash the car while also keeping an eye out for any lingering spirits. He settled on parking the car near the back corner, closest to the school. After throwing on a pair of latex gloves, he stashed the GPS in his jacket pocket and grabbed the driveway marker as the three of them walked down the gravel road leading back out to South Main Street.

Jackson stopped at the edge of the street and looked around. It was close to one o'clock in the afternoon on a Wednesday; at least, he thought it was Wednesday. He hoped everyone in the immediate vicinity had jobs because, in a small town like this, everybody knew everyone and would be quick to call the cops if they saw someone out of the ordinary milling about their house.

After he was sure no one was watching him, he made his way across the street and down the two-track. He needed to make this fast because the high school would surely be letting out in the next couple of hours.

"Once we get to the field, we need to head into the forest on the left. It's pretty overgrown, but about halfway down, there's a small opening," said Jessica, taking the lead. "It hasn't changed much," she added.

The house on the right side of the two-track had a long chain link fence running along the property line after the privacy fence ended. A large black-and-tan Doberman came running up to the fence and barked at them as they walked, causing Jackson to pick up the pace a little. The dog followed them all the way down the fence line and continued to bark. Jackson risked a glance over his shoulder and breathed a slight sigh of relief when he found no one staring back at them.

The long grass in the field touched Jackson's waist once he reached the end of the dirt path and was full of those small green sticky balls. The ones that always stuck to everything whenever you walked through them. Jessica pointed out the nearly invisible opening in the overgrown thicket of the forest's boundary. Jackson had to bend down pretty low in order to squeeze through it and wondered how Mark Karle must have done it while carrying Jessica's body.

Once they made it through the overgrowth, the small forest opened up, allowing Jackson to move about. A thick layer of leaves covered the ground while the green leaves of the tall trees swayed back and forth in the wind. Jessica led them to a spot near the back end of the forest, where Jackson found an old rusty metal fence separating the forest from a different field.

"This is the spot," Jessica said solemnly, tears welling up in her eyes.

Jackson pulled out the handheld GPS and turned it on. It took forever to acquire the satellite signal through the trees, but when it finally beeped louder than anyone had expected, they all gazed about in alarm. Jackson's heart literally skipped a beat as his pulse went from zero to sixty in half a second flat. He took several deep breaths when he was sure they were still alone.

"Got it," he said, saving the coordinates and pushing the reflective driveway marker into the ground, so the police would be able to find Jessica's body easier. "Now, let's get the hell out of here. This place gives me the creeps. No offense," he said, walking past Jessica.

They made their way back to the car, and Jackson wasted no time getting out of the small town. After making his way back to the highway, he eventually headed south, back toward Indiana. He saw a rest area coming up and pulled into it, so he could work on the second part of the plan. Putting on another pair of latex gloves, he opened the pack of pens. Picking a page from the middle of the notepad and ripping it out, he wrote down a specific set of directions, along with the GPS coordinates of Jessica's body. He also made sure to explain that he was *not* the killer but had come upon this credible information. He also provided Jessica's name and address, the names of her parents, and a phone number where they could be reached.

A quick internet search showed that the Village of Climax fell under the jurisdiction of the Kalamazoo County Sheriff's Department. Leaving the gloves on, he opened the pack of envelopes and wrote down the address of the sheriff's department on the front, carefully folded the letter, and placed it inside the envelope before pulling the tape from the back of the flap and sealing the letter up tight. After placing a single, self-stick stamp in the upper right corner of the envelope, he placed it above the sun visor for safekeeping.

For the second time in one day, Jackson drove through the town of Coldwater, and when he located one of those big blue mailboxes, he put on another pair of gloves and pushed the envelope into the mail slot.

"Satisfied?"

Jessica gave Jackson a slight nod. "It should take a couple of days for the sheriff's department to get the letter," Jackson said, putting the car in drive and heading back toward the highway.

"I still don't know why you couldn't have just called the police," Jessica wondered.

Chapter 20

Three's Company

Boonville, Indiana, was larger than the Village of Climax, but it was still just another small country town. Jackson stood in front of the mirror in the men's restroom of a gas station on the edge of town. He splashed some water on his face, but it didn't help much. He couldn't remember the last time he had slept, and every time he closed his eyes, the spirit of Harold Woodruff rushed from the darkness to greet him.

He took off his jacket and examined the spot on his arm where Harold had grabbed him. The area appeared slightly burned, and Jackson thanked his coat for taking the majority of the assault. The black leather appeared somewhat faded where the ghost had touched it.

A man entered the restroom and disappeared into a stall.

Jackson put his jacket back on and left the restroom. Perusing the isles of the gas station, he grabbed some snacks, caffeine, a map of the area, and a fresh pack of smokes before making his way back to his car. He slid into the driver's seat, unfolded the map, and took a long drink of some wake-up juice.

"You've been awfully quiet since we found Jessica," Lilly said from the passenger seat.

"Being attacked by ghosts and making a deal with a demon'll do that to guy," Jackson said. "This town isn't very big, but I've got no idea where we should start looking," he said, changing the subject. "There's a cemetery south of town. Maybe there?"

"I guess it's as good a place as any to start," Lilly said reluctantly. "Who knows, we might even get lucky and find her there."

The cemetery was small enough that the whole thing could be seen from the road. Jackson parked the car alongside the road and squinted against the bright afternoon sun. He saw several people wandering about the grounds but couldn't tell if they were gray. "Do they look like ghosts to you?" he asked, fighting back a yawn.

"We'll go check it out," Lilly volunteered, motioning to Jessica. "Why don't you stay in the car."

"And why is that?" Jackson asked, sounding a bit irritated at the thought of being left out.

"Oh, I don't know, maybe because the dead seem to know that you can see them," Lilly said with a bit of sarcasm. "Remember Mr. Morris?"

"Yeah," Jackson answered with a sigh of defeat.

Lilly and Jessica made their way into the cemetery under the watchful eye of Jackson. They met with several ghosts before running back to the car. "Allison lived in a big white house on West Walnut Street," Lilly said, passing through the passenger side door.

"And it has big pillars on the front porch," Jessica added, getting into the back seat.

Jackson got out the map and found the street. "Got it," he said, putting the car in drive and heading back toward town.

About twenty minutes later, Jackson pulled up in front of a large, two-story white house with large white pillars on the front porch.

"Well, this is the only house on this street with pillars," Jackson stated. "Why don't you two go in and see if you can find her, and I'll meet you in the park we passed a few blocks north of here."

~

LILLY AND JESSICA made their way up to the house's front door as they watched Jackson drive off.

"So, how do we do this?" Jessica asked.

"We walk through the front door," Lilly answered. "We're ghosts, remember. Besides, nobody in the house will even know we're here."

"Except for other ghosts," Jessica reminded her, her voice quivering ever so slightly.

Lilly wanted to tell her everything would be all right, but she knew better than to promise that. Especially after what they had been through. Instead, she said, "The way Tracy made it sound was like it was an all of us or none of us type situation, so we need to do this. You can stay out here and be my look out if you want."

"No, you're right," said Jessica, this time with a little more confidence. "You saved me from Leonard, so this is the least I can do," she added, stepping past Lilly and passing through the house's front door.

The house's interior was overflowing with old antiques and white lace doilies. Dark stained wood trim ran from room to room, as did the matching hardwood floor. In the living room, a large fireplace with a wooden mantel was set into the main interior wall. On top of the mantel sat two large pictures. The first was of a young woman with straight golden hair. She wore a purple graduation gown and hat. The second was of the same girl standing next to an older woman with gray hair. Both women wore large smiles and appeared to be having a good time.

They made their way upstairs, and after peeking into several doors, they found Allison's bedroom, as empty as the rest of the house. The room's walls had been painted pink, with slight splashes of orange. A heavy pink comforter covered a large bed, with at least twenty stuffed animals stacked on top of it. All about the room were pictures of the same blonde-haired girl from the picture downstairs. The girl appeared to be outside and enjoying life in all the photos. Rock climbing in one picture. Canoeing in another. Hiking a trail in yet another.

"She certainly enjoyed being outside," Jessica noted, going from picture to picture.

"Look at this," Lilly said, pointing to a race bib for The Scales Lake Park 5K.

"What about it?" Jessica asked.

"I saw that park on Jackson's map. If I loved the outdoors as much as she did, that's probably where'd I go. Beats being stuck in a house full of painful memories and reminders of what you used to be."

"Maybe," Jessica said. "I stayed at my house for over a year before it became too painful. Besides, if we don't find her there, we can always come back and check again later once someone comes home."

They returned to the car and found Jackson sound asleep. Lilly tried several times to wake him up, but it was no use. He couldn't hear her voice.

Jessica leaned forward and screamed, "Wake up!" into Jackson's ear. He shifted his position a little. "We don't have time for this."

"I know, but he hasn't slept at all the last few days," Lilly said in Jackson's defense.

"The thought of returning to *that* house never once entered my mind after I found out I had died. My afterlife representative told me about the golden light and that I would have to find its source to figure out what my unfinished business was. And I did. I made it all the way back to that house. I didn't know what it was at first or who even lived there. I went inside and found Tracy, who showed me the torture room in the basement," said Jessica, offering Lilly a slight glimpse of her own experience as tears ran down her gray cheeks. "Everything came flooding back in that very instant. The smell of that piss-stained mattress. The scent of Old Spice. The pain when he would hit me. The pain when he would rape me. And most of all, the smile on his face when he did it. I panicked. I ran from the house as fast as I could and never went back."

"And now I'm dragging you back there," Lilly said. "Thankfully. I wasn't awake for most of my ordeal. He must have hit me a little too hard when he took me," she added, rubbing the side of her bloodstained head. "I get flashes every so often, and I remember the smell of Old Spice, but that's it. I'm truly sorry for what happened to you, but..."

"But it must be done," Jessica said. "Mark Karle needs to be stopped once and for all."

"Maybe we can walk to the park," Lilly suggested.

"Do you know where it's at?"

"No."

"Then our only option is sound asleep," Jessica said. "Wake up," she screamed again, lunging forward and hitting the car's horn, causing Jackson to sit straight up and cry out in surprise.

"You guys find anything?" he asked, acting as if he had been awake the whole time.

"She wasn't in the house, but we might know where she's

at," Lilly answered before asking Jackson to unfold his map. "There," she said, pointing toward a green section of the map. "Scales Lake."

THE SCALES LAKE PARK campground had officially closed a few weeks ago with the beginning of fall. Jackson had done his best to park his car far enough from the main road but close enough to the campground so he wouldn't have to go on a major hike to reach it.

The three of them made their way up a long, winding dirt road until it ended at a large metal gate. A "closed for the season" sign hung loosely on the metal frame. Jackson made his way around the gate, keeping an eye out for any staff that might still be lingering around, but the farther they walked through the campground, the more apparent it became that they were alone.

The campground consisted of several large buildings, a couple of small cabins, and a large camping area across the lake. Sheets of plywood covered the windows of the buildings and cabins. There was a large, empty, covered pavilion. The volleyball courts had no nets, and the large metal canoe racks at the edge of the lake were empty.

"You guys see anything?" Jackson asked.

"Nothing," Lilly answered.

"Same here," replied Jessica.

"Why don't you two go and check out the buildings?" suggested Jackson. "I'll go and search down by the lake."

He lit a cigarette and took a deep drag as he reached the edge of the lake. Scanning the campsites across the water, he didn't see a single soul, living or dead. The lake was roughly half a mile wide and nearly three times as long, and according to the picture on the map, it had several finger-like bays, giving the ghost plenty of places to hide.

"Allison Murphey," he called out, listening as his voice echoed across the water.

"Hello?" an unsure female's voice answered.

Jackson couldn't tell where the voice had come from, but it sounded far away.

"Hello," he called back, looking out across the lake. Far to his left, coming out of one of the bays, a splash of color caught his attention. Squinting against the sun's reflection off the water, he spotted a bright red canoe drifting lazily across the lake. As it drew closer, he saw a young woman with long, straight, grayish hair sitting in the canoe's bow.

"Over here!" Jackson called out, waving his arms in the air.

"You can see me?" the girl asked.

"Yes," Jackson said, watching the canoe as it changed course, heading straight toward him.

"How?" the girl asked, the canoe gliding to a stop near the water's edge.

"I'm what'd you'd call a seer," Jackson answered, finding it a little funny that he was now introducing himself as something he hadn't even believed in a few days ago. "Are you Allison Murphey?"

"Why?" the girl asked, standing in the canoe. She was wearing a pair of jeans and a long-sleeved blue shirt with a picture of a turtle on the front. The colors of her clothes were like that of her skin: faded.

"Because if you are, we need your help."

"We?"

"He found her!" Lilly called out as she and Jessica ran down to join them at the water's edge.

"Who *are* you guys?"

"My name is Lilly."

"I'm Jessica."

"And you've already met Jackson," Lilly added, with Jackson giving Allison a wave. "And we need your help."

"Yeah, that's what he said," Allison replied.

"The three of us are connected," Lilly said, motioning to her and Jessica.

"He killed you too, didn't he?" Allison asked, her voice becoming a whisper. A look of terror crossed her face.

"Yes," Lilly answered.

"This isn't a good idea," Allison said, sitting back down in the canoe. "You should leave." The canoe drifted away from the shore as the ghost turned her back to the group.

"Wait," Lilly cried.

"Leave me alone!"

"We've found a way to cross over, but we need your help," Lilly said, stepping into the water and finding she could not walk upon it.

The canoe continued to drift farther out into the lake.

"He has another girl, and she'll die if we don't stop him," Jackson called out, praying the girl's sense of doing the right thing still lived within her. The canoe stopped, as if an unseen anchor had been dropped into the water. "I know you're scared," Jackson added. "They all are. Hell, so am I, but she needs our help, and we can't do it without you."

The canoe drifted back toward the shore but stopped a few feet from land. Allison turned around to face the trio. Her face was stern and unforgiving.

"You followed your golden light, didn't you?" Lilly asked. "You went back to the house?"

Allison stared at Lilly with unwavering eyes.

"When you went inside, did you meet Tracy Lafond? His first victim?"

"I never went back inside that foul place. I...I couldn't... Not after the things he did to me in there."

"We both know what you've been through," said Jessica, taking a few steps toward the water. "You're not alone anymore."

Tears fell from Allison's eyes.

"There's five of us," Lilly said. "Tracy told me to find you and to bring you back. She said if we combined our strength, we could stop him once and for all, and with our unfinished business complete, we *all* would be able to cross over."

"He can't hurt you anymore," said Jackson, still seeing the terror on the girl's face. "You have a chance to put things right, but we need to hurry. Did they ever find you?"

Mark Karle was good at covering his tracks. Allison's body was probably still right where Mark left it.

"No."

"We can help with that too," Lilly promised. "Your parents will finally be able to lay you to rest."

"My parents died when I was young. My grandmother raised me, but she's sick now. She doesn't have much time left."

"I'm sorry," Lilly said.

"You said if we can stop him, *we* all get to cross over? I'll be able to leave purgatory?"

"He's our unfinished business," Lilly answered. "We can all leave together."

"Count me in."

They made their way back to Jackson's car just as the sun began to dip below the horizon. Jackson put the key in the ignition and started the car. "I'm going to need a short nap," he said, reclining his seat a bit.

"So, what's your story?" Jessica asked Allison, sensing her tale would be quite similar to theirs.

· · ·

SEPTEMBER 15*TH*, 2016

"I'm so wasted," Allison giggled as her best friend, Betsy Parnell, parked her car about a block from Allison's house.

"Your grandma will ground you for a month if she catches you coming home like this," Betsy warned but giggled just the same.

"I'm eighteen years old and graduating in a few months," Allison argued. "I'm basically an adult, so she can't ground me," she added, opening the car door and stumbling onto the sidewalk. "Call me later," she said, trying to close the car door as quietly as possible and failing miserably. "But not too early."

Betsy's car pulled away, and Allison tried to put one foot in front of the other. She fell a couple of times on the hard sidewalk before finally making it to her house. Sneaking into the backyard, she made her way around to the far side of the house. The garage was on that side of the house. It was also where an old TV antenna used to be, with what remained of its metal scaffold-like tower still attached to the house right next to the brick chimney. An addition had been built onto the back of the garage a long time ago, and like the garage, it was only a single story high, while the rest of the house was two stories tall. Her bedroom overlooked the roof of the one-story add-on, allowing her an avenue of escape whenever she needed one. All she had to do was climb out her bedroom window, walk across the roof, then shimmy down the antenna.

Allison grabbed the old, rusty tower and placed a foot on the lowest rung. She made it up a few rungs when her world began to spin ever so slightly. Her foot missed the next rung, and she fell hard, landing on her back. The next thing she knew, she was gazing up at the stars. She let out a laugh, which she quickly silenced, not wanting to wake the neighbors. She rolled over and tried to stand when a gloved hand appeared out of the darkness, clamping itself across her mouth.

Allison tried to pull away, but the strong arm of the gloved hand pulled her tight against the body of whoever was behind her. She tried to scream. Tried to fight as hard as she could. She felt a sharp twinge of pain in the right side of her neck, and her world became as black as the void.

THE NIGHT SKY greeted Jackson when he finally opened his eyes. "How long was I asleep for," he said with a yawn.

"A few hours," Lilly answered. "We need to find Allison's body."

"I figured as much," Jackson said, lighting a cigarette and blowing a large puff of smoke out the crack in the driver's side window. "Where are we headed?"

"Woodbury Wildlife Area. It's north of West Bedford, Ohio," Allison said with a somber voice. "That's where he buried me three years ago."

"And where is the last girl?" Jackson asked.

"Laura Elliott. She was living in Oak Hill, Ohio when she disappeared," Lilly answered.

"He's smart." Jackson put the car in drive.

"What do you mean by that?" Jessica asked, her voice filling with anger.

"He takes you from one state and leaves you in another," Jackson answered. "It makes it harder for you to be identified if someone were to stumble upon your bodies. You wouldn't be in any local databases, and nobody would link him to the rest of you. They wouldn't be looking for one killer. They'd be treating all of you as separate cases."

Jessica screamed out in frustration.

A wave of energy passed through Jackson as the right headlight went dark. "Hey," Jackson yelled. "What the fuck was that?"

"Sorry," Jessica said, shrinking into the back seat cushions. "I just get so angry when I think of all the shit he's gotten away with."

Jackson saw a long driveway of a house coming up on his left and pulled into it. The driveway stretched at least a quarter mile long as the lights from a large house glowed softly in the distance. "That's what we're trying to change, remember?" Jackson asked. "Now the cops gotta reason to stop us," he added, getting out of the car and walking around to examine the headlight. After giving it a couple of whacks with his hand, it blinked back on. He was on his way back to the driver's side door when he stopped and stared out toward the road.

"What is it?" Lilly asked as all three girls looked out the back window of the Kia and stared into the darkness.

Jackson reached into the car and popped the trunk before making his way to the rear of the car. A few seconds later, he jumped in the driver's seat, wearing a pair of latex gloves and tossing a reflective driveway marker into the back seat.

"Hey," Jessica and Allison cried out as the plastic stick passed through them and landed on the seat.

"Relax." Jackson put the car in reverse. "It's not like it was going to hit you. Besides, we'll need it to mark where they can find your body, plus it saves me five bucks and a trip to the store," he added, slamming the car into drive and stepping on the gas. He took out his cell phone and typed Woodbury Wildlife Area in the search bar before sending it to the map app. "It's about a six-hour drive, so you all better get comfortable."

～

Woodbury Wildlife Area was over fourteen thousand acres, consisting of open fields, brushland, large forests, and wetlands. Jackson pulled into a parking area as the night sky lightened in anticipation of the morning sun. "I'm pretty sure this is the closest parking area," Allison said. "This looks familiar."

"How far is your...?" Jackson began to ask.

"A few miles," Allison answered.

"Can you lead me in the dark, or do we need to wait a few hours?"

Lilly peered out the window and looked at the pre-twilight sky. "It's never dark for us, remember?"

"Then we had better get moving," Jackson said, putting on another pair of latex gloves and grabbing the driveway marker from the back seat.

The morning sun was peeking out over the horizon, as the group trekked toward the burial site. A constant trickle of sweat ran down Jackson's back as he leaned heavily against a large oak tree. The area was thick and heavily wooded, with the only traversable path having been made by deer. "I need to get into shape," he said, taking out a cigarette and lighting it. "How much farther?"

"Just over that hill," Allison responded, motioning toward the steep incline about fifty yards ahead.

After resting for a few minutes, Jackson took one last drag of his cigarette and tossed it to the ground. "Let's get to it." He stepped on it for good measure, giving it a twist with his foot.

He was about halfway up the hill when he stopped and ran back down to the spot where he had been smoking. It took him a few minutes before he found the cigarette butt. "Don't want to leave any DNA lying around," he said, pushing the butt into his jacket pocket when he noticed the three girls staring at him.

They crested the hill and found themselves staring at an

even larger hill than the one they had just climbed. "Down there," Allison pointed toward the small valley between the two hills.

When they reached the bottom, the ghost of Allison Murphey led them to a small natural cave-like hole carved into the side of the hill. The entrance measured roughly a foot tall and maybe twice as wide. A pile of medium rocks covered the front of the hole. Small branches and leaves added to the concealment of the makeshift grave. Jackson did his best to clear off all the sticks and brush, but decided to leave the grave undisturbed. He placed the driveway marker into the ground in front of the rocks and saved the coordinates on the handheld GPS unit. The four of them stood there in silence for several long minutes before they headed back to the car.

Jackson drove into the small town of West Bedford and dropped off an envelope addressed to the Coshocton County Sheriff's Department at another roadside blue mailbox before getting on State Route 16 and heading south toward Mark Karle's fourth victim.

Chapter 21

Mirror, Mirror

Mark Karle pushed the snooze button on his digital alarm clock for the third time. After having one too many beers the night before, he found it almost impossible to get motivated to face the new day. It had been three days since his last visit with Norma Jean. Three days since she had stabbed him with a piece of glass from the baby food jar. He had to give it to the girl for her ingenuity. She was a real fighter. The most spirited one yet, and in a weird way, he had his mother to thank for it.

The thought of his mother lying in the room down the hall, with her diapers full of shit, made him sink deeper into his bed. Diapers he was going to have to change. His alarm went off again, catching him by surprise and making him jump. Grabbing the alarm clock, he threw it at the wall on the other side of the room, where it shattered into several pieces.

"Marky!" his mother's voice screeched. "I know you're awake!"

"Shut the fuck up!" he cursed, forcing himself out of bed.

After putting on a plain T-shirt and a pair of loose-fitting sweatpants, he lumbered out into the hallway and down to the bathroom. He turned on the cold water and splashed some onto his face. After drying off, he put some toothpaste onto his toothbrush and stuck it into his mouth.

"Marky!"

Jesus Christ, he thought, give it a rest for once.

"I'm hungry!"

"You should have done it a long time ago," his reflection told him, a reflection not brushing his teeth. A reflection not even holding a toothbrush. This was something new.

Mark took the toothbrush out of his mouth and stared at his reflection.

"You know I'm right. Imagine how stress-free our life would be without her," his reflection said. "You wouldn't even need to go down in the basement anymore. We'd be free to do whatever we wanted."

Mark leaned closer toward the mirror, as did his non-toothpaste reflection, and stared deep into his own eyes. Toothpaste oozed from his mouth and dropped into the sink. He blinked his eyes several times, but his reflection failed to mimic his movements.

"Marky!"

Mark's attention broke away from the mirror for a fraction of a second. Turning his head toward the door, he perceived, through his peripheral vision, that his reflection did not follow his movements again. Whipping his head back to the mirror as fast as he could, he found his toothpaste-filled mouth's reflection staring back at him. "Get a hold of yourself," he said, wiping the toothpaste from his mouth.

His mother kept calling his name, but Mark did his best to shut her out. He went downstairs and poured a bowl of cereal, which he ate in front of the television. When he finished, he ventured outside to feed Gunner. The dog had constantly been barking at something while Mark had been eating his breakfast, but when he made his way around to the back of the house, Gunner saw him coming and lay on the ground submissively, waiting for his master to feed him. After that, he made his way out to the mailbox and grabbed yesterday's mail and the paper before going back inside.

After placing the mail and paper on the kitchen table, he took a jar of carrot-flavored baby food out of the cupboard. Having wasted as much time as he could, Mark shuffled his way back up the stairs and down the hall to his mother's room. He did his best to walk as lightly as possible, avoiding the creaky spots in the old wooden planked floor. Standing in front of his mother's door, he listened intently as his heartbeat increased. He dreaded each and every morning in this house. Dreaded it with every fiber of his being, but he was a man of his word, he kept telling himself. He would be nothing without it. It was his one true compass point in life.

"Marky! I know you're out there!"

Mark felt his heart trying to beat itself out of his chest while anxiety crept through his veins. Taking a deep breath and putting a smile on his face, he opened the door to his mother's room. He hadn't even taken a full step into the room when the smell of shit slapped him in the face.

"I need a bath," his mother told him. "A real deep cleaning. Show mama how much you love her."

The pure rage that Mark had kept bottled up deep inside him finally reached its boiling point. His grip on the jar of baby food tightened as his knuckles cracked under the tension. He wanted nothing more in this world than to throw the small glass jar as hard as he could at his mother's head. He took a few strides into the room and raised the jar above his head before throwing it with all the might his arm could muster. The sound of breaking glass exploded throughout the room as the baby food jar crashed through the window next to his mother's bed. The old woman gazed upon her son with an expression of shock and fear as her mouth gaped open.

Mark pivoted on his heels and walked out of the room, slamming the door so hard that several pictures on the hallway wall fell to the floor. Before he knew it, he was standing in front of the special door in his basement. His heart raced like the wind, and he could feel a vein throbbing in his neck. Taking another deep breath and exhaling it loudly, he turned the doorknob.

Norma Jean woke with a jolt at the sound of the door opening. Her face was horribly bruised and swollen. Dried blood was smeared across her bare chest. She instinctively curled into a tight ball, her body shaking uncontrollably.

Mark slammed the door shut and screamed at the top of his lungs, careful not to let out all the rage he had been building up within him. He needed to save some for sweet Norma Jean, who began crying upon hearing Mark's primal howl.

"Why does she treat me like that?" Mark asked, his question causing Norma Jean to look in his direction. "I gave up everything for her. My entire life. Do you really think I want to be changing shit-filled diapers every day? God, it would be *so* much easier if I could just kill the fucking bitch!"

"Why don't you?"

Mark slowly shifted his eyes and brought his full attention to sweet Norma Jean. "What did you say?"

"If you hate her so much, then why don't you kill her? It's obvious you've done it before."

"Oh, you have no idea," Mark said, licking his dry lips. "It'll be your turn soon enough," he promised. "As soon as you outlive your purpose."

Norma Jean stopped crying and sat up. "It doesn't sound like she's being a very good mother if you ask me. A mother is supposed to care for her children, not the other way around. They are supposed to cook for them and clean for them. Make them feel loved and protected."

Mark let out a loud, boisterous laugh. "Not in this house. My mother never had time for any of that nonsense. Always too busy trying to relive her past, and now she's nothing more than a waste of oxygen who does nothing but eat, shit, and make my life a living hell," he said, walking over and taking a seat on his throne.

"I could take care of you," Norma Jean said, the words struggling to pass her lip.

Mark's ears perked up.

"I could do all those things for you if you let me," she said. "And more..." she added, hesitantly spreading her legs.

Mark glared at Norma Jean for a while, tapping his fingers on the chair's armrest. "There's two problems with your plan," Mark finally said. "First, I promised my father, upon his deathbed, that I would watch after my mother, and I am a man of my word, if nothing else. The second problem is that your sole purpose in *my* life is to allow me to do the things that I can't do to her to you," he added, standing up and removing his shirt.

Tears ran down Norma Jean's blood-smeared cheeks.

"The sex is an added bonus," he told her, taking off his pants. "I have no inclination to fuck my mother. I'm not a pervert. It's just...the act of taking you by force arouses me like nothing else. So the minute you let me have you is the minute my interest in you is lost, and that is when I will end your life, which is something else I will take great pleasure in doing, and then I'll simply find another plaything to spend my time with," he said, coming to stand above her.

Norma Jean raised her foot as hard as she could, kicking Mark square in the balls, causing him to double over in pain as he quickly backed out of her reach. Scrambling to her feet, she took a defensive fighting stance, putting her hands out in front of her.

Mark took in several deep breaths and exhaled them just as fast. "Whoooo!" he exclaimed. "That'll get the blood flowing." He took a large step toward her.

Norma Jean grunted hard and threw a right hook, putting her weight behind the punch.

Mark took the punch with ease, his head barely turning. "That's more like it," he said, slapping her so hard across the face that her knees buckled.

Norma Jean knew he would win in the end. He would take her, and there was nothing she could do to stop him. However, when faced with the prospect of death, people find themselves willing to do anything to survive, and Norma Jean wanted to live now more than ever, so she dug down deep and fought with all of her strength. Whatever he did to her, she would take it. She would make sure he did not lose his interest in her. That she did not lose her purpose.

Chapter 22

We Don't Do Tests

Jackson reached the city limits of Oak Hill, Ohio, right around dinnertime. The small town had one local diner, and it was packed. Jackson walked in. The smell of french fries made his mouth water and his stomach growl.

An older, slightly overweight woman, dressed in a tight pink skirt and matching shirt accented with a white apron and a name tag that read Linda, greeted Jackson near the front door. "How many?" she asked, grabbing a handful of menus.

"One," Jackson answered. "Can I get a booth by chance?" he asked, trying to ignore the three ghosts who had accompanied him into the diner instead of waiting out in the car like he had suggested.

Linda gave Jackson an "are you kidding me?" look.

Jackson shrugged.

"You better leave me a gracious tip," she said, leading him toward the rear of the diner. "I'll give you a few minutes," she told him, placing a single menu on the table and watching Jackson slide into the booth and move over to the wall.

"No need," he said, handing her back the menu. "I'll take a

bacon cheeseburger with just barbeque sauce. A side of fries and a vanilla malt."

Linda scratched his order down on her pad before disappearing into the kitchen.

"Ok, so what's our game plan on this one?" Lilly asked.

"Same as before," Jackson said, taking out his phone. "Find out where she lived, and go from there." He realized several people seated around him were giving him a sideways glare. "I wish you girls would have stayed in the car."

"We're not dogs," Jessica snapped angrily as the lights in the diner flickered.

Jackson stared up at the lights.

Jessica, who appeared visibly upset, glared at the young man with dark eyes.

"That's not what I'm suggesting," Jackson said, trying to keep his voice as low as he could.

"I believe what Jackson is trying to say is that he doesn't want people thinking he's crazy when it looks like he's talking to himself," Lilly said.

"Sorry." Jessica took in a deep breath. "I've been in purgatory too long. I just need to cross over. I had all but given up hope, and then you guys showed up, and now it's all I can think about, and all we're doing is zig-zagging back and forth between Indiana and Ohio when we need to be on the road heading to Michigan, not sitting here in some huck suck diner."

"You need to calm down," Allison butted in. "We'll get there. We're all in this together, remember?"

Again, the lights flickered.

"Excuse me for not being dead," Jackson said as Linda appeared with a tray of food.

"Did you say something?" the waitress asked.

"I said looks great."

"You do know I'm doing this out of the kindness of my

heart," Jackson pointed out as soon as Linda was out of earshot. He grabbed the ketchup bottle and splashed the tangy red sauce on the fresh-out-of-the-fryer fries.

Jessica glared at him even harder than before as the lights flickered again.

"Enough with the lights!" Jackson's outburst caused everyone in the diner to turn and give him a nervous look. "Sorry," said Jackson, feeling like a fish out of water. "It's been a long day, and I have epilepsy," he lied. "The flickering lights are bugging me out. Can I get this to go, please," he added, waving to Linda.

Jackson stormed out of the diner, then slammed the car door shut as he slid into the driver's seat.

"I'm sorry," Jessica said again. "It's...it's getting hard for me to concentrate on things. I shouldn't have lost my temper like that. I really appreciate what you're doing."

"No, I'm sorry." Jackson took out a cigarette and lit it. "I shouldn't have snapped at you. You girls have all been through your own personal hells, and I can't even begin to imagine what it's like to be dead." He stuck the key in the ignition and gave it a turn. The car started up, and the headlights automatically turned on. "Well, I guess I can, but my outcome was a tad bit different, and I'm not the one stuck in-between worlds, so let me eat real fast, and we'll figure this out."

Jackson nearly jumped out of his seat when a knock came at his car window. The cigarette fell out of his mouth and landed in between his legs. He jumped up again and quickly grabbed the cigarette from underneath his crotch. When he finally looked out the window, he found an unamused police officer staring at him. "Good evening, Officer," Jackson greeted, rolling down his window. "Is everything all right?"

"I was about to ask you the same thing," the officer said. He was an older man with gray hair and a matching mustache, who stood at least six feet tall. His two-hundred-pound frame wore a brown uniform with a big, shiny gold badge and matching nameplate, which read Chief Vaughn. "Folks in the diner called. Said you were acting a little peculiar."

"Me?" Jackson said. "No, can't say that I was. Just trying to get some food." He held up the to-go bag. "Must have been someone else."

"Son, this is a *real* small town. The kind where everybody knows everybody, and nobody in there knows you. So, I'm pretty sure I've got the right guy. Besides, I could hear you talking to yourself when I approached your car."

All Jackson could do was stare at the chief. He was all out of smart-ass answers. He could always try to tell him the truth, but he had a strong notion of how that conversation would go. "Yeah, that... I apologized for the outburst in the diner. I've got epilepsy, and the lights were flickering, and my eyes started to bug out..."

The chief held up his left hand and shined his bright flashlight in Jackson's face. "Are you on drugs?"

"No," Jackson answered. "I wish I was, to tell you the truth, but I've been clean for almost three weeks now."

"Where you headed to?"

"Michigan, just needed to grab a bite."

"We're so busted," Jessica blurted out, and the headlights on the car flickered.

Jackson muttered something under his breath as Chief Vaughn's gaze shifted to the front of the car. "Need to see your driver's license," the chief ordered, resting his right hand on his service weapon.

"Yeah, sure thing," Jackson said, fishing out his wallet and handing the chief his ID.

"Long way from South Dakota," the chief said. "Said you were headed to Michigan?"

"Yes, sir."

"Why don't you step out of the car for a minute young man?"

The pistol in Jackson's jacket pocket suddenly weighed a ton. "Sure thing," he said, slowly opening the door and stepping out of the car. As soon as he did, the chief spun him around and had him place his hands on the top of his car. The chief patted him down, starting at the ankles and working his way up. He had just cleared Jackson's waist when a woman's voice blared out from the chief's police radio.

"Chief, you there?"

"What now?" Chief Vaughn muttered under his breath, stepping back from Jackson and grabbing his radio. "Go ahead, Myrtle. I'm here."

"Chief, Mrs. Elliott's back on the phone. She's sounding crazier than ever. Something about wanting a priest to cleanse her house of evil spirits. What do you want me to tell her?"

Jackson glanced over his shoulder upon hearing the last name of Elliott. How many Elliotts could there be in this small town where everybody knew everybody?

"Poor woman," the chief said when he saw Jackson heard the radio traffic. "She hasn't been the same since her daughter went missing about two years ago."

"What happened?"

"Nobody knows. But now her mother keeps insisting her house is haunted or something."

"You believe in that kinda stuff?" Jackson asked, trying to see where the chief sat on things concerning the supernatural.

"You better believe it," Chief Vaughn answered with a straight face. "I retired from the Cincinnati Police Department. Spent my last ten years as a homicide detective, so I've seen my share of dead bodies. Enough to know that I get this certain feeling every once in a while that tells me something might be lingering about."

"Like a ghost?" Jackson asked, turning around to face the chief.

"I'm not going to say that I've ever seen one, because I haven't, but I do believe I'm sensitive to the supernatural. I get this feeling like the air around my head gets heavy, and I can feel the pressure change. Kinda like I'm feeling right now, standing next to your car."

Jackson peeked into the car and found the ghosts of all three girls staring back at him.

"This time might be different," Lilly said.

"And what if it's not?" Jackson said.

"What if it's not what?" Chief Vaughn asked.

"Ok...fine," Jackson blurted out, throwing up his arms. "I'm what some people in the supernatural realm call a seer."

"And what do you see?"

"Ghosts."

The chief frowned at Jackson.

"You wanna know what I'm doing here in Oak Hill? I'm here looking for Mrs. Elliott's daughter. Well, not her actual daughter, but her daughter's ghost."

"Is that right, now?"

"I know it sounds crazy, and you probably think I'm on drugs."

"No," the chief lied while shaking his head.

"Listen, I know how this sounds, but it's the truth. If you take me over there, I can prove it to you," Jackson insisted.

"First off, I'm not just gonna up and take you over there because you say you can see dead people. Mrs. Elliott has been through enough as it is, and I don't need some crackpot showing up at her front door and claiming that her daughter is dead. Is this some kind of scam or something? You gonna tell her that you can see her daughter, and for a small fee, you can pass on a loving final message? I ought to lock you up right now."

"No, no, no... Nothing like that," Jackson pleaded.

"Then what's it like, hm? Why are you even looking for Laura in the first place?"

Jackson glanced into the car, searching for help.

"Tell him," Lilly said.

"Might as well," Allison said. "He already thinks you're crazy."

"There's a guy up in Michigan named Mark Karle, and he's a serial killer. He's killed five girls so far. All blonde. All young. He's smart too. He takes them each from a different state, and then buries them in another, that way..."

"Local agencies can't find a pattern. We don't share much info with other states, just other agencies close to us," the chief said, finishing Jackson's sentence.

"And he's got another girl in his basement right now."

"Have you called the police in that jurisdiction?"

"And tell them what?" Jackson asked. "That a ghost told me what he's doing? Without any physical evidence, they'll never get into that house. It'll just tip him off that they're on to him, and he'll get rid of anything he's got that can tie him to any of the murders. Besides...there's something else that needs to be done first."

"And what would that be?"

"From what I've been told about the afterlife, some spirits are put in this place called purgatory when they die. It's a place..."

"Between heaven and hell," Chief Vaughn said.

"Yeah, and a spirit is placed there because they have some unfinished business left here on earth, and to prove they are worthy enough to enter heaven, they have to complete that business before they can move forward, and it's nearly impossible because ghosts can't communicate with the living."

"So what, they're just stuck *here* until they can prove themselves?"

Jackson nodded.

"And if they can't?'

"Like you said, they're stuck here," Jackson said.

"All of this doesn't explain why *you're* looking for Laura."

"Bringing Mark Karle to justice is the unfinished business of *all* his victims," Jackson said. "And for them all to cross over, they all need to be present when it happens, so me and the three ghosts in the car are here to find Laura Elliott's spirit so she can cross over with the others."

"So, where's her body?"

"Beats me," Jackson said. "I haven't talked to her yet. Lilly Barnes, she's the one in the front seat—"

The chief bent down and studied the empty front passenger seat.

"She was found in a forest in Greenville, Ohio. Jessica Watkins and Allison Murphey, they're in the back seat, haven't been found yet, but they did take me to where their bodies were buried. I wrote down their coordinates using a handheld GPS and mailed them to the local police, so it's only a matter of time before they're found."

"And you'll do the same when you find Laura Elliott?"

Jackson nodded again. "They deserve to be laid to rest. Their families deserve to have some closure."

"How do you even know Laura's ghost is here in Oak Hill? She moved to Cincinnati the minute she turned eighteen and disappeared a few months later."

"Well, like the others," Jackson said, motioning to the car. "They always tend to return to their loved ones once they realize they can't complete their tasks. So, how about it, Chief?"

"Ok, get back in your car and follow me," Chief Vaughn said, walking back to his cruiser.

Jackson jumped in the driver's seat of his Kia. "Guess you were right," he said to Lilly. "For once."

"OOOHHH," Jessica and Allison said at the same time.

"Ha-ha, very funny," Lilly said. Though a smile graced her face, Jackson could tell by her voice that she was only smiling on the outside.

"Relax," said Jackson flashing a big smile. "I was kidding," he added, putting the car into gear and following the chief down the street. He reached into his jacket pocket, took out the small revolver he had found underneath Harold Woodruff's bed, and placed it under his seat.

"Where did you get that from?" Lilly asked in a shocked tone.

"Back in the house where we found Jessica. Thought it might come in handy somewhere down the road."

"That's not what you said when I suggested..."

"That's different and still not an option," Jackson said.

"What's not an option?" asked Jessica.

"Killing Mark Karle," Lilly answered.

"That would solve our dilemma," Allison added.

"I'm not going to go and murder someone so you three can cross over," Jackson scolded them. "I still have to live with my actions, and knowing what I know now, I'm not doing anything that will put me on anyone's scale or worse. Not saying I'm an angel by any stretch of the imagination, but from now on, I'm on the straight and narrow."

"You're right," Lilly told him. "And I'm not going to put you in that position. I'm just surprised you've got a gun is all."

"I didn't go out and look for one. It kinda found me. I thought for sure he was going to find it. He *would* have locked me up for sure," Jackson pointed out. "That's a felony right there. We're talking prison time. Can we just drop it?"

The chief took them to the other side of town and pulled over in front of a large, two-story green house with red shutters.

"Is this it?" Jackson asked, getting out of the car and joining the chief on the sidewalk in front of the house.

"No," Chief Vaughn answered. "This is my house. I've had that *feeling* for a while now every time I walk in there. So, you're gonna go in there and see if there's a ghost."

"Who is it?"

"That's for you to tell me," the chief answered. "Consider this a test. You pass it, and I'll take you over to the Elliotts'."

"And if I fail?"

"Jail."

~

THE INSIDE of the house appeared clean and well-organized. The living room had pink carpet, as did the rest of the house, with a white-and-pink, floral-patterned wallpaper accenting it. Jackson walked into the living room and began to feel nauseated. "It's a very flattering color," he said as the chief walked in behind him and closed the front door.

"Well?" he asked.

"Well, what?"

"Where's the ghost?"

"Not in here," Jackson answered. "The pink carpet probably scared it away."

"And you're failing the test."

"I ain't failing shit," Jackson said. "Just saying there aren't any ghosts in this room." He began to wander about the house, peeking into each and every room. The main bedroom had a queen bed and two dressers. He peeked in the closet and found men's and women's clothing. He made his way down the hall, looking into the guest bedroom, and then into the room across the hall. Both contained numerous boxes of quilting supplies but no ghosts. From there, he made his way back downstairs and into the kitchen, then down into the basement. After searching the entire house, he had yet to find any signs of a supernatural presence. "I got nothing."

Chief Vaughn took out his handcuffs.

"Hold on." Jackson took a step back. "Maybe *your* feelings aren't real," he suggested. "You ever think about that? Maybe you're feeling what you want to feel."

"That doesn't make any sense, and I know what I feel," defended the chief.

"And are you feeling it now?" Jackson said. "Because there ain't no ghost in your house."

The chief looked around as an unsure expression crossed his face. "You're not feeling anything, are you?" Jackson asked. "Maybe they've moved on..." He trailed off as he looked through the kitchen window out into the backyard. The sun was dangerously close to the horizon, but there was still enough light for Jackson to see the large wooden privacy fence running along the yard's border.

Nestled in front of the fence, in direct view from the kitchen window, rested a wooden bench with green-painted metal armrests and matching legs. It sat in the middle of a small clearing, free of grass and covered with red cedar chips. Several large flowering plants had been planted on both sides of the bench. They were showing signs of the fast-approaching fall season. But the thing that caught Jackson's attention was the older woman seated on the bench, staring up into the sky. She appeared to be about the same age as Chief Vaughn, and she was a bright shade of gray. Jackson had no idea what color her clothes had been, but even from the kitchen window, he could make out the large floral print on her shirt.

"A woman is sitting on your bench."

The chief looked out into the backyard and to the empty wooden bench. "Don't fuck with me, young man," he said in a stern voice.

"You're the one who brought *me* here, remember?"

The chief made his way to the back door. "After you," he motioned.

Jackson opened the back door and entered the well-manicured backyard. The trees had all begun to lose their leaves, but not one could be found on the green grass. The woman's attention was drawn to the back door as soon as it opened. Her face brightened upon seeing Chief Vaughn.

Jackson sat beside the woman, whose eyes were still staring intently at the chief. "Hello," he said.

The woman looked at Jackson, her eyes widening in surprise upon realizing he could see her. "You can see me, can't you?" she asked, reaching out and placing a hand upon his arm, her expression saddening when her hand passed through Jackson's flesh.

"Yes, I can."

"What is she saying?" the chief asked, taking a few eager steps forward.

"You're his wife, aren't you?"

The woman nodded. "My name is Helen."

"Well?" asked the chief.

"Nice to meet you, Helen. I'm Jackson. You've got some unfinished business, I presume?" Jackson inquired.

"Are they with you?" she asked, watching Lilly and the others.

"Yes, they're...my friends. We're on a secret mission."

Helen gazed up at the bright golden ray of light engulfing

her house. "It's a beautiful sight," she said. "One I never get tired of looking at, though it seems like I've been looking at it for a long time."

"The golden light? I've heard. When did you...die?" Jackson asked, trying to sound as sensitive as he could.

"Two thousand and eight," she replied. "What year is it now?"

"It's been quite a while."

"Wow," Helen replied. "I had no idea."

"What happened, if you don't mind me asking?"

"Cancer, and it wasn't the quick kind. I felt so bad for Jim having to see me like that. Having to watch me fade away and being unable to do anything about it. He always wore such a strong face, even around the kids."

"Do you need to tell him something? Is that it?"

"It's time for him to move on. Time for him to stop living in an empty house."

"You better start talking," the chief warned.

"She said that she's sorry for putting you through her sickness. She knows it was hard on you. That, even though you always wore a brave face, especially around the kids, it tore you up on the inside. She also says you need to move on. She's mad that you're still sitting in this big house all alone after all these years."

"I'm not alone," Chief Vaughn argued.

Helen told Jackson a few more facts.

"Your kids are living on each coast, and you're stuck here in the middle," Jackson continued. "You don't have any friends, and the only woman you talk to is Agnes, from across the street, when she brings you over some food a couple of times a week to make sure that you don't starve. Agnes likes you, you know. Helen says you're kind of slow when it comes to those things. She says you need to ask her out to dinner."

"I can't do that," said the chief, with a hint of anger.

"Why not?" Jackson and Helen both asked at the same time.

"Because...because I'm a married man!"

"No, you're not, Chief," Jackson said. "Not anymore. Helen says she can't move on, knowing you're not happy. That you're here all alone. She didn't want to leave, but she had to. She didn't have a choice. She needs you to know she didn't give up on you or the kids. She fought as long as she could."

A tear welled in the chief's eye as his stern face began to soften. He quickly wiped it away, and his face became like stone once more. "How do I know you're not making this shit up?" he asked.

"Seriously?" Jackson asked. "Again, you're the one who brought me here."

"You could have googled me or something on your way over here. Or maybe you could have figured it out from walking through my house."

Jackson spoke one single word. "Suzzy."

The expression Chief Vaughn made upon hearing that name reminded Jackson of someone who had just gotten kicked in the balls. Hard. "Excuse me," he said with a "how dare you say that name" look.

"Suzzy. That was the name of your first daughter. She was a miscarriage late in Helen's second trimester."

The tear ran down the large man's face. "We never told anyone her name. That was our little secret. I thought about her for a long time after that day, and I still do. She really is here, isn't she?"

Jackson nodded, fighting back his own tears. He had no idea how emotional it was to get involved with the grief of others. He had spent most of his life only taking things. Only caring about himself, and while he had helped Darnell and

Joshua cross over, neither of their experiences had been so personal. This was way out of his comfort zone. Even helping Lilly and the others hadn't been this taxing, not yet anyway, but he knew they were far from being finished. He now began to believe that he had been given a second chance at life, and what he initially thought of as a curse now felt more like a new purpose.

"Ok," Chief Vaughn said, wiping away his tears again. "I'll ask out Agnes. I only ever wanted to make Helen happy. That was my single purpose in life, and now it will be my purpose in her death. I love you, Helen."

Tears fell from Helen's eyes. They were of joy and grief. "Tell him we'll be together again someday in the distant future."

"I will," Jackson said.

Helen Vaughn's spirit turned into specks of golden light, which were wafted upward upon the wind.

"She's crossed over," Jackson told the chief. "She said you'll be together again someday in the distant future."

"Ok, ok," Chief Vaughn stammered, trying to compose himself. "I suppose you passed the test," he said, straightening his uniform. "And now it's my turn to honor my end of the bargain."

Jackson let out a hard, exhaustive breath as he turned to the girls and found their eyes were as wet as his.

Chapter 23

Gotta Pay the Rent

"Mrs. Elliott, I brought someone here I believe might be able to help you," Chief Vaughn said as Laura Elliott's mother opened her front door.

"It's about time," Mrs. Elliott said, ushering them into her house.

Jackson had asked Lilly, Jessica, and Allison to stay in the car this time. He didn't want to overwhelm Laura if she was in the house, and from what Chief Vaughn had told him before knocking on the front door, it sounded like she was.

Barbara Elliott had not been doing well since her daughter had disappeared. Having been diagnosed with schizophrenia in her early twenties, she had been able to maintain her sanity through a strict regimen of medication and therapy, and as fate would have it, Laura had been diagnosed with the same mental illness before moving out and was not handling it well. The two of them had gotten into a knockdown, drag-out fight, causing Laura to storm out one night and never come back.

A few months later, her parents received a call from a girl

named Janey, who said Laura was living with her in Cincinnati and thought they should at least know their daughter was ok. She was also the one who gave the police their phone number when Laura went missing. Barbara's life forever changed the night the police called to tell her of her daughter's disappearance. She stopped taking her meds. Stopped talking to her therapist. Her husband had tried his best to get her back on track, but it wasn't until she started talking to Laura, who was not there, that he'd had enough and left as well.

The inside of the house was a mess. Dirty dishes were stacked up in the kitchen sink and piled on top of one another on the counters. Bags of trash were scattered throughout the house, and dirty clothes covered most of the floors.

"Come in, come in," Barbara said, leading them into the living room and throwing a handful of dirty clothes from the couch, so they could have a place to sit down. She turned on a lamp sitting on top of an end table between the couch and an old leather recliner.

Sitting on the edge of the recliner was a girl with long blonde hair. The left side of her head was shaved bald, and while her color was still there, her overall appearance was becoming slightly tarnished. She had a small hoop nose ring, like a bull, and several tattoos on her neck and arms. A black Ramones band shirt, a short denim skirt, and black fishnet stockings completed her ensemble. The black eyeliner caked around her eyes matched her black lipstick. She sat stiffly on the edge of the cushion with her arms crossed across her stomach as she rocked back and forth slightly, mumbling incoherently.

Jackson sat on the couch while the chief made his way to Barbara's side. "What's going on today, Barbara? How are you doing?"

"It's Laura again," she said, glancing nervously at the old recliner. "She's upset about something, but I can't hear her. How can I help her if I don't know what she needs?"

Chief Vaughn gave Jackson a questioning stare. "I feel something," he mouthed silently as Jackson nodded, telling him his intuition was spot on.

"My friend Jackson here is real good at handling these kinds of things. Why don't we step out onto the porch and give him a couple of minutes?"

"Laura, why don't you talk to me?"

Laura stared at her mother with distant eyes. She let out a loud scream, and the light bulb in the lamp exploded. Barbara screamed in turn and began slapping her forehead repeatedly. Chief Vaughn placed his hands on her shoulders and gently pushed her toward the front door.

"Laura, can you hear me?" Jackson asked once they were alone.

If she could, she didn't act like it. She just kept rocking back and forth.

"I can see you, and I know about your unfinished business."

Laura stopped rocking for a second or two before resuming.

"I also know about Mark Karle."

That did it. Upon hearing the name of the man who had taken her life, Laura's rocking came to an abrupt halt. The glare in her eyes was nothing short of pure hatred. Jackson's breath became visible in the air in front of him as the temperature in the room took a dramatic drop. Frost formed in the bottom corner of a mirror on the other side of the room before stretching itself across its entire reflective surface. The rest of the lights in the house began to flicker off and on.

"Hey, take it easy," Jackson said, looking nervously around the room. "I'm here to help you."

Her eyes continued to glare at Jackson. Springing from the

chair, a primal shriek escaped her black lips. A large crack ripped through the mirror, and all of the lightbulbs in the house exploded.

From out of nowhere, Jessica appeared and moved between them, as she slapped Laura hard across the face. "Snap out of it!"

Laura stopped screaming. "Ouch," she said, placing a hand on her cheek. "What the fuck?"

"Sit down and shut up," Jessica ordered, pushing Laura back into the recliner.

Flopping down like a rag doll, Laura's eyes appeared lost. "Who are you guys? Where's my mother? I've been trying to talk to her for the longest time, but she can't hear me for some reason. I think she might be off her meds again. I need to get her to her doctor."

"You're dead," Jackson told her, hoping to jog her memory. Given their sense of urgency, he hoped that taking the "ripping the Band-Aid off" approach was the best way to proceed.

"I'm...what?"

"Dead, like me," Jessica said.

"And me," Lilly's voice added.

"And me," said Allison.

"I remember..." Laura said, her gaze dropping to the floor. "I have to..." Her voice trailed off.

"Complete your unfinished business?" Jackson asked.

"Yes, but it was..."

"Too hard to do by yourself," said Lilly, walking over and placing a gentle hand upon Laura's shoulder.

"Yes."

"Well, you're not alone anymore," Jackson assured her.

"You're not dead, are you?" she asked, studying Jackson's face.

"Not yet," Jackson answered with a quick wink.

"I went…"

"Back to his house," said Allison. "We all have."

"And we all failed," Jessica added.

"There was another girl there," Laura said. "I think she said her name was Tracy."

"Tracy Lafond," Lilly said. "We met her too. She told me to find you. Said that together we could bring *him* to justice and get the hell out of purgatory."

"I don't want to go back to that house. You don't know the things he did to me."

"He did them to us too," Allison said.

"It's the only way," Lilly said. "If you don't come with us, you'll be trapped here forever when we cross over."

The words found their way through Laura's disturbed mind as she nodded in understanding. "What about my mother?" she asked, standing, her eyes becoming a little clearer.

"Leave that to me," Jackson said.

Chief Vaughn led Laura's mother back into the house, and both stared in disbelief at the damage.

"Laura?" her mother said, walking into the living room and seeing her daughter.

"Mom, can you hear me?" Laura asked.

"I can see her lips moving, but why can't I hear her voice?" Barbara asked, tears welling in her eyes.

"Honestly, ma'am, I don't think you should even be able to see her at all," Jackson speculated. "But who knows? I'm pretty new at this stuff too."

"Tell her I love her," Laura insisted. "And that I'm sorry."

"Laura wants you to know that she loves you with all of her heart and that she's sorry," Jackson relayed the message.

"She's dead, isn't she?" her mother asked.

"Yes," Jackson answered.

"Where is she? Her body, I mean. I need to have her laid to rest."

"And I promise I'm going to do everything I can to make sure that happens," Jackson said. "But we must be leaving," he added, ushering Chief Vaughn toward the front door.

"You're going to go and find her body, aren't you?" the chief asked, walking down the driveway.

"Do you remember where you're buried?" Lilly asked Laura, whose confused eyes were transfixed on the sky and the fast-moving dark clouds.

"Ichabod Crane," Laura responded cryptically.

"What's that supposed to mean?" Jackson asked Lilly, who could only shrug.

"You're buried where Ichabod Crane is?" Jessica asked.

"Where he was," said Laura, still holding her gaze upon the sky, her lost eyes darting back and forth.

"I'm sorry, but I'm not following you," Jackson confessed. "Let's start with what state you're buried in?"

Laura held up her hand, palm out.

"Yes. Hi. We've already met," Jackson said, becoming a little irritated.

"She's not saying hello," Lilly said. "That means Michigan."

"Ok, but Ichabod Crane wasn't from Michigan, was he?"

"I don't think so," Lilly answered.

"He wasn't," Jessica said. "*The Legend of Sleepy Hollow* took place in New York."

"What does Ichabod Crane have to do with Michigan, then?" Allison asked.

"What's going on?" asked the chief. "I'm feeling a bit left out over here."

"Sorry," Jackson said. "Laura says she's buried in Michigan. Somewhere Ichabod Crane was?"

"Sleepy Hollow State Park," Chief Vaughn answered. "It's off US 127. Helen and I honeymooned on Mackinac Island. I remembered seeing a sign that read Sleepy Hollow State Park. Helen made such a big deal about it. She even made me turn around so she could get a picture of the damn thing," he told them, taking out his phone. "Here it is. It's in Laingsburg, Michigan. It'll take us about six and half hours to get there."

"Us?" Jackson asked. "I don't know if that's such a good idea, Chief."

"I watched that girl grow up here," Chief Vaughn said. "And the thought of her being out there like that doesn't sit well in my gut. So, if there's something I can do to help remedy that situation, I'm going to do it. Besides, I could come in very handy if you run into any local agencies up there. I assume you've had some trouble in the past?"

Jackson gave Lilly a look, remembering his time with Detective Brandt. "You're in charge," she said. "But for the record, I think you should let him come along. It could help bring him some closure too."

"Fine," Jackson said, answering both Lilly and the chief simultaneously.

"Why don't you come back to my house first?" the chief offered. "It's getting late, and I'm sure you could use some food since you didn't get to finish your meal from earlier, and that'll give me time to pack some stuff."

It had been a long time since Jackson had had a good home-cooked meal. Chief Vaughn called Agnes and told her he had a guest and wondered if she would be interested in helping him out. She showed up with a large pan of homemade lasagna and garlic bread. "I was going to bring this over in the morning anyway," she said, setting the food down on the kitchen table. "You just won't have anything to eat tomorrow."

"Well, I'll have to take you to dinner then," the chief said. His words caught Agnes by surprise. She gasped aloud before holding her breath in embarrassment. "If you're interested," the chief added.

"I would be, yes," Agnes said, sitting with the chief at the dining room table.

Jackson went upstairs and took a shower before lying down on the bed in the guest bedroom. He was asleep before his head hit the pillow. The ghosts of the girls sat in the living room for a while, listening to Chief Vaughn and Agnes talk, but they soon felt a little weird for eavesdropping on their conversation and ventured out to the bench in the backyard. Lilly, Jessica, and Allison each shared their stories with Laura. Then it was her turn.

May 4th, 2017

"I don't need to take any medication," Laura told her mom after they had gotten back from her doctor's appointment. "I feel fine."

"But you're not," her mother said. "Trust me. I've been there, remember?"

"Yeah, I remember," Laura told her with a bit of anger rising in her voice. "I remember the outbursts and weeks on end you spent locked away in your bedroom. I remember the fits of rage and always getting yelled at for nothing."

"That wasn't me," her mother tried to explain. "It was the sickness. Because I didn't take my meds."

"The same meds you want me to take?"

"They will help you in the long run, trust me."

"You keep telling me that," Laura yelled. "But you're the crazy one, not me. The best thing for me is to get as far away

from you as possible!" She ran to her bedroom and slammed the door shut behind her, making sure to lock it.

"Come pick me up!" she texted her best friend Janey, who had moved to Cincinnati about eight months ago, leaving her here to fend for herself.

Laura had been so mad at her for doing it. Janey had all but begged Laura to go with her, but Laura had been too afraid to leave the nest then. Now was a completely different story, and with Janey's roommate, Maria, having just moved out, it seemed like fate was finally pushing her out the door.

"On my way!" Janey texted her back. "Pack your shit!"

Janey arrived in the middle of the night. "Let's go," she texted.

Laura crept through her house with the stealth of a teenager, leaving a note on the kitchen table telling her mother not to worry. She ran out to the awaiting car and jumped in with a scream of freedom as Janey sped off down the street. Laura peered over her shoulder at the only home she had ever known and began to have second thoughts about the whole thing.

She had been so mad at her mother. She was the one with schizophrenia, and she was the one who had given it to her. Passed it on through her genes. She had told her mom the truth about what she remembered as a child, and now feared she would end up the same way. The medication the doctor had given her rested heavily at the bottom of her purse. She had thought about taking one pill earlier, but if she started taking the medication, that meant she was indeed truly mental.

"Relax girl," Janey told her, handing her a joint. "Take a hit and chill. You can do whatever the hell you want now. This is gonna be epic! You and me back together again!"

Janey's apartment had one bedroom, so Laura had to sleep on a broken-down couch in the living room. There was also only one bathroom, meaning she had to share almost everything with

Janey. Rent was a thousand dollars a month and would be split down the middle, which was something Janey could not have been affording on her own, working as a waitress at a pizza place a couple of blocks down. When Laura asked her about it, Janey had confided that the landlord was a real creep, but he would knock off a hundred bucks for every blowjob she gave him throughout the month. That usually meant that her half of the rent was three hundred a month instead of five, which was still a bit on the high side for anyone working for tips.

Laura searched the wanted ads and found nothing she liked for the first two weeks. The third week, she had an interview at a clothing store and got the job. The only problem was that she would be working for commission, and being the new girl, she wasn't selling as much as the more experienced salespeople. By the time rent was due, she only had two hundred dollars to her name.

"You can always go and knock on Stanley's door," Janey told her. "We can't afford to get kicked out of here. Maria always did her share too."

"Do I have to?"

"No," Janey answered. "If you can come up with three hundred bucks another way, I'm all ears."

"How do you always have money? Tips can't be that great at Sal's Pizzeria."

"The tips there are shit," she said. "I work a night job on the weekends."

"I thought you were working at Sal's on the weekends. What's your second job? Are they hiring?"

"I'm what you would call a...lady of the night."

"You're a fucking hooker," Laura said.

"Call it what you want, but there's no way in fucking hell I'm going back to Oak Hill."

"What do you do?"

"What the fuck do you think I do? I suck dick and get fucked by lonely old married men."

"How can you do something like that?"

"Don't fucking judge me," Janey argued, her voice taking a defensive tone. "Living here ain't cheap, and there's no fucking way I'm going back home. You remember dear old Tom, don't you? He got real friendly after he and my mom got married. I was twelve and didn't have a choice. At least now I get paid for it."

"Jesus."

"Jesus has nothing to do with it, because if he did, he would never have allowed it to happen in the first place, right?"

Laura didn't say anything. She just stared at the person she thought had been her best friend but was now becoming a stranger before her very eyes.

"You got one week to come up with three hundred bucks, or I find a new roommate," Janey said coldly before walking into her room and slamming the door shut.

A week later, Laura stood nervously in front of Stanley's apartment door. Janey made her drink a half pint of blackberry brandy to give her some much-needed liquid courage. She knocked softly, hoping the landlord wouldn't be home. Her heart sank into her stomach when the door opened.

"What do we have here?" Stanley asked, taking a good, long, lingering look up and down Laura.

"Hi," she said, a wave of nausea washing over her. "I live in apartment 3B with Janey."

"And?"

"And we're a little short with our rent this month," Laura told him.

"How short?"

"Three hundred..."

"Your friend has been late before, so I can't give her any

more extensions," *Stanley said. "Did she tell you about our...
special arrangement?"*

*Laura nodded as Stanley opened his door wider. Laura took
a deep breath and walked inside the apartment. When she
returned to her apartment, she ran straight to the bathroom and
threw up into the toilet.*

"So?" asked Janey.

"Rent's paid in full," Laura answered between gags.

*"Good job," Janey congratulated her. "See, that wasn't so
hard, now was it? No pun intended."*

*Laura laughed. She didn't know why. Maybe it was the alco-
hol, but the joke had been funny because Stanley barely got hard,
and when he did, thankfully, he didn't last long. "What's it like
on the weekends?" she asked.*

*"Kind of like Stanley but cleaner," Janey answered. "And
they're in a car and usually have a wife to get back to, so it's
quicker too. Why? You want to make some extra money?"*

"Maybe?"

*That Saturday night, Laura stood anxiously next to Janey.
They were under a bright streetlight, so the Johns could get a
good look at them as they drove by. Laura had borrowed a short
denim skirt, a black T-shirt, and matching fishnet stockings.*

"You got the rubbers in your purse?" Janey asked.

Laura nodded.

*"Remember, fifty bucks for a blowjob. Seventy-five if they
want to fuck, and if they do, they always wear a rubber. Got it?"*

Laura nodded again.

*A car pulled up and honked its horn. "This is one of my
regulars," Janey said. "I'll be back in a bit. Good luck. Take
another drink," she told her. "It helps."*

*Laura took the bottle of blackberry brandy out of her
handbag and took a long swig. As she slipped the bottle back into
her purse, an old wood panel station wagon pulled up and*

honked. Laura timidly walked over to the car, and as she did so, the front passenger window rolled down. She bent over and looked into the car.

"Hello," said the driver, a middle-aged man with a mustache and thick glasses.

Laura tried to convince herself he appeared harmless enough.

"Why don't you get in so we can talk?" said the man.

Laura climbed into the passenger seat, and the car slowly drove away from the curb.

"Sorry," said the man. "I'm a little nervous. I've never done this sort of thing before."

"That makes two of us." Laura laughed. "What are you looking for?"

"Someone like you," the driver said with a large smile. "Name's Mark."

"Nice to meet you. I'm Laura. I meant, what were you looking to do tonight?"

"Oh, that...um...I guess... a blowjob. How much for one of those?"

"Fifty."

"Sounds like a good deal," Mark said, pulling into a dark alleyway. "Is here fine?"

"Looks like a good spot," Laura answered.

Janey hadn't told her anything about finding a spot or where to go, but this spot looked deserted enough that she was sure they wouldn't get caught by the cops.

"So, do I unzip?"

Laura nodded.

Mark undid his pants and pulled them down a bit, exposing his half-erect penis. Laura glanced nervously around, making sure the coast was clear before leaning over and putting Mark's *manhood into her mouth. She had only been sucking for a few minutes when she felt a twinge of pain in her neck.*

"What the fuck?" She sat up. "What the hell was that?"

She saw a syringe in Mark's right hand as the world around her grew fuzzy and dark.

Chapter 24

I Gotta Quit Smoking

"What time is it?" Jackson asked when Chief Vaughn nudged him awake.

"It's 3:00 a.m.," the chief answered, handing Jackson a cup of coffee. "If we leave now, we can make it there with plenty of daylight left. Are we alone?"

Jackson didn't understand what the chief was asking.

"The girls?"

"Oh," Jackson said, taking a look around the room. "Yeah."

"I'm guessing by the way you were talking to Laura earlier that she might not be all there?"

"Yeah." Jackson sighed. "Being stuck in purgatory hasn't done her any favors."

"If she can at least get us in the general vicinity, I can make a few phone calls and get the state police out there with a cadaver dog."

"Are you sure you want to get *that* involved?" Jackson asked, taking a long sip of caffeine. "You know they're going to be asking you a lot of questions that you're not going to be able to answer. At least if you want to sound sane."

"You let me worry about that," the chief said. "Besides, figured I'd be the one calling it in, anyway. I'll tell them I got an anonymous tip with a vague location."

"All right," Jackson said, standing up and holding his hand out. "I really appreciate the help."

"Anything to bring Barbara's little girl home," the chief said, shaking Jackson's hand.

They made their way outside into the cold brisk night air. The girls quietly got into Jackson's car as the young man walked to the end of the chief's driveway.

"What are you doing?" the chief asked.

Jackson grabbed one of the two reflective driveway markers sticking out of the ground at the end of the chief's driveway. "Getting supplies," he answered.

THEY DROVE IN SEPARATE CARS, with Chief Vaughn driving his police cruiser and Jackson in his Kia. The chief called in his part-time deputy and told him he needed a few personal days and to call him if anything major happened, which he was sure wouldn't.

Jackson hadn't said many words during the trip, and neither had any of the girls, except for Laura, who kept mumbling incoherently. Jackson tried to listen to the dead girl's one-sided conversation but found it gave him a headache, so he turned his attention elsewhere.

They passed a brown road sign that read SLEEPY HOLLOW STATE PARK with an arrow. Jackson turned the car in the direction of the arrow, and a short time later, he turned into the park's main entrance. The road ended at a small welcome center. In front of the building stood a statue of a large wooden black bear, with the word *Sleepy* painted on the base of the statue.

"The bear!" Laura giggled.

Jackson pulled the car into a parking spot as he and Chief Vaughn, along with the girls, made their way up to the building.

"This is a pretty big place," Chief Vaughn said, finding a park map on a large wooden display stand. The park consisted of over thirteen miles of hiking trails, not including the horse and multipurpose trails. A large lake with multiple camping sites all nestled on twenty-six hundred acres.

"Ok, Laura, it's up to you now," Jackson told her. "Can you show us where you're buried?"

Laura gazed upon the map and shook her head.

"What can you remember?" asked Lilly, placing a hand on her shoulder to reassure the ghost that she was not alone.

"Water."

"The lake?" Jackson asked, studying the size of the lake on the map and thinking this would be like finding a needle in a haystack. "Are you buried near the lake?"

"No," Laura answered. "Something smaller."

"Something smaller," Jackson repeated softly.

"There's two spots where a river feeds into the lake." Chief Vaughn pointed. "In the northwest corner of the lake and southwest corner."

"What else can you remember?" Jackson asked.

"Boats."

"There's a boat launch," said Allison, pointing toward the southeast side of the lake.

"It's closer to the southern river bend," Jessica said.

"You wanna fill me in?" asked the chief.

"Sorry," said Jackson. "I keep forgetting that you can't... never mind. We've narrowed it down to being near the river, but she's not sure on what side of the lake. She also remembers boats, but I don't think that's going be much help."

"Sure it is," the chief said.

"It is?" asked Jackson. "How?"

"If she remembers boats, that means she passed the boat launch, which would suggest she's buried somewhere near the north end. She would have walked past the boat launch on her way back to the main road. But, then again, I am looking at this from the vantage point of a living person who would have followed the trails."

"Chief, you're a freaking genius," Jackson replied. "Following the trails would have been second nature to her too, right, not having been dead that long?" He looked to the trio of spirits, who all agreed with him.

Chief Vaughn grabbed a second map, and they all rushed back to their cars and made their way over to the boat launch. Before Jackson could even put his car in park, Laura jumped through the door and ran off into the woods.

"Hey," he yelled, slamming the car into park. "Laura, come back here," he called out, trying to undo his seat belt, his voice drawing the attention of two fishermen pulling their boat from the water. Lilly, Jessica, and Allison took off after Mark Karle's fourth victim, who was no longer in sight.

Chief Vaughn, hearing Jackson, jumped out of his cruiser. He grabbed a backpack from his trunk and easily caught up to the young man, who was already moving down the nearest trail headed north.

"What happened?"

"Beats the fuck out of me," Jackson said, holding the chief's driveway marker in one hand. "Laura jumped out of the car and ran off before I could get it in park."

"What about the others?"

"They took off after her, but I can't see any of them either."

"Why are you wearing latex gloves?" the chief asked, noticing the driveway marker in Jackson's right hand.

"Stay in your lane, bro. I know what I'm doing. I just need to figure out which way she went, and we'll be back on track."

"She should be heading toward the river, right?" the chief said, taking out his map. "Looks like there's a dam at the mouth of the river. Let's concentrate on making it that far first. I'm sure the others will be waiting for us somewhere along the route."

They had been walking for several miles; at least Jackson's heaving lungs thought so, anyway. The smell of soil and dry leaves filled his nostrils and lungs, making him cough. "Hold on," Jackson called out, leaning heavily against a large tree, as a weird sense of déjà vu played across his mind. "I *really* need to quit smoking," he said, sweat trickling down his back. "How much farther?"

"About another half mile or so," the chief answered, looking at the map. "Come on, we need to keep moving."

A cement dam had been built at the mouth of the river, which helped regulate the water flow entering the lake. The river stretched nearly fifty feet across and was at least waist-deep. On top of the cement dam was a steel catwalk with handrails, allowing hikers to get from one side of the river to the other.

Jackson sat down on the wet steel bridge and tried to catch his breath. Chief Vaughn took out a water bottle and handed it to Jackson, who took a hard, long drink. "Thanks," he said after taking a second drink and placing the water bottle into his jacket pocket.

"Jackson, hurry up," Allison called out from the other side of the river.

"This way," Jackson told the chief, wearily getting to his feet and heading out across the steel catwalk.

They reached the other side of the dam and continued down the path. They found Jessica about a mile and a half later. She was sitting on a knee-high tree stump, waiting impatiently for them. "Jesus Christ, you guys are slow," she said, arms folded across her chest. "This way." She left the path and ventured into the woods.

Jackson and Chief Vaughn fought through the thicket and underbrush, taking an occasional branch to the face. Chief Vaughn estimated they had traveled about another mile into the heavy forest when they came upon a small clearing between a large cluster of trees.

The first thing Jackson observed upon entering the small space was the absence of noise. He, like so many other people in life, had become accustomed to the everyday noises of the living. The sounds of cars and people moving about. Even on the trek to reach this place, he had been bombarded with the constant sound of his breathing, and his bitching about his breathing, but now, he could only hear the wind rustling the red fall leaves of the trees. Then he saw Laura. She was kneeling at the center of the clearing, crying uncontrollably.

Lilly placed a solemn hand upon her shoulder, trying her best to provide some much-needed comfort.

"This is the spot." Jackson took the driveway marker and stuck it into the ground.

"What do we do now?" the chief asked.

Jackson took out the handheld GPS unit and turned it on. "Once I get the coordinates, I'll write a letter to the local sheriff and put it in a mailbox, and then you can go home. Case closed."

"I didn't come all this way to just go home. I'm here to see this thing through to the end. You know who's responsible for this, and you know where to find him, so let's go get the mother fucker."

"Can't ask you to do that, Chief," Jackson said.

"I'm not asking for your permission here, Jackson," the chief said.

"Listen, I don't even know how we're going to end this yet," Jackson said honestly. "This guy is pure evil, and if something happened to you, Helen would probably come back and haunt my ass till the day I die. Besides, how will you explain yourself to the authorities up here? You gonna tell them you're just following some guy who claims he can see dead people? You know that won't go over very well. And I might have to resort to committing several felonies, which is something I know you won't want any part of."

"Yes, but I've got a lot more experience in dealing with evil people than you."

"Not arguing with you there, Chief," Jackson said as the GPS beeped, signaling it had found its mark.

"Tell him you won't be alone," Lilly said.

"Tell him that this is something we need to do on our own," Jessica added.

"Tell him that we won't let anything happen to you," Allison promised.

"Tell him that I want him to be the one to bring me home," Laura said, getting up from the ground and wiping the tears from her face.

Jackson relayed the girls' messages, and the chief found he wasn't in any position to refuse Laura's last request. "I'll make the call," he said with a heavy sigh. "If you need me for anything," he said, "all you gotta do is call, and I'll bring the cavalry. Understand?"

Jackson nodded and extended his hand toward the chief. Chief Vaughn reached into his waistband and pulled out a black Glock pistol. "Just in case," he said.

"Got that covered," Jackson said with an awkward smile.

"Ten-four," the chief replied, returning the gun from where he got it.

Jackson gave the chief a surprising hug, catching the old man off guard, before walking back toward the trail.

"Jackson," the chief called out to him before he got too far away. "Thank you."

Jackson nodded and disappeared among the trees.

Chapter 25

The More, the Merrier

It was a relatively short drive from Sleepy Hollow State Park to the small town of Harrison, Michigan, given all the other places Jackson had been driving to over the past week. He pulled into town a little after two in the afternoon. The downtown area had several historic buildings, giving the center of the village a quaint feel. Jackson parked in front of an old-school mom-and-pop hardware store.

"We need to come up with a plan," he said, putting the car in park.

"The plan is we go inside and meet up with Tracy," Lilly answered. "She's the one who said we needed to all come together, so I'm sure she'll know what to do."

"Don't take this the wrong way, but you're all just ghosts." Jackson winced at the thought of the arguments he knew were coming. "Flickering the lights or cracking a mirror isn't going to save Norma Jean or stop a guy like Mark Karle, which means I'm going to have to get involved."

"You mean with that gun?" Lilly asked.

Jackson didn't answer as he thought about the old revolver

stashed under the front seat of the car. "If it comes to that, I guess."

"Only as a last resort," Lilly reminded him. "Remember what Carol told you?"

"How do you even plan on getting into the house?" Jessica asked. "I remember he kept that placed locked up pretty tight."

"She's right," Allison said. "*We* can walk right through the door, but how are *you* going to get in without alerting him?"

"Maybe one of you girls can try to unlock a window or something," said Jackson. "Or else I'll have to try to break in. This hardware store should have something I could use. Stay here and talk this plan out a little bit more. I'll be right back."

The small bell above the hardware store door came to life when Jackson walked in. An elderly woman greeted him from behind the counter as the smell of freshly popped popcorn filled the air. The old planked hardwood floor of the store creaked and popped as Jackson made his way up and down the aisles. He picked up a hammer and a flathead screwdriver but stopped there when he drew a blank on what other things he might need to break into a house. He wondered if he was really going to break into a serial killer's house while searching for anything else that might come in handy. He was getting in way over his head. Seeing ghosts was one thing, but Mark Karle was very real. A very real serial killer. What were ghosts going to be able to do against him?

Dan, the soldier, had punched him pretty hard, and Harold Woodruff had played with his reality, while Larry Finton had possessed Madam Denesha and tore his own poor brother apart. All those spirits were full of hate and anger, unlike the ghosts of the girls, and while Jessica was getting there and Laura had caused some minor damage back at her house, Jackson couldn't fathom that it would be enough to stop someone like Mark.

Jackson took his phone out and checked the time. Shoving it back into his pocket, he felt something he had all but forgotten about. Carol's business card. Taking the cell phone back out, he stared at the number printed on the card. Against his better judgment, he made the call and felt a sigh of relief when it went to voice mail. He pondered for a few seconds about leaving a message but ended the call abruptly. "Nobody here on her list."

"Help you find anything?" asked a man wearing a red vest under a long sleeve flannel shirt.

Jackson remembered Lilly saying that Norma Jean had a chain tied around her ankle. "You got anything that'll cut through a chain?"

The man gave Jackson a funny look before shaking it off. "Hack saw or bolt cutters. Take your pick."

Jackson walked out of the store with a pair of bolt cutters under one arm, a hammer, and a flathead screwdriver in each of his hands. He popped open the trunk and placed the tools inside when some yelling from across the street caught his attention. A heavy-set man, wearing a baseball hat, was yelling at a middle-aged blonde woman holding a handful of flyers.

"I thought I told you not to be hanging these things up anymore!" the man yelled, ripping down the flyer the woman had taped to a light pole.

The woman shrank back a few steps before trying to side-step the man, who moved to block her path.

"Hey! Leave her alone." Jackson rushed to the woman's defense. "What's going on here?" Jackson grabbed the flyer out of the man's hand. It was a missing poster of a young blonde girl.

"Not like it's any of *your* business, but this crazy lady has been hanging these damn things all over town for the last twenty years, and we're all sick of staring at 'em. Everybody knows she ain't missing. She ran off with some satanic cult," the man said.

"That's Tracy," Lilly said from behind Jackson, making him jump at the sound of her voice.

"Wish you'd stop doing that," he said.

"That's what I'm saying," said the man.

"I wasn't talking to you," Jackson said. "And how do you know she ran off with a satanic cult? Got a lot of those around Harrison?"

"No," answered the man. "But John Rivers told me he found her one day out in the woods on the back end of his farm. She had his cat in one hand and a butcher's knife in her other while sitting in the middle of a ring of candles. Now if that ain't satanic, I don't know what is."

Jackson glanced at the flyer and then at Lilly, who didn't say a word. "You still should leave the woman alone," Jackson said, taping the flyer back up to the light pole. "Or maybe I could call the police and tell them how you're harassing her."

"Whatever," the man said with a dismissing wave as he turned around and walked away.

"Thank you," the woman said. "She's been missing for a long time, but I've never given up hope. I know my Tracy had some issues, but..."

Jackson placed a sympathetic hand upon the woman's shoulder. "I know how you feel," he said. "Never lose hope," he told her, not having the heart to tell her that her daughter was indeed dead and not that far from home.

The woman made her way down the sidewalk, stopping at each lamppost. Jackson watched her for several minutes, lost in thought, before making his way back to his car. "This ends tonight."

❧

Jackson parked his car about a quarter mile down the road from Mark Karle's house. The digital clock on the radio told him it was three minutes after three in the morning. Turning off the headlights of his car about a mile out, he slowly made his way down the dirt road, using only the light of the moon to steer by. "We'll approach on foot from here," he said, reaching under the seat and retrieving the pistol. He knew nothing about guns, so he checked it one more time for a safety. Not finding one, he stuffed it into the inside pocket of his leather jacket.

"Last resort," Lilly warned him again.

They slipped into the woods on the opposite side of the road. The trees gave way to a cornfield a short distance later. Tall, brown stalks still waiting to be pulled from the ground and turned into feed gave Jackson plenty of cover as he peered at the killer's house through the first few rows.

"Let's go over this one more time," he said quietly, kneeling down.

"We'll go first," Lilly said. "And find Tracy."

"I'll try to unlock a side window," Jessica said.

"Once we figure out how to distract him, we'll give you the signal," said Allison.

"Flickering lights," Jessica said.

"That's when I'll make my move," Jackson said. "Once inside, I'll make my way to the basement and free Norma Jean...if she's still alive."

"She will be," Allison said.

"She has to be," Lilly said.

"Good luck, everyone," Jackson said.

Jessica, Allison, and Laura started across the dirt road while Lilly hung back momentarily. "I want you to know how much this means to us," she said. "To me."

"Glad I could be a part of it," Jackson said. "This is the most meaningful thing I've done in my entire life. I believe now, because of you, I've been given a second chance, and I'm going to make the most of it."

Leaning forward, Lilly kissed him on the cheek. He knew her lips would pass through his flesh but felt that the overall act should not be wasted. She and Jackson were both surprised when her lips became solid, as they pressed against his skin.

All four of the girls stood in a line, shoulder to shoulder, at the edge of the front yard and stared at the bright ray of golden light shining down and engulfing the house. "This is it," Lilly told them. "Tonight, we cross over. Tonight, we can finally rest."

Jackson watched from the safety of the corn as the spirits of the four girls walked up to the house and disappeared through the front door. The entire front side of the house was cast in darkness except for a single illuminated curtain-covered window on the second floor. He took a few steps back and concealed himself with a few more rows of corn while pulling out his pack of cigarettes.

Using his hand to block the flame from his lighter, he took a long drag of smoke and held it in his lungs for a few seconds before blowing it out. Using his cell phone, he checked the time. It had already felt like an eternity since the girls had entered the house, but he knew it had only been a few minutes.

THE INSIDE of the house looked just as all the girls had remembered. Rays of bright golden light poured in through the house windows, their closed curtains doing little to curb the brilliance of their unfinished business.

"I'll try to unlock a window," Jessica said, moving into the living room. She found a side window and reached out a hand to push apart the curtains, but her hands passed right through them. She tried several times more, but each attempt ended with the same result.

Lilly could tell the girl's frustration was getting the better of her. "Take a minute," she said. "If you get angry and the lights start to flicker, Jackson will think we're giving him the signal."

"If I can't push some curtains out of the way, how can I unlock the window? Just go and find Tracy," Jessica said. "I'll figure something out." She blew out a frustrated breath.

"It's about fucking time."

The girls all turned to the sound of the voice and found Tracy Lafond standing on the first step of the stairs leading to the upper level of the house, glaring at them.

"I found them." Lilly moved toward her.

"Follow me upstairs," Tracy said. "He's taking a shower right now. We can catch him off guard."

"Wait," Lilly said. "Jackson is waiting outside. We need to try to unlock a window, so he can get in and rescue Norma Jean."

"Seriously?" Tracy asked, with a hint of annoyance in her voice.

"What's your plan, anyway?" Lilly asked.

"Follow me upstairs, and I'll show you," Tracy answered, walking up several steps before turning to see if Lilly and the others were following her.

"I don't think we can do this on our own," Allison said.

"You won't have to," Tracy promised. "Once we join forces, we will be able to stop Mark Karle from ever hurting another girl again."

"I'm in," said Laura, walking to the stairs. "Let's make that bastard pay."

"Me too," said Jessica, forgetting all about the curtains and Jackson.

"We're still going to need Jackson's help," Lilly pleaded.

"I'm with her," Allison said. "We need to stick together on this. First, we deal with the window, then Mark Karle."

Tracy's lips curled in a snarl as her dark eyes filled with hate. "This is *my* house bitch, and you'll do what I say." She extended her hand to Laura, who reached out and took it. Tracy pulled the spirit of the girl *into* her as Laura disappeared. "Together, we are strong," she said, extending her hand to Jessica.

"Let's do this," Jessica said, accepting Tracy's hand and merging her essence with the other two.

Tracy closed her eyes and took in a deep breath. Her dark gray appearance slowly saturated with color once again as she began to take on her living form. The red drops of blood that dotted her face, neck, and bare legs glowed with the color of life against her pale white skin. When she opened her eyes, they were an icy shade of blue. She let out a scream as the lights in the living room flickered on before all of the bulbs exploded.

"We need to get out of here!" Allison made a mad dash for the front door.

Tracy moved with supernatural speed and blocked the ghost's path, as she reached out and grabbed Allison by the wrist. Allison tried to pull away, but with one quick yank, Tracy pulled Allison off her feet, and her form disappeared.

"What are you doing?" Lilly moved behind Mark's recliner, trying to put some kind of barrier between her and Tracy.

"What needs to be done to make that bastard pay."

Chapter 26

A Man of His Word

A shiver ran down Jackson's spine as the cold night air finally made it through his thick leather jacket. He had already smoked three cigarettes and was reaching into his pocket to get another when the lights on the first floor of the house flickered on and off. His heartbeat instantly increased, and his mouth became as dry as the desert. He did a quick mental check. The screwdriver was in his back pocket. The hammer was in a belt loop on the side of his jeans, and the revolver, which he would only use as a last resort, was in the inside pocket of his jacket. Reaching down, he picked up the bolt cutters. The cold metal stung his hand, but he sucked it up and moved out from the safety of the cornfield.

He reached the left side of the house and tried to lift the first window he came to. When it wouldn't budge, he cursed under his breath and moved to the next one. "Fuck," he cursed again when that one wouldn't open either.

The curtains to both windows were drawn shut, but Jackson found a sliver of visibility within the center of the curtains of the second window. Putting one eye up to the tiny crevice and peeking into the house, he could tell he was looking into the living room. The only light came from the stairway light, whose faint brilliance cast itself sparingly over the living room. Jackson thought he heard voices coming from inside the house. He strained to peek through the thin opening, and after moving his head to just the right angle, he found Lilly standing on the opposite side of a recliner, with Tracy standing in front of her. Tracy lunged through the recliner, catching Lilly off guard. Jackson watched as Lilly drew her fist back, but before she could throw a punch, Tracy hit her with a strong backhand, sending Lilly flying through the air before coming to stand directly over her.

The necessity for Jackson to gain entry into the house took over all other plans he had. "Fuck it," he said, smashing the window with the hammer. The sound of breaking glass echoed through the living room as he reached in and undid the latch. Pushing the window open, he could only watch as Tracy raced up the stairs and disappeared from sight.

MARK KARLE STEPPED out of the shower and dried off. He slipped on a pair of comfortable sweatpants and a plain white T-shirt. Wiping the condensation from the mirror, he gazed upon his reflection. His mother had finally fallen asleep, with a little help from her medication. Mark had spent a better part of an hour cleaning up the caked-on shit from her diapers. He knew he brought this punishment upon himself by not changing her more often, but he could only clean up so much feces from a grown adult in one day.

He had given her a little extra medicine tonight because he wanted to be able to sleep in. Norma Jean had put up a good fight tonight, he thought, studying the new bruises on his knuckles, and he wanted to be fresh and recovered for his next visit. The sound of breaking glass echoed from somewhere downstairs. Thoughts of his plaything escaping rushed through his mind. He stepped toward the door but stopped at the sight of his breath becoming visible in the air in front of him. The bathroom temperature changed so drastically that ice began to gather around the mirror's edges. He stared at the ice in utter confusion, his mind unable to comprehend what was going on around him. Then something in the reflection of the mirror made his heart stop. Standing directly behind him was Tracy Lafond.

Mark stared at the reflection of the first life he had ever taken. "What are you...? How are you...?" he stammered, the sound of his own beating heart drowning out the volume of his voice.

What he was seeing was not possible. There was no way in hell *she* was standing behind him. She was right where he had put her all those years ago. Buried in the backyard under the birdbath. This had to be some kind of weird hallucination, he thought, but the sound of breaking glass had been real.

"Get a hold of yourself," he said. "Stay strong."

Tracy lunged forward and placed her hands on both sides of Mark's head. "But you're so weak," Mark's reflection said as her image vanished from sight.

"Stop saying that," Mark yelled at his reflection.

"But it's true."

"No, it's not!"

"If it wasn't for me, you wouldn't even have anyone to play with," his reflection said with a mocking smirk. "Who do you think was egging you on for all these years? Pushing you. Prodding you. Gentle nudges here and there. Bending your will to mine so that you would do all of those horrible things. It has always been me."

"You're lying," Mark told his reflection. "I wanted to do those things! I did those things! Me, not you!"

"You wanted to do those things, but you didn't have the balls to follow through, now did you?"

"I killed *you*, didn't I?" Mark asked. "Buried you right in my backyard."

Mark's reflection gave him a smirk. "That was different, and in a way, I made you do that too. And what happened after that? Nothing. Nothing for twenty years until you came back to this shit hole. Back to *her*."

Mark's eyes widened at the realization of the words being spoken to him.

"I followed you, you know, when you left home. When you moved into that piss-poor studio apartment in Los Angeles. I was there watching all your failed attempts at love. Heather. Joellen. Mary. I was there when you trolled all those high schools, looking for your next precious rape fantasy to jerk off to."

"Shut up!"

"It wasn't until we returned home to care for your dear old mother that I finally discovered how I could end my never-ending hell."

"Shut up!"

"I found that the more anger I had, the more persuasive I could be. And the more persuasive I could be, the more influence I had on you. It became quite easy once you began to loathe your mother."

"Shut up!"

"I still remember the night I pushed you over the edge. Remember? We were watching that stupid movie. She sat down in the row in front of us. The smell of her flowery perfume choked me out when she walked by with her friends. She had that long blonde hair, just like mine. Just like your mother. I kept catching you leering at her, and I knew what your perverted little mind was thinking. Even after stalking her and disabling her car, I still didn't think you had it in you, so I began to whisper words of encouragement into your ear. Things that I knew you wanted to do to her. I knew I had you when I saw that hard-on you had going on in your pants."

"Get out of my head!" Mark slapped the side of his face.

"You want to say hello?" his reflection asked. "She's here with us."

Jessica took the place of Mark's reflection, her dead eyes glaring at him with such hatred. "And let's not forget about Allison Murphey." The image in the mirror changed to that of Mark's third victim. "Laura's here too." The image of Allison changed to Laura Elliott.

Mark closed his eyes as his breathing became erratic. "This isn't happening. This isn't happening," he told himself. "This isn't real. Get a hold of yourself."

"You did everything I suggested." His reflection returned.

Mark resisted the temptation to look, but for some reason, he could not pull himself away from the mirror. The sound of breaking glass was still at the forefront of his thoughts, but his feet would not move.

"Everything, except for the one thing I wanted you to do the most. The one thing that would bring me the most joy in my afterlife. The one thing that would make you mine forever. Why won't you kill your fucking mother? You hate her with every fiber of your being, but you just won't do it. No matter how hard I pushed. I've even pushed *her*, and still, you wouldn't kill the bitch."

"Don't talk about her!"

"Her fragile mind was so easy to manipulate. I barely even had to try. She was putty in my hands. I had no idea someone could even produce that much shit, and you just cleaned it up. Every fucking time. You even gave her her special bath time. Mommy really does get your rocks off, doesn't she?"

"No, no, no," Mark stammered. "This isn't happening!"

"Oh, it's happening. You took everything from me that night. I only turned you into the man you are now because I honestly thought you weren't smart enough to have made it this far without being caught. I wanted to take your life away from you, like you did to me, and I have ensured that now, haven't I? You will spend the rest of your life in a small cell because of me. But, before I'm done, I'm going to take away the only purpose you have left in your pathetic little life, and I'm going to make *you* be the one who does it."

Tracy's reflection reappeared behind Mark. Her blue, hate-filled eyes glared at him from the other side of the mirror. She blew him a kiss before running through the bathroom door and disappearing out into the hall.

Mark regained the ability to move just in time to hear his mother scream his name.

Jackson crawled through the open window, careful not to cut his hands. His feet crunched against the broken glass on the floor as he made his way to Lilly's side. "What the hell is going on?"

Lilly slowly got to her feet and looked around the room anxiously. "Tracy...she absorbed the others. I tried to stop her, but she's strong now. Really strong. I think she's going to try to kill Mark."

"Good," Jackson said. "Let her do the work for us."

"No," Lilly replied. "You said it before. You can't go and murder someone. That will mark your soul forever. If Jessica,

Allison, and Laura are still inside her when she does it, I don't think they will be able to cross over."

"What do you want me to do?"

"Stick to the plan," Lilly said, heading to the stairs. "Get Norma Jean out of here. I'll try to stop Tracy the best I can," she added, not giving Jackson time to argue as she rushed up the stairs and disappeared from sight.

Jackson found the door to the basement and flicked on the lights before descending into Mark Karle's inner sanctum. At the bottom of the steps, his eyes fixed upon the door on the other side of the basement, for he knew what lay beyond it. His sweaty palm slowly turned the doorknob as he did his best to keep his heart from leaping into his throat at the anticipation of what he might find.

Norma Jean lay tucked up into the corner as far as she could. Curled up in a ball on the mattress, her body was visibly shivering, although the temperature in the room was as hot as hell from the bright lights. Her brown hair was a tangled mess of dried blood, and dirt covered most of her face, while her naked, blood-smeared body overflowed with small cuts and large bruises.

Jackson spotted the heavy chain attached to the thick eyebolt on the cement floor. He followed the chain to the metal shackle wrapped around Norma Jean's ankle. "Norma Jean?" he called out to her from the doorway. Jackson could not imagine the hell this poor girl had been through, and the last thing he wanted to do was overwhelm her by rushing into the room, but time was of the essence. "Can you hear me? My name is Jackson, and I'm here to rescue you."

Norma Jean slowly lifted her head and stared at Jackson through her tangled hair. Realizing it wasn't Mark, she rushed to Jackson with open arms, only to be knocked to the ground when she reached the end of the chain.

"Hold on." Jackson moved to her side and took a better look at what was keeping Norma Jean a prisoner. "The chain links are too thick to cut through," he said, grabbing the chain and gauging its weight. Running his hand up the chain to the metal shackle around Norma Jean's ankle, he turned it slightly and spotted the padlock keeping the whole thing together. "Now this is something I can work with," he said, placing the metal shank of the lock into the open jaws of the bolt cutters. He pushed the handle together with all his might and watched as the cutters barely bit into the metal. He pulled them apart and pushed them back together again. "Come on," he said, his arms shaking from the exertion.

"Again!" Norma Jean yelled, placing her hands upon Jackson's and adding her strength to his. They did this again and again, over and over, until, at last, they heard a snap, followed by the sound of the metal shank bouncing off the cement floor. "You did it," she squealed, hugging him tightly around his neck and hanging on for dear life.

"We need to go." Jackson pulled Norma Jean to her feet. "Can you walk?"

"No... I can run."

Mark turned the doorknob of his mother's bedroom and panicked when it would not open. "Mom!" he yelled, pounding desperately on the door.

"Marky! Help me!"

Adrenaline surged through the large man's veins as he took a few steps back and kicked the door hard, right under the doorknob. The wood of the doorframe splintered and cracked as the door flew open from the force of the assault. Mark stepped into the room and could not believe his eyes. His mother was standing in the middle of the room. She was completely naked. Shit stained her hairy vagina and flabby inner thighs. Her chin was tucked into her chest, with her hair covering the majority of her face. Her shoulders hung low, and her body swayed slightly back and forth. "Mom?" he asked, cautiously stepping into the room. "Are you ok?"

"Marky!" her voice cackled before a wicked laugh bellowed from her mouth. She slowly raised her head and glared at Mark with eyes as black as the night. Dark veins stretched across her face, neck, and chest. "Time for mama's bath," she said, smiling, revealing a mouth full of sharpened fangs.

"Leave my mother alone, you bitch!" Mark screamed, surging into the room. His mother lunged at him with supernatural speed. Acting on pure instinct, the large man punched her as hard as he could, square in the face, snapping his mother's head back and halting her charge.

"Marky, you ungrateful little shit. How dare you hit your mother." She laughed, lunging forward again, her sharp fangs aiming for the soft skin of her son's throat.

Mark's powerful hands grabbed both of his mother's shoulders in an attempt to hold her at bay as her razor-sharp teeth came within inches of his neck. He couldn't believe how much strength his mother now possessed as he felt himself being overpowered, leading him to the only course of action he could think of. He tilted his head back and snapped it forward as hard as he could, headbutting his mother right in her nose.

The world around Mark became fuzzy. A sharp pain shot straight through his brain. The room began to spin, followed by the sensation of flight as he soared across the room. He slammed into the wall hard and felt the air purge from his lungs before falling heavily to the floor. He fought to get to his feet, but his heavy head kept him pinned to the floor.

"You can't stop me," his mother said.

Mark knew she was right. His eyes began to regain focus as his mother stood facing the empty doorway.

"Join us," she said.

Mark wondered *who* she was talking to before his mind went black.

"Don't do this," Lilly pleaded. "If you kill him, none of you can cross over. Murder is a mortal sin."

"I'm not worried about that," Tracy said. "Once I'm finished with him, there's no golden ray of light keeping me here."

"Jessica, fight!"

"She can't hear you."

"Allison!"

"No one here by that name."

"Laura, can you hear me?"

"That schizophrenic twit was the easiest to consume. So much raw anger in that one."

"I'll stop you," Lilly promised. "Jackson will stop you."

"I nearly forgot about your *living* boy toy. Where is he? Ah, you sent him to the basement, didn't you? Clever girls, but I can read their thoughts. I know all of their deepest, darkest, twisted little secrets." Tracy lashed out and wrapped a hand around Lilly's throat, lifting her into the air easily. "I'm going to make you watch as I tear your little boyfriend limb from limb." She rushed from the room and literally flew down the stairs.

"We need to move," Jackson said with a sense of urgency. He put a strong arm around Norma Jean's waist and led her toward the door. They had just crossed the threshold when an old, naked woman with long gray hair and black eyes came storming down the stairs. And if the black eyes didn't freak him out, the fact that the old woman had a hand wrapped around Lilly's throat did.

"Lilly!" Jackson yelled, watching his friend try her hardest to break free from Norma Karle's grip.

The old woman flashed a fang-filled smile at Jackson. "She's not the one you should be worrying about," she hissed. "Mama's hungry and has a craving for fresh meat." She threw Lilly to the ground and leaped at Jackson.

Jackson swung the bolt cutters through the air and kept the momentum going when the metal tool made contact with the old woman's face. The blow did little to stop her, though. Norma Karle shrugged off the attack and punched Jackson hard in the chest. The force of the blow knocked him off his feet and sent him flying back into her son's pleasure room.

Jackson hit the floor hard and skidded all the way to the back wall. The hag was on the move. Before he could get back to his feet, the possessed form of the old woman breached the doorway. He only had seconds to act before his throat would most certainly be ripped from his neck.

Lilly jumped through the air and landed on Norma Karle's back. Wrapping an arm around the old woman's throat and putting her in a headlock, she began to squeeze with all her strength. The old woman staggered a few steps into the room. Flailing her arms about, she landed a hard elbow to Lilly's face, causing her hold to falter just enough that Norma could pitch her from her back, throwing her across the room, where she landed hard, right next to Jackson.

"Little bitch," Norma hissed as her black eyes locked on to Jackson. She bent her knees slightly, getting ready to pounce.

Jackson frantically reached into the inside pocket of his

jacket and drew forth the pistol he had found under Harold Woodruff's bed. Not having time to aim, he pointed the gun toward the charging woman and pulled the trigger two times as fast as he could.

Both shots hit the woman in the chest but did little to slow her down as black blood gushed over her saggy bare breasts. Jackson raised the barrel of the revolver a couple of inches and squeezed the trigger a third time. The old woman's head snapped backward with a hard crack, causing her momentum to slow to a crawl. A single bullet hole was visible in her forehead as a line of blood trickled down her face. Black eyes glared at Jackson as the old woman's mouth full of razor-sharp teeth formed a wicked smile.

"Nice try."

A strange, rapid, clicking noise filled the room. The old woman raised up on her tippy toes and arched her back. A scream of agony escaped her lips. The clicking sound stopped, and the old woman's body collapsed to the ground, leaving Tracy Lafond standing in her place and visibly stunned.

"You've gone and gotten yourself into all kinds of trouble, haven't you," Carol asked, holding her Taser out in front of her. The reaper walked up behind Tracy and grabbed a fistful of her hair before slamming her hard onto the concrete floor.

Jackson staggered to his feet and stared down at Norma Karle's dead body. The revolver slipped from his fingers and clanked hard against the cement ground. The utter fact that he had been responsible for her death became a cognitive thought.

"Don't do that to yourself," Carol told him. "That was not *your* fault. Hold this," she added, handing the Taser to Jackson. "If she tries anything funny, make her ride the lightning." She took out a pair of handcuffs and slapped them onto Tracy's wrists. "Now, let's get the hell out of here," she ordered, extending a helping hand to Lilly, who graciously accepted it.

Jackson took off his jacket and wrapped it around Norma Jean before helping her to her feet as Carol dragged the now-compliant ghost of Tracy Lafond toward the basement stairs.

Once they were free of Mark Karle's twisted fun house, Jackson led Norma Jean to a large tree near the road and sat her down. "You're safe now. I'll be right back. I promise."

Carol's black, windowless van sat at the end of the driveway. The reaper led Tracy to the back of the van and opened the doors. Lilly began to tell Carol what Tracy had done, but before she could open her mouth, the reaper reached into Tracy's chest and pulled out the spirits of the others, one by one. When the girls were free, Carol pushed Tracy into the silver cage and slammed the doors shut.

"How?" Jackson joined the others.

"I traced your call, duh. Figured you might be in some kind of trouble, even though you didn't leave a message. You really should have left a message."

"Sorry," Jackson said. "I didn't want to bother you. Figured you had more important things to do."

"Rookie mistake." Carol placed her Taser back into her holster. "After I found out where you were, I had Kenny cross reference this area with any outstanding bouncers, and Tracy Lafond's name popped up."

"I thought she was a purg like us," Lilly said, confused.

"Did she ever say she was? Or that she had unfinished business like you?"

"Now that you mention it, no."

"What about us?" Jessica asked. "Is it over?"

Carol checked her watch. "Almost."

~

Mark struggled to get to his feet. His head was still spinning, but he had to find his mother, or whatever was pretending to be his mother. He made his way down the stairs, bouncing hard off the walls before reaching the kitchen. When he finally reached the basement, he found the door to his private sanctum wide open. From where he stood, he could see a pair of bare, dirty feet stretched out upon the cold concrete floor. Cautiously, he went to the doorway and fell hard to his knees when he gazed upon his mother's dead body lying on the floor in a pool of black blood. It took several minutes for his mind to register that Norma Jean was gone. Tracy was right. His life *was* over. He would spend the rest of his life in a tiny cell.

Crawling to his mother's side, he pushed the hair away from her face. He had failed to keep her safe. He had failed to keep his word. The word he had given his father. The reflection of something metallic on the floor caught his eye. Crawling over to it, he picked up the revolver Jackson had dropped. The revolver that had killed his mother. A tear trickled down his cheek as he gently placed the barrel of the gun into his mouth and pulled the trigger, splattering his brains all over the wall behind him.

The spirits of Jessica Watkins, Allison Murphey, and Laura Elliott glowed with a bright golden aura. The golden rays of light that had once been their unfinished business blinked out of existence as the souls of the dead turned into a swarm of glowing embers. The embers swirled about Lilly and Jackson for a few seconds before floating upward upon an unfelt wind.

"You did it," Lilly told Jackson, a smile of pure joy forming upon her lips.

"We did it," Jackson corrected her. "But why are you still here? I mean, I don't mind you being here, but with your unfinished business being complete, it's your turn to cross over."

"I think I might have one more piece of unfinished business to attend to," she said, finding a new golden glow in the sky to the south.

Chapter 27

One Last Task

Jackson sat in the brightly lit interrogation room, his right hand cuffed to the table. The thought of déjà vu played across his mind. A detective, wearing a pair of blue dress pants and a white button-up shirt with a blue tie, entered the room and sat down on the opposite side of the table.

"Let me tell you what I've got," the detective said. "I've got one huge cluster fuck and no real good answers, so why don't you help me clear some of this up?"

"I'll do what I can, but you might not like all of my answers."

"Try me."

"I was driving down the road when I heard gunshots, and then that girl ran in front of my car. I almost hit her," said Jackson.

"Bullshit. I know when I'm being lied to. I suggest you don't do it again."

"Fine."

"So why don't we begin with something easy? Who's the girl, and where did she come from?"

"Her name is Norma Jean, and she's from Warsaw, Indiana," Jackson answered.

"Is that where you and Mark Karle took her from?" the detective asked.

"Whoa! Time out! I didn't take anyone. That was *all* him."

"So, he takes 'em, and you just play with 'em?"

"I don't play with shit. I was there rescuing Norma Jean. Ask her. She'll tell you."

"And you just happened to know she was there?"

"Yeah," Jackson answered.

"And why didn't you call 911?"

"There wasn't any time."

"Bullshit," the detective said again. "I've got two dead bodies and one tortured young girl who's in no condition to talk right now. You know how I know that? Because she keeps talking about monsters. Monsters with fangs and black eyes. So, if you don't start filling in some of the blanks, I'm gonna throw you in one of my cells, and you can take the fall for it all."

"Except none of it'll stick."

"So, you're a lawyer now? How's this, Mr. Lawyer? I've got you at the crime scene. Your right hand tested positive for gunshot residue, which means you fired the only gun found at the scene, and I'm pretty sure at least one of the other victim's blood will be on your jacket. How am I doing so far?"

Jackson let out a loud sigh. "You wouldn't believe me if I told you the truth."

"Only one way to find out."

"Fine, I'm what's called a..."

"Don't you dare say psychic," the detective warned.

"I can't read minds," Jackson said. "I'm a seer."

"And what do you see?"

"Dead people."

"You see dead people?"

"I see dead people."

"Ok, I hope you're looking forward to spending the rest of your life in a prison cell." The detective stood and walked toward the door.

"Tracy Lafond."

The detective stopped a few feet from the door before turning to give Jackson a skeptical stare. "Gotta do better than that. That's one of the biggest things to ever have happened around here. Everybody knows about her."

"Did you know that Mark Karle killed her twenty years ago and buried her in his backyard under the birdbath?"

The detective narrowed his eyes as Jackson motioned toward the empty chair. "Mark Karle was a serial killer. There's evidence of this in his bedroom. Look under his bed, and you'll find a box with lockets of hair from all his victims."

"Is that so?" The detective sat back down.

"His second victim, Jessica Watkins, went missing from Sault Ste. Marie. He buried her in Climax, Michigan. Next, Allison Murphey. He took her from Boonville, Indiana, a year later. She's buried in Woodbury Wildlife Area near West Bedford, Ohio. Then there's Laura Elliott. He took her from Cincinnati and buried her in the Sleepy Hollow State Park in Laingsburg, Michigan. His fifth victim, Lilly Barnes from Olivet, Michigan, was found in Greenville, Ohio."

The detective stared at Jackson. "They already tried to blame me for her death when I told them where she was buried, but I was locked up when she was killed, so they cut me loose. You can call Detective Brandt from Greenville and ask him."

"What about Chief Vaughn?"

"He's the chief of Oak Hill, Ohio. That's where Laura lived with her mother before she moved to Cincinnati."

"Yeah, he called here vouching for you. Said you weren't

involved in any of this, but yet here you are. Still doesn't tell me why you didn't call us if you knew Norma Jean was in this guy's basement."

"If I'm being honest, it's like this. All of the ghosts of his victims were stuck here, in a place called purgatory, and needed to bring Mark Karle to justice to cross over. Once I got them all there, I didn't think Norma Jean had that much time left. Besides, you wouldn't have believed me then, especially with no evidence, like I'm sure you don't believe me now, but it's the truth."

The detective pushed away from the table and, without saying a word, walked out of the room. He came back a few hours later and undid the handcuff keeping Jackson tethered to the table. "I did some checking. All of the victims you named off have been recovered, which to me, means that either you're telling the truth or you were working with Mark Karle, but Norma Jean insists that you shot Norma Karle in self-defense because, and I quote, 'she was possessed or something.' And for the record, I don't believe in any of that mumbo jumbo shit, so I think you're full of it, but without any hard evidence linking you to any of the missing girls and Norma Jean's testimony, the prosecuting attorney has ordered your release."

～

Jackson shifted his car into park and stared out at Lilly's house. He took the last drag of his cigarette and flicked it out the crack of the open window. "Are you ready?" He picked up a notepad and pen.

"I can never thank you enough for doing this," Lilly said him from the passenger seat.

"Sure you can. You can show me around when I get up

there. Take me to all the interesting places, and introduce me to all the cool people."

"Deal." She slid over and disappeared into his body as Jackson's hand began to write. When she was done, she returned to her side of the car.

"Wow," Jackson said, taking out another cigarette. "That was so...weird." He sat there, staring at the house for nearly half an hour, before finding the courage to get out of the car and walk up to the front door. The butterflies in his stomach churned hard as he pushed the doorbell.

"You know you can leave it in the mailbox," Lilly said.

"Can I help you?" asked the middle-aged woman who opened the door. Jackson could see hints of Lilly in the woman's face—or was it the other way around?

"No, but I can help you." Jackson handed the woman a folded piece of paper. "This is from your daughter, Lilly. We were...friends. She said I could leave it in the mailbox, but I thought I should deliver it in person and tell you that your daughter is an amazing person, and she's at peace now."

"I don't understand."

"Just read the letter, and you will," Jackson answered before walking back to his car alone and driving off.

Lilly's mother unfolded the piece of paper and saw words upon its surface were in her daughter's handwriting.

Dear Mom and Dad,

I never thought my life would end the way it did. I can only imagine the pain and grief I have caused you over the six months you had no idea where your little girl was. I'm so sorry that I won't be able to be a part of your life anymore.

Dad, I'm sorry you won't be able to walk your little girl down the aisle. I fought as hard as I could, but it just wasn't enough. In the end, when it truly mattered the most, I found the courage I needed because of you. Because you always pushed me to be the best I could be, and for that, I can never thank you enough.

Mom, I'm going to miss our little talks the most. I loved sharing with you everything that was always happening in my life during our late-night ice cream binges. The bad break-ups, the new crushes. You were more than my mother. You were my best friend.

Know that you gave me a good life and that you taught me how to live a good life. A life filled with hope and kindness. A life filled with a daughter's love for her parents. A love that I will never lose. A love that will be reunited one day, far in the future, when we meet again.

You both must promise me that you will move on. To not dwell in the past, or in the what could have beens. Live your lives, and be happy together, and remember that this is only temporary. Until then, know that I will always be looking down upon you with a smile on my face and love in my heart.

Your loving daughter,

Lilly

Tears began to dot the paper as Lilly's mother wiped her eyes. Holding the paper to her chest, she fought to get her breathing under control. Lilly placed a hand upon her mother's shoulder before being reborn as tiny embers of light.

The End.

About the Author

L. N. Costley has been in Law Enforcement for over 20 years. He lives in Michigan with his wife and children. He is an avid reader of both Fantasy and Science Fiction, and has been so for the majority of his life, with authors such as R. A. Salvatore, Dean Koontz, and Kevin J. Anderson fueling my imagination. When not writing he enjoys knife and sword forging, wood working, and playing video games.

Afterword

Congratulations! You made it to the end of the book! Hopefully you read the book to get here, so if you haven't, hint, hint, I'll wait. First, I want to thank you for taking time out of your life to read Lilies on Her Grave. That means a lot. Now, I would like to ask for one more favor from you. Could you leave this book a review? Indie Authors need reviews like a yellow lab needs water. If done right, an indie book costs a pretty penny to publish, and in order to make that money back, so that they can write and publish more books, hint, hint, we need to sell more books, and reviews are the most important part of that process. If you can't, you can't. I understand. What if you didn't like the book, or didn't like certain parts? Still leave a review. If you didn't like something, I need to know. So, what's coming next you're asking? Check out Quillandinkpublishing.com and find out. Hope to see you again.

L.N. Costley